Praise for

the SOMEDAY BIRDS

"Sally J. Pla does a wonderful job of weaving humor and humanity into this tale of one boy's triumph."
—Cammie McGovern, author of *Just My Luck* and *Say What You Will*

"Sally J. Pla's heartwarming debut novel zings with humor, spot-on characters, and a poignant exploration of the effects of war."
—Edith Hope Fine, author of *Under the Lemon Moon*

"A truly wonderful, unique story. This celebration of family, individuality, and nature will remind you to always be on the lookout for wonder."
—Wendy Mass, *New York Times* bestselling author of *The Candymakers*

"Offering a mixture of suspense, mystery, tragedy, and humor, Pla's story captures both the literal and figurative meanings of journey."
—*Publishers Weekly* (starred review)

"Achingly real. Charlie's unique voice and his quest to understand the world around him will resonate with readers dealing with their own pain. Hopeful, authentic, and oddly endearing."—*Kirkus Reviews*

"A delight from beginning to end."—ALA *Booklist*

"Readers will genuinely be captivated and touched by Charlie's soft and sensitive demeanor and amused by his pondrous exploits across the country. A strong addition to most middle grade collections."
—*School Library Journal*

the SOMEDAY BIRDS

SALLY J. PLA

HARPER

An Imprint of HarperCollinsPublishers

ISBN 978-0-06-244577-3

Typography by Michelle Gengaro-Kokmen
19 20   BRR   10 9 8 7 6
First paperback edition, 2018

For my family.

CONTENTS

MIGRATORY GEESE

FLOCKERS
and LONERS

1

My hands aren't really clean until I've washed them twelve times, one for each year of my life. I *soap-rinse-one-soap-rinse-two-soap-rinse-three-soap-rinse-four-soap-rinse-five-soap-rinse-six,* open my palms to scalding water, and repeat. I do it quick, so no one notices, and I'm usually done in about the same time it takes Joel and Jake to spray water at each other and throw towels on the floor, which is what *they* call washing up.

This time I gotta go faster because Gram's already yelling from the driveway, "Charlie, get your bee-hind out here! Your father's waiting!"

But he's not really waiting. Dad never knows if we're in his hospital room or not.

Gram does something my sister, Davis, calls sideways swearing. Gram says words like *bee-hind*, *flipping*, *heck*, and *gosh-dang*. Davis, who's fifteen and a half, says, "Gram, just curse normally like the rest of the world." Then Gram says, "Davis, I ever hear that kind of talk outta your sassy teenage mouth, I'll swat your dang bee-hind so hard you'll think twice about talkin' in general."

I used to be scared of Gram. Davis says that's just Gram's way, tough love, but I don't get how tough equals love. Dad's love wasn't tough. He never lost his temper, or freaked out with worrying, or tried so hard to control everything we did. Or sideways swore. Still, I have to admit I'm no expert on love. Or hate. Or really anything that has to do with feelings. I rely on what Davis tells me—she's the expert on that kind of stuff.

The doctors are supposed to have some news for us today about Dad's condition. So when Gram crams us all into her little MINI Cooper to go visit the hospital, the sideways swearing really cranks up.

"Finally, here's our Lysol Louie," says Gram when I open the back door and wait for Joel and Jake to scoot over.

"My name isn't Lysol Louie; it's Charlie," I say.

Joel and Jake say, "You think we don't know your name, Droid?"

"My name isn't Droid; it's Charlie." I say it quietly and hope they'll drop it. My twin brothers are up to something. I'm not the best at reading people in general, but I know evil when I see it in those identical pairs of eyes.

"GET IN, CHARLIE! DAD'S WAITING!" yells Davis from the front passenger seat. Meanwhile, the twins snicker, waiting for me to sit down in my spot.

"Dad's not really waiting," I say, taking a Kleenex out of my trusty supply pack and brushing away the dead flies and clumps of dryer lint my brothers have strewn over my seat. I used to get upset at their little booby traps of contamination. But Davis told me that's exactly what they want. She told me not to react, not to give them the satisfaction. So I just shoot the twins a dead-fish-eye look and sit down carefully, making sure no part of me touches any part of Joel.

"Dad's not really waiting, because he doesn't know whether we're there or not," I explain.

Davis and Gram don't like hearing this. But if something's a fact, it's a fact, and I don't think it's wrong to say it out loud. Dad's got a brain injury, and he stares straight ahead like he's looking at something really far away. He doesn't say much, or seem to see us. Gram says that brain injuries like Dad's are unpredictable things, and we don't know anything for sure. She says we have to treat him normally, tell him about our day, even if he just sits there most of the time.

She says, "Charlie, that's how we got you to start talking when you were little. You were just like your dad, in a way, all sealed off in your own little world. But we broke through to you, finally, didn't we? We talked your gosh-dang ears off. We talked and talked, and we made you do stuff, go to therapy. We wouldn't let you off the hook. So now we won't let your dad off the hook either."

Off the hook is a weird expression. I imagine being a really little kid, just wanting to be left alone. And there's a big fishhook holding me up by the back of my collar while I dangle, and a whole crowd of people—my family, therapists, doctors—watches me squirm. Is that how Dad feels in the hospital? Inside, where we can't tell what's going on, is he squirming, too?

Dad got hurt in Afghanistan. He's not in the military, though. He's an English teacher and a part-time journalist. He was over there to do a profile on some soldiers, to write about what their life was like. But a bomb went off while he was riding around in a jeep. The doctors said Dad was really lucky, because he got thrown into the air away from the explosion.

Gram covered her eyes and said "Holy Jesus!" when the doctors first told us that. But I asked them more questions. I needed to picture what that moment was like, with my dad flying through the air like a bird. I tried to draw it once—how high the flames could have reached, which direction Dad flew (up high, and then straight ahead into the road, they think). I drew him flying. I wish I could have drawn him a better place to land.

Dad sustained a head injury. That's the word they used, *sustained*. It means you've had to withstand something. But it also means something is stretched out, like a note of music, just played and held constant for a long period of time. That's what it's like now, with Dad in the hospital. Like this strange invisible hum is in the air around us, and Gram and the twins and Davis and I just have to keep listening to it, and none of us know how long it will go on.

2

Human and bird behavior share similar qualities
when it comes to the issues of family and survival.
—Tiberius Shaw, PhD

The hospital's basically our home away from home. I used to get anxious about it, but not so much anymore. First you go in these huge sliding glass doors, and there's a bunch of orange couches and coffee tables and potted palms. It's like they're trying to pretend it's some sort of nice hotel—one with hand-sanitizer dispensers all over the place, and people wearing scrubs, and others pacing around with their phones.

"Can we go down to the cafeteria?" asks Joel, dragging on Gram's arm. "Please? We're *starving*!"

Joel and Jake love the hospital cafeteria. It's called the Garden of Eatin.' I try to tell them it's actually pretty much the opposite, but they never listen to me. They are ten, and always squabbling and wrestling with each other.

"Shush!" says Gram to the twins. "We're not going to the cafeteria. Stand up and walk straight, like normal human beings."

"But we're starving! STARVING!" They limp along, moaning.

That cafeteria is taste-bud torture. The sandwich bread has seeds like little pebbles. The soup has blobs of orange scum, and the oatmeal's a lump of sticky paste. Their scrambled eggs leak a soggy puddle of egg juice that ends up seeping into all the other stuff on your plate. Just thinking about it makes me gag.

It doesn't take much to make me gag—I even do it when I brush my teeth, which is why Dad always let me use a wet washcloth over my finger. But now Gram makes me use a toothbrush. She stands over me while I gag, and she doesn't even care. I don't know what the big deal is, toothbrush or washcloth, if your teeth get clean.

The hospital cafeteria is torture overall, but I admit it usually does have fairly decent chicken nuggets. The coating is crispy and kind of bland, which I like. I've figured out that no matter where you get dragged in this world, you can usually survive by ordering the chicken nuggets.

I'm hungry right now, too, but I don't say anything because I don't want to sound like Joel and Jake.

"Oh, for the love of Pete." Gram is yanking Joel along the hall while he holds his stomach and wails loudly. Jake joins in, and the two of them stumble along, doubled over and groaning like they're going to die of starvation at any minute. I hang back and stay behind Davis, walking close to the wall, my hands held up like surgeons do on television.

A nurse in purple scrubs and white clogs stops in her tracks when she sees the twins, doubled over and moaning. "Oh my. Are you looking for the urgent care?" she asks.

Gram puckers up her already wrinkly face. "Heavens, no, thank you!" When the nurse is past, Gram smacks Joel on the back of his head. "See how you behave? Shut those traps, the pair of you."

Right before the elevator bank, I tug on Gram's jacket.

We are by the propped-open door of the gift shop.

"*Two* minutes, today, Charlie," Gram says, holding up two of her bony, wrinkly fingers in a *V*. "We're in a hurry." I could argue, because I usually get five or ten minutes in the gift shop. But something about Gram's face keeps me quiet.

Joel says, "If we're in such a hurry, how come we always have to wait for *him*?"

Jake says, "Let's get candy!"

Davis rolls her eyes, folds her arms, and slumps against the wall outside the shop to wait.

There's a bunch of lady stuff in the shop—scarves and jewelry. Also these teeny tiny little T-shirts for newborn babies, and candy and gum, and toy dinosaurs and Lego sets for all the bored kids that get dragged around.

But what I'm after is on a shelf behind the counter.

Perched on that shelf are the coolest, most realistic little bird sculptures ever. There's a screech owl, a quail, a parrot, a bald eagle, a dove, and a ruby-throated hummingbird in flight, posed on this little wire stand stuck into a chunk of wood. When I look at it, I can almost hear its wings whirring. (From fifty to two hundred beats per second, faster than any other bird.)

The sculptures were hand carved by *Legendary Ornithologist, Artist, and Philosopher, Dr. Tiberius Shaw, PhD.* An old, folded notecard says so. It has a gold feather stamped on it, as well as a photo of Dr. Shaw, who looks carved from wood himself: dark, piercing eagle eyes, brown leathery skin, and big white eyebrows that stick out like feathery wings.

Tiberius Shaw knows everything about birds, and has written tons of books. I don't have any of them yet. Someday, I hope I will. But what I do have, with me right here always, in this blue canvas backpack of supplies I always carry, is my own notebook, my own sort of Bird Book. It's where I copy sketches of birds, write down facts I learn about birds, and other stuff, too. My Bird Book comes with me everywhere.

And actually, back at home, I have this other really cool old book Dad got me at a garage sale. It's huge, and it weighs a ton. It's called the Audubon baby "elephant" folio. There are no elephants in it, just giant full-color paintings of birds—shore, marsh, forest, birds of prey, ocean birds, waterfowl—that someone named John James Audubon painted, back before even Dr. Shaw was born. Long, long ago, when America was mainly wilderness.

When I was younger, I would only talk about birds and nothing else. I mean, if you had asked me when I was six, "How are you today, Charlie?" I might have replied, "Did you know that hummingbirds are actually really nasty and territorial and fight with each other all the time?" or "Did you know that there are feral peacocks in Southern California?" I'd talk bird stuff at you until you felt like asking, "What does all THAT have to do with the price of tea in China?" (That's what Gram always asks, when I go on and on about bird facts.)

But I'm way better about that now. Now, when you ask, "How are you, Charlie?" I will say "Fine," even if I'm not fine, even if I know this amazing thing about starlings that would fascinate you to hear, instead of just hearing the boring old word: "Fine."

But if that's what people want, then fine. Okay. I'm fine.

Ellie is behind the gift shop counter today. I like her. She never minds showing me the shelf of bird sculptures. She says, "Take your time, Charlie boy. You want me to take 'em all down for you?"

I don't have to answer that question; she knows. She puts the birds on the counter.

Ellie told me that *Legendary Ornithologist, Artist, and Philosopher, Dr. Tiberius Shaw, PhD,* used to be a lot more famous. "Folks don't know him as much now, but he was a big shot. Wrote those kinds of self-help sorts of books, about what birds can teach us about people, about life. Big-name scientist guru; got on all the talk shows."

Someday, I am going to buy all his books.

I wish I could stay here in the gift shop and sketch the little bird statues. I'd rather do that than go upstairs to see Dad. I love my dad, but that hospital room makes my feet rumble and my stomach feel like a washing machine. Meanwhile, seeing the birds makes me feel quiet and orderly. The birds are beautiful. The basic facts about them don't change. Bird behavior is pretty consistent.

You can write it down, know it, understand it. No matter how hard you try, you can't do that with people.

Someday, when I meet *Legendary Ornithologist, Artist, and Philosopher, Dr. Tiberius Shaw, PhD*, I will ask him what he means, that birds can teach us about people.

Ellie is the gift-shop person on Monday-Wednesday-Fridays. She is about six feet tall and maybe four feet wide, and her blue vest is as big as a tent. Ellie has wild curly black hair, dark brown skin, and big dangly earrings that swing back and forth when she talks to Gram. They talk a lot. They whisper, thinking we don't hear, but we do. And as always, they're whispering away about one thing and one thing only: Ludmila.

Ellie whispers to Gram, "Well, I don't know, but if I were to guess, I'd say that Ludmila, well, she's got issues, is all I'm saying. What's she *doing* in his room like that all the time? Sitting around staring at him like a vulture. What's she waiting for?"

Gram widens her eyes and looks up at Ellie. "But no, that's not how Ludmila is, Ellie. Not at all! She watches over him like a hawk. The other night she caught one of the new orderlies about to give him the wrong meds!"

Ellie nods. Her earrings sway like clock pendulums. "Mm hmm, oh dear," she says, crossing her arms across her big chest. "Dear, oh dear. The whole situation is rough. But why's that Ludmila even involved? Why'd she just show up in his room one day out of the blue? It's strange, if you ask me."

Gram shrugs. "It's strange, yes. But I don't want to pry. There's a story there. It'll all come out in good time."

Gram buys chocolate bars for Joel and Jake. I say good-bye to the bird sculptures, and then we don't delay anymore. We take the elevator up to Dad. They've put him up with the stable patients on the sixth floor of the hospital now.

The elevator doors open, and boom, who do we see standing there? Ludmila herself, waiting to go down. We all jump a little. She has a blue wig on today, electric blue, with straight bangs that stick out over her thick black glasses. I know that her normal hair under that wig is bright pink. She nods to Gram, and says, in her deep, slightly Russian-sounding accent, "He didn't want anything this morning. Not even the coffee with lots of sugar."

"Well, you sure are gettin' to know him," says Gram.

No one else says anything. We all look down.

"So," Ludmila says, nodding to herself. "Well. I'll be back a little later."

Davis snorts loudly, folds her arms, and looks away. When Gram's not around, Davis calls her "Ludmila, the Intruder Gorilla."

"*Thank you*," Gram answers, in the same sort of voice

she uses to talk to Aiden, the three-year-old kid who lives next door. "We *so* appreciate your help."

Ludmila gets on the elevator going down.

One thing about Ludmila? She doesn't feel the need to force a smile or talk all loud and cheery, like some people do.

The first time we met her, it was one of the early days—when we were sitting around Dad's bed, listening to the machines beep and trying not to look at that pressure monitor thing sticking out of his head. And suddenly there she was—a lady in maybe her twenties or thirties, with bright pink spiky hair and thin silver rings in her nose and ears. She had on thick glasses, an old flowery dress, black leather vest, heavy boots, and lots of tattoos up and down her bare arms. There was a scabby-looking new tattoo on her right hand: the word *Amar,* with lots of tiny red hearts and angel wings fluttering all around it. All red and puffy.

Joel and Jake jumped back a little when they saw her at the door. She just walked right in. "I'm Ludmila," she said, offering the hand to shake. Gram shook it. Then Jake pointed to it and said, "Your tattoo is bleeding."

And Ludmila had squinted her small eyes behind her heavy glasses, put her puffy hand over her chest, and said in a deep voice, "Yes. So is my heart, bleeding. For your sorrow, and for mine." Then she bowed to us all, and left the room.

Gram's mouth was hanging open. That's a visual cue that means a person is surprised.

Anyway, that was the first time we met Ludmila.

3

*For some birds, survival means the flock. For
others, life is a solitary proving ground in the wild.*
—**Tiberius Shaw, PhD**

Dad's room is a private one, with a window overlooking the parking lot. He's sitting by it right now in his wheelchair. It's still weird to see him in it. But at least he's out of bed and those machines are gone, with all their beeps and buzzes.

For a while, all anybody talked about was something called his "intracranial pressure." That's what happens when your injured brain swells up and bleeds, and the inside-the-brain bleeding puts too much pressure on your skull. Dad's brain pressure was so serious, they had to remove a piece of his skull to relieve it. Plus, he's had something called *aphasia*. That means he has trouble speaking and writing. It could all get completely better.

Or not. It's tricky. We just don't know. It's what they're calling, "Wait and see."

Dad's eyes watch us enter, but the visual cue on his face—or what you can see of it under the protective bike helmet he wears—doesn't seem to change too much. At least, not that I can tell.

"Hey, Dad, it's us!" Joel and Jake yell, and they sort of swipe their fingers along the back of his wheelchair before they start bouncing around the room.

"Hey, Daddy-o, it's Davis," says Davis in a soft voice, kissing her fingers and then touching the top of his helmet.

Gram rests her hands on Dad's shoulders. Then she asks, as usual, "Well, Charlie? Aren't you going to say hello to your father?"

I look down at my shoes, my black outdoor Crocs, and inspect for dirt or scuffmarks. They are fine. "Even if I did say hello," I say, "Dad doesn't hear me."

Gram stomps her foot. "For crying out loud, Charlie!"

There is a hand-sanitizer dispenser in the corner of Dad's room. I put my palms under it, first one, then the other, and the dispenser whirs. I coat every finger, one-two-three-four-five, and repeat. Alcohol gel is horrible, but it's better than nothing. Hospitals are hotbeds of germs. I think about microbes crawling up the walls. My skin is twitching and itching.

Davis takes a book out of her bag and settles on Dad's bed. She pats the spot next to her and calls me over, but I stay by the dispenser. She shrugs, and starts to read in that loud and cheery voice the nurses use. It's a book she pulled off Dad's office shelf by someone called Dave Barry that Dad used to think was funny. Davis thinks laughing is *therapeutic*, but only she and the twins ever laugh at the book, never Dad, and he's the one who needs the therapy.

Davis used to also insist on bringing Dad his cup of coffee every morning. We'd stop at Klatch, his old favorite spot, for a caramel latte to go, and Davis would spoon him little foamy sips. Dad would smile at her out of the right side of his mouth. Once he even winked, and everyone got all excited. Dad used to be a big winker, back in the day.

But one morning, when Davis came in with her cup, Ludmila was already sitting in the chair in front of Dad. And she said to Davis, "The milk in that latte is no good; it upset his stomach. Do not bring it anymore. No more milk. I'm just giving him half a cup of plain black."

Gram said later that she thought Davis was going to throw that cup at Ludmila.

Gram rebuttons Dad's pajama shirt. She says to Joel

and Jake, "Behave yourselves." She tells Davis, "You're in charge, doll-baby. I'm gonna corner that dang doctor for an update."

When Dad first came here, I made him a drawing for the wall by his bed. I drew him a red-tailed hawk sitting on a branch, and I surrounded the picture with all the facts I could find about red-tailed hawks, which I wrote in perfect lettering. My handwriting's so weirdly good that Mr. Simpson, my sixth-grade teacher, used to call me the Human Typewriter.

I try not to think about what my seventh-grade teachers are going to call me. I have enough to worry about this summer.

It took a long time to do the drawing. I chose a red-tailed hawk to remind Dad of the ones we've spotted together near our house, swooping around the canyon, looking for mice. Now and then Dad would make me go walking on the trails with him. He'd force me, even though I hate to be outside. It's dusty and dirty out there, and there could be ticks. I have this thing about ticks. I can handle most bugs—I even think they are interesting. But ticks are evil parasites that steal your precious blood. I live in mortal fear of ticks.

Still. I wish I'd gone walking with Dad a little more often. He liked to try to point out all kinds of nature things to me.

"Some birds are flockers, Charlie, and some birds are loners," Dad said to me once. "Now, that hawk up there, wheeling around, he's a magnificent loner. Look how powerfully he flies. He just makes the whole blue sky his own." We watched the bird coast on a thermal up, up, up till he looked like a pinprick. Then down he swooped, like he was doing it just for fun.

Dad had looked at me then, and asked, "Are you a flocker or a loner, Charlie?"

I told him, "I'm a boy, not a bird," and Dad just smiled and almost ruffled my hair, before he remembered how much I hate that. Then we started walking back home so I could decontaminate myself. And inspect for ticks.

But while we were walking, Dad stopped me to say one more thing. "You like to make lists, right, Charlie? Well, here's a thought: Why don't we make a list together? Let's write down the names of all the birds we want to see out in the wild someday. Would you like that?"

I am not a fan of "out in the wild." So I just shrugged.

"All right!" Dad said. "I'll take that shrug as a yes! So, if you could choose any birds to put on our list, what would they be?"

I'd just read *The Trumpet of the Swan*, so I said a

trumpeter swan. And Dad said that it would be the coolest thing to see a bald eagle, and I should put that down.
He added sandhill cranes, because he'd heard that they
had an interesting, babbling call. We both thought great
horned owls should be on the list.

"You know what's also a cool bird?" Dad asked. "A
big old turkey vulture. People just don't understand the
importance of vultures to society."

He didn't have to tell me. I totally agreed.

"And maybe we should get a little ambitious with our
list, Charlie," Dad had said. "Let's get a little crazy. Let's
throw some really exotic bird on there, something totally
unique, strange, and different."

"Like what, Dad?"

"A wild card. Like an emu. Or even more crazy: a
passenger pigeon."

"Well, for one thing," I said, "emus live in Australia.
And passenger pigeons are extinct."

"Oh, I know, I know." Dad smiled. "We'll just put
them on there for the challenge. Don't you like thinking
that maybe anything could happen?

"When I was a kid in South Carolina," Dad went on,
"I remember hearing how, once upon a time, there were
tens of thousands of these little green parakeets living
in the fields around my house. Carolina parakeets. They
got hunted into extinction, because the farmers didn't

like them getting into the crops." Dad shook his head. "Still, when I was young, I'd always look for them in the woods. Just kind of hoping against hope, you know. It made life exciting."

"I already told you. You can't see extinct birds, Dad."

"I know, kiddo." Dad laughed softly. "I'm just talking through my hat."

That's an expression that means "impossible dreams."

When we got home, I wrote down all the birds we'd listed, even the impossible ones, in my Bird Book. Here is our Someday Birds List:

Bald Eagle
Great Horned Owl
Trumpeter Swan
Sandhill Crane
Turkey Vulture
Emu
Passenger Pigeon
Carolina Parakeet

One Australian bird, and two extinct birds on our list! Good grief. And we didn't put the red-tailed hawk on it, I think, as I look at my old drawing on Dad's hospital room wall. He's all too common around here, that loner, always circling the sky somewhere nearby.

My old hawk drawing on the wall is faded from all the San Diego sunlight that's been streaming in the hospital window since Dad got here in March. But the weather's gray and cloudy today. It's mid-June, and school just let out. In Southern California they call this weather "May Gray, June Gloom." It's super-sunny around here for most of the school year, and then, just when school's about to end, boom. June Gloom.

When Dad first got to the hospital, the doctors thought he'd be home by June. But nobody's talked about Dad coming home for a while. That's the real gloom hanging over this June.

I hear voices in the hall, then Gram steps back into the room. Davis stops reading. I leave the hand sanitizer alone, and we all look up and wait.

"Well, they finally told me the scoop," Gram says, rubbing her hands together like she's cold. "Your dad's stable now, which is wonderful. But he's a special case, and they're a little stumped. They're recommending we send him to a new place for a few weeks, where they can do much more specialized tests. Apparently, there's a bunch of big shot neurology experts in Virginia who are willing to take a gander at your father's noggin for free," Gram says, her voice cracking. She tries to smile, but it comes out kind of twisted. I can't read the visual cue on her face at all.

"It's a world-class research hospital. In Virginia." Gram takes a deep breath. "We sure as heck can't pass up an opportunity like this, now, can we? Isn't it great?"

Gram is teary. It doesn't make sense to say happy words like "Isn't it great" while your eyes are teary.

"*Virginia?*" Davis scrunches her nose.

"Just outside Washington, DC. He'll get top treatment there, honey. I'm going to start making the arrangements right now." Gram rustles in her purse for her phone. "Thing is, I think I'll probably have to leave you all, to go with him. He'll need me with him more than ever, being so far away."

"Virginia?" Davis repeats. She shakes her head back and forth in quick little jerks, like she's trying to shake Gram's words out of—or into—her brain.

"I know, honey-bunnies. It's another big change," Gram says, looking around at us all. "But it's the best decision for your father. And it's just for a few weeks. We'll find a way to make this work."

"Okay, Grammy," the twins say. They are standing perfectly still for once, shoulder to shoulder, eyes riveted on Gram.

I stick close by the hand-sanitizer dispenser. And Dad just sits in his chair, looking bewildered by everything. Which is pretty much how I feel most of the time these days, too.

4

For young birds and hatchlings, a nest that is
relatively safe from marauding intruders—both of the
four- and two-legged variety—is a matter of life and
death. Nothing is more important than that nest.
—Tiberius Shaw, PhD

They flew Dad to the special Virginia expert neurology place yesterday morning. Gram left with him, nagging Davis up until the last second to "Please be responsible" until Mrs. Bertolo could get here to watch us.

Davis said of course she would. But what do you think? The minute the cab left, she called Jonathan Dylan Daniels. And he has been sprawled on our couch eating Doritos ever since.

Oh, and Mrs. Bertolo never showed up.

Our house currently resembles an "Environmental Protection Agency Superfund Clean-Up Site." That's what Dad used to say when things got extremely messy around here. So I am staying in my bedroom with the door shut most of the time. At least it's clean in here, and I don't have to bump into Jonathan Dylan Daniels.

Jonathan Dylan Daniels is Davis's fourth boyfriend, but this time she says she's *really* in love. He is tall and hairy. He only ever talks to me when he has to. And then, he will only ever ask me, "How's it going, Charlie." And when I say "fine," he looks super-relieved and walks away. Plus, he bosses Davis around. "Hey, babe, could you get me this; hey, babe, could you get me that?" If I talked to her like that, she'd clobber me.

I wonder what it's like in Virginia.

I've never been outside California, except once to Colorado Springs for this stupid "Special Snowflake" camp Gram signed me up for as a Christmas present. Some present. It was basically a lot of clapping and useless awards. There was this song we had to sing: "*Every snowflake's special, and so . . . are . . . you!*" And they made us point to each other when we said the word "you!" If you ask me, snowflakes are nothing special. They melt. They're just water.

Out there far away across the whole country, in a place I've never seen, my dad's supposed to be having more and better tests of his brain. And he is starting something called *intensive rehabilitation*. Gram told us she's staying in a hotel right across the street from the new hospital.

"Good griefus," Gram said last night on the phone, "I don't know if I'm more frantic about your father, you kids, or poor Mrs. Bertolo!"

This is because on her way over here to take care of us, Mrs. Bertolo tripped over her grandson's skateboard in her driveway and broke her hip.

Gram freaked when she found out. She yelled, "Jesus H. Christ, will it never end?" Then she yelled at the twins over the phone, warning them that they better start keeping *their* skateboards off the dang driveway, as if Mrs. Bertolo's accident was somehow doomed to be repeated by Joel and Jake.

Now Gram's trying to find someone else who'd be willing to stay with us for a few weeks. And it isn't easy, because Mrs. Perry's in Florida at her sister's, and her friends Linda and Denise are on "one of those special cruises," whatever those are.

"It's too bad your mother didn't have any people," Gram says. She sighs about this every time she gets frustrated because she can't find a sitter for us.

By "any people," Gram means relatives. My mother had only one relative—her Tía Marta, who raised her and put her through college and medical school in Mexico City, which was where my mom was from, and where she met my dad, way back when. Davis says she can remember both Mom and Tía Marta. But the twins and I can't.

When Davis was five, I was two, and the twins were newborn, Mom was driving Tía Marta to an eye doctor appointment, and a drunk driver hit and killed them. I can talk about it totally fine, and it doesn't make me sad, because I was so little that I don't remember a thing. It's just a sad fact, to me. Gram says it happened in the middle of the day, which brings up another sad fact: drunk drivers strike at all hours.

Since then, it's been just my dad and Gram coming over from her old people community to take care of us when Dad goes on his magazine-writing assignments. Gram grumbles about it. She thinks single fathers should stay home with their kids, and protect the nest.

Also, we make Gram "bone-tired with all our shenanigans." Still, if we need her, she comes. Even though she likes to tell us it's like trading Peaceful Palms (which is the name of her retired community) for Casa Chaos (which is her name for our house).

Anyhow, while Gram tries to find someone to take poor broken-hipped Mrs. Bertolo's place, here at Casa Chaos, the dishes are piling up, the floor is sticky, and the living room smells like Doritos and old socks.

Actually, Doritos sort of smell like old socks.

Joel and Jake are on a gaming marathon and they haven't changed out of their pajamas since Friday. Their thumbs, orange from Dorito powder, fly on the controllers. *Click-click-click, kapow, bang, bang, click-click-click.*

I try to concentrate on drawing birds and writing in my Bird Book, but it doesn't calm me down at all. I go in the kitchen for a snack and see Gram's number, written in smudgy pen on a yellow Post-it note, stuck on the fridge.

I call it.

"Who's this? Charlie? Baby, when you call someone, you're supposed to start by saying 'hello.'"

I know that.

"Hi, Gram. This is Charlie."

"Well, *hello*, Charlie. How are *you*?"

"I am not so good."

"Oh no? Why?"

Hearing Gram's voice, I get a hot lump in my throat and my eyes burn. I am not sure where to begin. I want to ask about Dad, want to know how he is, if he's comfortable, if they are taking care of him, what his new room looks like, if they hung up my picture of the red-tailed hawk for him. Do people talk different in Virginia? Do the doctors look the same? Is there a gift shop?

But I can't get any words past the lump in my throat. Finally, I croak out the only thing I can: "Davis doesn't get how to microwave."

"Yeah? Tell me about it, sport."

"She made the chicken taste like a dried-out sponge. And Jonathan Dylan Daniels spilled Mountain Dew."

"Lordy, is *that boy* hanging around?" (Gram always calls Jonathan Dylan Daniels *that boy*.)

"Yes. He tells her 'Hey, babe, bring me another soda' and she does it. He puts his hand on her knee when they sit on the couch. You know what else?"

"Great heavens, what."

"The twins put Doritos in my bed. And they hid the soap, so now I have to use dishwashing liquid to wash, and the skin on my hands is starting to crack again."

I don't mean to complain so much. It all just comes out.

"Oh dear. Okay, Charlie boy. Sit tight. I'm gonna call someone right now to take control of that madhouse. I've got a last resort phone number here, and apparently I'm going to have to use it. Put your sister on the phone."

I yell upstairs, "DAVIS." She doesn't hear. I bring the phone up while Gram is still going at it:

"—And tell Davis to make sure the guest bed's still nice and neat," she says. I knock on Davis's door. "—coming to straighten you dang noodle-heads out," I hear.

Davis turns quickly from where she's sprawled across her bed, phone in hand. Her long brown hair whips across her face as she turns, and she's making her mushed-up-eyebrow face at me, a visual cue of anger that means: "How dare you barge in my room."

Davis and Dad used to give me mirror lessons, to instruct me about visual cues. "Look, Charlie," Davis would say, peering at us both in the mirror. "When my eyebrows smash together and my lips curl down like this? That's a visual cue. It means I'm in a crummy mood, okay? Visual cue, leave me the heck alone."

"Charlie! When will you ever learn to knock?"

I lob the phone onto Davis's bed. "Gram found a babysitter of last resort." I slam her door.

On my way back downstairs I hear Davis shriek, *"You've got to be kidding!"*

Gram does know some totally loopy old ladies. I wonder who she got.

5

An hour later, I find out. The twins, now joined by Jonathan Dylan Daniels, are clicking their controllers and grinding chips into the couch. Davis is upstairs, probably experimenting with her makeup or spraying her hair or something. I'm sketching a trumpeter swan into my Bird Book. I wanted to sketch him with his long neck outstretched, but the Audubon print I'm copying from only shows him with his neck all bent down by his feet.

Fun fact: Audubon painted his long-necked birds all contorted because otherwise they wouldn't fit on the paper. He had to make things fit the printer's page size. So a bunch of his long-necked birds are painted all hunched over, like they're squashed into invisible cages.

Which is a feeling I can sort of identify with.

Anyhow, I've just about given up on getting his long neck right, when I happen to look out the window, and there's a strange little gray car turning into our driveway.

My stomach does that washing machine chug-and-flip, like when the teacher says, "Take out your homework," and you realize you left it at home.

Behind the wheel of the strange car, I see a flash of shocking pink. Intruder-Gorilla pink.

Something tells me Davis is not going to like this.

6

*When you see a new and unusual bird, think like
a scientist. Be systematic. Note the crown, face,
throat, and body. Move from there to more subtle
qualities of voice and behavior.*
—Tiberius Shaw, PhD

Ludmila has a green leather dog collar with silver
studs strapped around her neck, and black lace gloves
with no fingers. She has leather shorts and black boots
with wobbly high heels. She is carrying a leopard suit-
case. Probably not real leopard, although you never
know. There are tattoos on her ribs—I can see them
through horizontal slashes in her shirt.

A guy riding by on his bike turns and stares at her.
He's wearing a skintight, bright yellow biking suit, so, to
be honest, I don't know why he's staring. His outfit's just
as strange as hers.

I don't understand why people wear weird, tight stuff
with buckles and belts and zippers and laces, when it's

so much more comfortable not to. I always wear plain T-shirts, no tags, collars, or buttons. Loose cotton sweats or shorts, no drawstring, buttons, or zippers. A pair of blue indoor Crocs, a pair of black outdoor Crocs. A perfect, simple system.

Ludmila is pretty much the opposite kind of dresser.

I open the front door and we stare at each other for a second. "You just smoked a cigarette," I say. I have a crazy-keen sense of smell. It is a burden, not a talent.

"I do not smoke. Hello, Charlie." Ludmila points a short, poison-green fingernail at me. She has thick black lines on top of her eyelids that flick up and out in three sharp lines at the corners, like how Dad drew eye pencil on Davis once when she was a cat for Halloween.

"Why are you wearing a dog collar?" I say.

She shifts her leopard bag again. "Don't worry, okay? I don't smoke. My roommate, she does. I yell at her for it. You smell that, really?"

We just stand there, looking at each other. I sniff the air a few times to make my point.

"Let me in, Charlie. I'm here to help out."

I hear Davis open her bedroom door a crack. She calls out in a high, tight voice that doesn't sound like her. "Hello? Who's there?"

I stare at Ludmila's dog collar.

"Charlie." She looks at me hard. I have a tough time

looking people in the eye, but somehow Ludmila sucks me into a hypnotic vortex. She might be some kind of witch.

"Your grandmother said come quick. Three boys out of control, young girl with boyfriend doing who knows what, emergency, emergency, house in uproar. So here I am."

She peers over my shoulder at the family room, where the twins and Jonathan Dylan Daniels are still on the couch, *click-click-clicking*. They haven't even looked up.

"I promise I don't bite." She smiles, and I notice pointy, crooked eyeteeth.

Maybe it's because she has put me into a witch's trance with her hypnotic vortex gaze. Or maybe it's because I am mad at Davis and the twins for ignoring me. Or because the house is getting more contaminated by the minute. Anyhow, I let her in and close the door.

Davis has finally come downstairs. She stands on the bottom step, a hand on her hip. "My grandmother has clearly made a mistake. Why would she call *you*?"

"Apparently, to supervise a madhouse," Ludmila says in her strange, husky voice, looking all around at the mess. Then she walks past Davis into the kitchen. She doesn't even take off her shoes. The rule is to take off your shoes. She looks around at the dirty dishes, the crumbs and clutter everywhere, Jonathan Dylan Daniels's collection of empty fast-food wrappers.

"Listen," says Davis, following. "We're fine, okay?"

Ludmila waves her arms around, flapping flustered hands, almost like I do.

Davis's mouth is opening and shutting but she isn't saying anything.

Jonathan Dylan Daniels comes into the kitchen, his eyes half closed, scratching his stomach—until he sees Ludmila. Then his eyes open wide.

"Well, hello, there," says Jonathan Dylan Daniels to Ludmila, standing up straighter and smiling. "How's it going?"

Davis's face gets even redder.

Ludmila scrunches up her eyebrows at him. "You, sir, are going. Now." She takes him by the shoulders and spins him around so that he's facing the front door. "Good-bye!"

Davis's mouth is hanging open. She starts making little gasping sounds. Finally, she says, "You can't tell him to leave. You have no right!"

"I have every right," says Ludmila, looking down at Davis. With her deep voice, spiky hair, spiky collar, and spiky heels, she is tall, and mean, and scary. And spiky.

When the front door clicks shut on Jonathan Dylan Daniels, Ludmila goes to the TV and turns off the game, just as Jake was about to win his level. There is a flurry of orange cheese dust.

"HEY!" both twins shout at the same time.

Ludmila hands them the garbage pail. "Time to clean up, boys. And you. Charlie. Please to show me the guest room."

I look at Davis, but she is still standing there, making gasping goldfish noises. So I show Ludmila to Dad's office, where Gram had left the pull-out couch all made up nice and neat for poor old Mrs. Bertolo. Ludmila puts down her old cigarette-smelling leopard bag on what was supposed to be poor old Mrs. Bertolo's pillow.

Davis wants Dad's office to stay exactly the way he left it, so it's ready for him to work in again, when he gets better. She has his favorite coffee mug on his desk. His pencils sharpened. His green grading pens (he never uses red ink) at the ready. The rest of the house is a disaster, but Davis dusts in here. She didn't even want poor old Mrs. Bertolo to stay in here.

"Seriously?" Davis shouts. "First you take over my dad's hospital room, and now you take over our house? You think you're staying in his *room*?"

Ludmila sits down in Dad's desk chair. She looks tired. She swivels around to face Davis. "I forgive your rudeness," she says. "These are tough times, no?"

Davis's eyes bulge out a little bit. Then she explodes

into this weird screaming noise and waves her arms around uselessly, sort of like a T. rex imitation. Then she stomps away upstairs.

Ludmila takes off her thick black glasses, rubs her eyes. I notice the *Amar* tattoo on her hand has healed up, in the weeks since we first met her. The wings and hearts look like they've been curling around her wrist forever.

Davis says *amar* means "to love" in Spanish. There's nothing much to love about Ludmila, though.

She runs her hands over Dad's desk and the shelves above it, full of journalism awards, photos of students, photos of us, stacks of messy folders. She picks up one of my favorite photos of Dad. She touches his face with her poison-green fingernail, and then puts the photo carefully back. "Nice room," she finally says. "Lucky kids, to have nice father. Nice house."

Something about the way she says it—something about the way she touched Dad's face in the photo with her finger—it just doesn't seem right, even to me. Maybe Davis's suspicions are correct. Maybe there is something strange going on, with this already strange Ludmila person. Should we worry about having her here? Was Gram right or wrong to send her?

Something's wrong. It is. But I can't put my finger on it.

7

Bird migrations start with a single bird. One little creature senses that conditions have changed, something is off, not quite the same in their world, and it is time to be on the wing. Once a single bird senses it, the others quickly join in, as if destined to follow.
—Tiberius Shaw, PhD

After it gets dark, I put away my sketch of the trumpeter swan and wash up as usual, *soap-rinse-one-soap-rinse-two-soap-rinse-three-soap-rinse-four-soap-rinse-five-soap-rinse-six*, and repeat. I get into my clean pajamas and settle in between my left and right pillows, lying straight down the middle of my bed, the covers pulled up evenly to my chin. If I just keep doing it this way every night, with no variation, no change, then the odds are better that Dad will get better.

I doze off right away. I am just starting to dream I am a little green bird, gliding over the water of a marshy glade, looking down at the tops of pine trees . . .

Then, my super senses detect a disturbance in the Force.

There's someone in my room, poking my arm.

The rule is: no one touches me without my permission. Everyone knows this. If I don't have enough warning before a touch, I'll jump out of my skin.

So I flail out with my hand—and hit something warm and soft.

"Ow! Jesus, Charlie!" I hear Davis's hoarse whisper in the dark. "You just punched me in the face!"

"Whaaa?" I am still half thinking I am a green dream-bird.

"News flash, we're winging it out of here, kiddo. I already packed your clothes."

Wait. I must still be dreaming.

"Jon's parked his car just down the block. We've got to sneak out super quietly. Here are your clothes. Get dressed quick."

I rub my eyes. "What are you talking about?"

Davis sits on my bed and makes the whole mattress slope down. I hate it when she does that. "I'm talking about a road trip. Why should we be stuck thousands of miles away from Dad, with that—that—evil witch?!

Because Ludmila is evil, Charlie. She's got some hidden agenda. I've been spying on her. She's been snooping around down there. She's been looking at all of Dad's old photos, and crying! Who does that? What kind of strange—I mean, who the heck is she, anyway? The whole thing gives me the creeps. I'm not gonna stay in this house with her."

I don't say anything.

"Why does she have to stay in his office? It's a total invasion of privacy. Who knows what she'll do? It's one thing to rifle through his photos. Next, she could decide to go through his private papers, or his computer files!"

I still don't say anything.

"Well, I'm taking action. I'm protecting Dad. When she went to wash up, I saved most of his work files on this." She waves a flash drive under my nose.

"What?"

"Also, I locked his file cabinet and took the key. I mean, he's defenseless, and she's *in his office*!" Davis says. "She could be some kind of Russian spy."

I think about this. It seems unlikely.

"She's got Gram wrapped around her finger. What right does she have to be in Dad's office? And what right does she have to kick out *Jonathan?* Really!" Davis's voice gets totally shrill when she says Jonathan's name.

I am too tired for this.

But she whips the covers off of me. "So, Charlie, come on, get your stuff." She turns on my desk lamp and I wince. "Ludmila's fast asleep. Now's our chance. And we're leaving. We're all of us going to drive to Dad and Gram."

"Davis, that's crazy!"

"No, it's not. It's totally within reason. Jonathan's a great driver. He drove to Michigan all by himself last summer; he's good on the highways; he's eighteen already, anyhow. And I have my debit card and my phone. We could be with Dad and Gram before you know it."

Davis knows there are two very important things about me. They are: I hate change. And I hate travel.

"Charlie, come on. The twins are already out in the car."

I pull a pillow over my head.

"Charlie! It'll be fine. *You can do this thing.*"

I pull another pillow over my head.

"You can wash your hands as many times as you want. We'll only stop to eat where *you* want. We'll be very quiet in the car." She is whispering louder, and faster. She pulls on my arm and leg so that I slump over and slide— *kerthunk*—onto the floor.

"If you don't come now, Charlie, I swear to God, I'll—I'll take toilet water and sprinkle it all over your bed. I'll contaminate your shoes. I'll put dog poop in your bird folders. I'll—I'll—"

"Stop. Wait. Did you say the twins are *already in Jonathan's car?*"

She nods. "I knew we had to wake you last. We're all packed."

I swing my legs out of my comfortable, perfect bed. I look around quickly. I make sure my supply backpack is stocked with my soap, special towel, antibacterial wipes, Kleenex, and my *Star Wars* Velcro wallet stuffed with money and my old school ID card in it, even though it's expired. I leave the Audubon baby elephant folio behind.

I add in some clothes. Grab my favorite pillow. Most importantly, I pack my Bird Book and sketching pencils.

Dad once asked me if I was a flocker or a loner. Well, I guess for now I'm a flocker, because Davis has already gotten her clutches into my brothers, and I'm not staying here alone. If I am going to keep us all together, there is only one thing I can do, and it's to follow Davis quietly, fearfully, out to the car.

8

No one knows for sure why birds fall silent when
their cages are covered. All we know is that they do.
—Tiberius Shaw, PhD

When I ride for a long time in a plane or a car, I conk
out. Dad and Gram used to think I was actually fainting
dead away, but I wasn't. I just shut down my systems to
avoid sensory overload. And barfing.

I'm out for hours, in the backseat of Jonathan Dylan
Daniels's grubby old Honda CR-V surfer car. It smells
crabby, like low tide, and there's sand in the cracks of
the upholstery that stick to the backs of my thighs. My
neck has that tired ache, and I can vaguely sense that I'm
drooling now and then. But gradually, after eons, heat
starts seeping into my brain. It starts to coat my skin and
glaze my glued-shut eyes. The light's different now—
under my eyelids it's not black anymore, but bright red

and pulsing. Too bright to sleep. Too bright to pretend to sleep. Too . . . hot.

I open my eyes to a glaring, beige world. Sand stretches away, flat as a pancake, on both sides. San Diego's palms and flowery plants are history. The world is now a parched, pulsing desert.

"Where are we?" Davis stretches and yawns, then rests her hand on the back of Jonathan Dylan Daniels's head and strokes his hair with her fingers.

Ick.

"Almost to Vegas, babe. Gimme your card; we gotta get gas." He jerks the wheel and we jolt onto crunchy gravel toward the big red ball sign of a 76 gas station. Heat waves ripple off the top of bright orange pumps.

Jonathan Dylan Daniels hops out and holds out his hand for Davis's card, then slides it through the pump slot. The twins are starting to rouse in the back. He raps on their window. "Yo, little buds. You gotta pee, do it now."

Joel raps back. "Hey! I can pump the gas, Jon," he says. "Want me to? I know how; my dad taught me."

The twins think Jonathan Dylan Daniels is so cool. Once, he brought over a whole stack of M-rated games and they played for hours while Gram was in the kitchen making cookies. Gram had no idea what was going on. Dad would never have let them play those games. Dad says once an act of bad violence is stuck in your head, you can't un-see it or ever get it out of there. So you have to be very, very selective about what you decide to allow into your brain.

Jonathan Dylan Daniels thinks I'm an old grandmother. A priss. He said exactly that to Davis once, said, "Hey, why's your brother such a priss?"

Priss.

Old grandmother.

Kook.

Droid.

Lysol Louie.

Charlie.

Nerd.

I go by a lot of names, because no one really knows me that well.

"We're almost to Vegas!" says Davis, smearing gunk on her lips from a little pink plastic container. "Let's stop off, just to drive through and see it! No reason why we can't enjoy the trip, right? We could pretend it's a family vacation—Jon and I will be like the parents and you guys will be like our kids!"

Even the twins gag and groan.

"No, really!" She smiles, and tiny sparkles in her pink lip gloss glisten.

But she has dark, tired skin under her eyes, and so

does Jonathan Dylan Daniels, who's actually been the one doing all the driving.

"Does Gram know?" I say. "When do we get there? Did you call Gram? Will she have to get an extra hotel room for us or something?"

Davis looks at me from the visor mirror, where she's putting a tiny wand of black stuff on her eyelashes. Mascara. Like from the word *mask*.

"Don't worry, Charlie. We've got a ways to go first. I'm gonna talk that over with her real soon," she says.

Jonathan Dylan Daniels gets back in and chucks a bag of Twizzlers to Joel and Jake. He doesn't give anything to me.

We keep driving and driving and driving and driving through the hot beige wasteland, listening to horrible drum-bashing radio music . . . And then, a few billboards start cropping up. A few more. Billboards showing fancy-dressed people laughing around a casino table. Billboards showing magicians, and sequin-dressed singers, and the American flag.

Finally, the city of Las Vegas just kind of rises up out of the sand. One minute you are in this big, monotonous desert, nothing but beige. And then: bam! You're on this big wide fancy boulevard, with all sorts of sights clamoring for your attention.

"Look! The Eiffel Tower!" Davis says. "I've always wanted to go to Paris!"

"I'm hungry!" says Joel.

"This is Vegas—not Paris—right?" Jake asks, and Joel shoves him.

"How could it be Paris, you dork?"

The twins look sweaty. Their eyes are big and round. Something about them seems much younger this morning.

Jonathan Dylan Daniels keeps driving. There are these huge fountains, giant walls of water spurting up and down in different rhythms and colors. And plazas, and sculptures, and huge hotel entrances—all this stuff jumping in front of your eyes. And it's still early in the morning, just past dawn, so there's practically no one out yet. All this "look at me look at me!" craziness is competing for the attention of hardly anyone right now.

"Hey, check it out!" Joel shouts. "That guy's puking!" Sure enough, on the sidewalk up ahead, near a bar, a businessman in a rumpled suit is on his hands and knees.

"Ugh, his tie is hanging in it!" Davis says.

We're still shouting "eewww," when we notice a runner, a lady, rounding the corner. She's so busy fiddling with her headphones and trying not to break her stride, that she doesn't notice the puking guy. At the last second, she decides to hurdle over his back. She leaps high in the air and lands, stumbling, on the other side of him.

Everyone thinks this is hilarious, and they're laughing and clapping and looking back down the street, and that's when Jonathan Dylan Daniels doesn't notice something. He doesn't notice that there is a huge, black, truck fender, looming into view in his driver-side window, about to hit us.

THE FLIGHT
of the
BAR-TAILED GODWIT

9

BAM!

A jolt.

Time stops while the car silently spins.

We land backward, halfway up the curb, just past a sushi bar. I peer forward through the cracked windshield and notice we are facing the wrong way down the wide Las Vegas boulevard. I crane my neck sideways; someone is running toward us. It's the jogging hurdler lady. I don't know how to describe her face.

A weird feeling. A sick feeling. A few other cars pull into view in the small area of cracked windshield. Their car doors open. I can't see Davis's or Jonathan Dylan Daniels's faces. Just two big white air bags.

A car alarm is going off. Maybe it's ours. A strange man is yanking open our doors and yelling, "Don't move! Just answer if you're okay!"

Davis says yes in a super-high, needling kind of voice. The twins are crying, but they manage to say, "Yeah, uh-huh!" I say, in a hoarse, weird voice that doesn't seem like me: "Yes. I am okay." Jonathan Dylan Daniels groans.

A siren.

We are surrounded by EMTs. They yell, "Stay where you are! Don't move!" It's like we're in a police drama. But they just want to examine our medical situation thoroughly before they let us out of the car. Which they eventually do.

Davis's face floats next to me, so white—except for a big purple mark on the side of her forehead.

I am angry at her. So angry I don't know what to do with what I am feeling. The twins come and stand next to us. They are shaky and pale, but okay. Just very silent.

Joel suddenly turns and throws up all the Twizzlers he'd eaten at the gas station, right there onto the sidewalk. That's the second puking I've witnessed this morning.

EMTs take Jonathan Dylan Daniels out of the car and help him get on a stretcher. He is complaining. "I'm fine! Really man, this is . . . ," he starts to say, but his voice sounds half swallowed. Then he stops protesting when he sees his arm. We all stop when we see his arm. His left hand is bent from his wrist at a weird angle and there is a really strange-looking bone-lump under the skin. Also, the left side of his face is starting to swell up.

"Whoa, dude!" says Jake.

The trucker who hit us comes over. He is the biggest person I have ever seen. He seems completely fine—not a scratch. "Thank God you stopped in time," an EMT says to him.

More paramedics and firefighters appear out of nowhere. They look us all over, tell us how lucky we are, a glancing blow, how good that we were all buckled in. No one is seriously hurt except Jonathan Dylan Daniels, who is being loaded into a small ambulance. An EMT guy is helping Joel wipe Twizzler-puke off his face, giving him water.

A policeman is talking to Davis, who is by the curb now, her arms crossed over her chest, shivering, even though it is a really hot morning. It looks like the policeman is asking her questions, but she is not answering.

"Where are your parents?" That is what the one policeman is asking, but Davis only scrunches up her face funny. "I need to call somebody to tell them what happened to you. If you don't give me a number, I'm calling social services to come get you. So can you talk to me, please, miss? Who should I call?"

Davis is whimper-crying and staring at Jonathan Dylan Daniels's stretcher, which is disappearing into the ambulance.

I walk over to the policeman, calm and quiet, like I am in a movie about myself. I stare into the officer's mirror sunglasses, and tell him the only number I know by heart. Gram made me memorize it only a few weeks ago, when she found out I didn't know any of my contact information. "Jesus H. Christ, Charlie," she'd said. "What if there's an emergency?"

It wasn't hard to memorize. It's no problem to tell him our home phone number. I can see it like it's burned in the air, right in front of me.

10

No one would guess, looking at this unassuming little shorebird, the astounding long distances he's willing to travel.
—Tiberius Shaw, PhD

Jonathan Dylan Daniels's family doesn't have insurance, so he wouldn't let the EMTs bring him to a fancy expensive Vegas hospital. We went to a free clinic almost out of town, far away from the strip. In the crowded urgent care, I can hear people arguing in Spanish, medical equipment clanging and beeping, a vacuum cleaner, phones. It smells like toilet cleanser and machine oil.

Jonathan Dylan Daniels is pretty much all right, except for a new, bright blue cast up to his elbow, and a black eye. His face is all twisted-looking. Which is either because he's in pain, or because Davis and he are having a huge fight. Or both.

I tug at my sister's shirt, but she pays no attention. I

want to tell her that the twins got sick of waiting around in this place, and they've completely disappeared, and I'm worried.

The police left us here in the care of this lady who is a registered social worker. She filled out a bunch of forms and made a bunch of phone calls, and then she told us we're supposed to stay *right with her* until an adult comes for us. We're supposed to stick tight and wait for our ride. But about an hour after she said that, the social worker lady got an emergency phone call that sounded way worse than our emergency. Now, she's nowhere to be found.

And the twins are gone.

And Davis doesn't seem to care. She is only interested in yelling.

"We should have left your stupid brothers behind," Jonathan Dylan Daniels says.

"Like it's their fault that you *hit a truck*?" Davis shouts. She has something called a "butterfly" bandage on a little cut on her temple. It is not as pretty as it sounds.

They hurt my ears, so I leave them to go look for Joel and Jake. The sidewalk outside the clinic is filthy: there's cigarette stubs and dented old beer cans and dirty, soggy old plastic bags. It's quiet, though. Despite everything that's happened to us so far, it's still pretty early in the morning. We've only been gone from home about seven or eight hours, which is almost impossible to believe.

Where are my brothers?

"JOEL! JAKE!" I call down the street.

Nothing. My stomach feels strangely tight.

Where did my brothers go?

11

*If I study bird behavior, I am hoping I will
eventually increase my understanding of
human behavior as well.*
—Tiberius Shaw, PhD

I wander down the street, calling and calling for Joel
and Jake.

A few doors away, I see a shabby junk shop with a
dirty front window. Above the door is a big old-fashioned
sign, with two black crows painted on it, along with the
words: *Twa Corbies Curiosities.*

My brothers love junk. Maybe they went in here.

Twa corbies means "two crows." It's from an old Scot-
tish poem—I learned this because Dad's an English
teacher, and learning boring poetry trivia is what Dad
calls an "occupational hazard" of having to be his kids. I
don't mind, really. In the poem, two black crows plan on

how they're going to eat the body of some dead guy in a ditch. Pretty creepy stuff.

Most people think corvids, such as crows and ravens, are scary death symbols. But what they don't realize is how smart and cool corvids actually are. For example, they have incredibly long memories. If you hurt a crow, it will remember your face, or the shirt you were wearing at the time, and avoid you every time it sees you again. Every single time. Forever. I like this fact a lot, because I, too, have an incredibly long memory.

Also, I read about this crow incident that happened in Ontario, Canada. Hundreds of thousands of crows would migrate through this one small town, and they'd cause such an awful ruckus, that one year the townsfolk decided to have a crow-hunting day to try to shoot them and get rid of them. Well, one hunter shot one crow. ONE CROW. And guess what happened then? Every other crow flew off—and get this: they stayed away, *forever*. Talk about "getting the message." Those hundreds of thousands of crows somehow got the word out to each other never to fly over that particular unfriendly town ever again. They all changed their whole migration pattern, forever. Because one single crow got hurt.

I wish flocks of people would look out for each other like that.

Also, there's this girl in England who has been feeding the crows around her house, every day, for years. They are grateful for the food, so they leave her gifts. They bring shiny little bits of broken glass and beads and stuff, as if to say thank you. She has boxes full of crow-gifts.

Seriously. Crows.

So. The Twa Corbies. Curiosities. Junk. My brothers. I open that shabby, creaking shop door and go in.

"Joel?" I whisper. "Jake?"

Nothing. It's totally silent in here. Behind a tall wooden desk, no sign of anyone.

There aren't even aisles in this junk shop. It's crammed to overflowing with boxes and books, crates of old dishes, glass cases of jewelry, rickety chairs. A mangy old stuffed raccoon sits on a shelf, his marble eyes dead and dusty. For some reason I don't like, that makes me think about Dad.

In the back room, a giant stuffed raven with sleek black wings sits on a top shelf. I get the feeling that wherever I turn, he's looking at me. Below him is a wall of old, dusty books. Each shelf has a category: Biographies. Nevada history. The Wild West. Philosophy, Another wooden crate of dusty old books sits on the floor.

On top of a random pile in the crate something catches my eye: it's a faded green book, with a gold feather painted on the cover.

I've seen that particular gold feather before. On the old yellow card, by the birds on the shelf in the hospital gift shop.

That gold feather looks like the logo of *Legendary Ornithologist, Artist, and Philosopher, Tiberius Shaw, PhD.*

I pick up the book and crack open its dusty spine. On the first page is an old, faded pencil sketch of a mallard duck.

Mallards are the most common duck in America, you know. People ooh and ah when they see their shiny green heads, but they are really no big deal. Sometimes the most exotic-looking things are common underneath, and the most boring-looking things turn out to be rare.

An old bookmark is stuck in the pages: it shows the same photo as back in Ellie's hospital gift shop! Brown leathery skin and white tufted eyebrow wings. Underneath the photo, it says:

One of this nation's foremost authorities on ornithology and human nature, birds, and mysticism, the reclusive Dr. Tiberius Shaw, PhD, lives, writes, sculpts, and paints from his abode within the world-famous Sanctuary Marsh in the state of Virginia.

I turn to the first page in the journal, and get a shiver. In neat handwriting that's not too different from my own Human Typewriter lettering, in old blue ink, are words that—could it be? Yes, it could!—words that must be—*have* to be—from the very hand and pen of Dr. Tiberius Shaw, PhD, himself:

> *Dec. 26, 1969*
> *If I study bird behavior, I am hoping I will*
> *eventually increase my understanding of human*
> *behavior as well. . . .*

My heart leaps. I hug the book tightly and jump up and down. I feel shock pangs leaping through my veins, but in a good way. What a find! I can't believe it. I know my mission right now is to find my brothers, but I have to take a minute out to buy this book. I run to the wooden counter, clutching the green journal.

A dusty old shopkeeper dodders out of the darkness of the back room. He looks like a wax figure—bald, with wisps of white hair. I hand over my treasure, and he turns it around in his skeletal hands, peering at it, frowning. I feel breathless while it's out of my grasp. I need that book back. Now.

He holds it out at arm's length, peering. He gets out a pair of rimless glasses. The suspense is killing me. His mouth hangs open with the effort of trying to find a price. I can almost see my heart knocking against my T-shirt.

I whisper a prayer that it costs less than a dollar. I only have the money that's in my pocket. I left my backpack with Davis in the clinic!

He says, "Well, this is an interesting old volume."

I swallow and nod.

The shopkeeper peers at me, opens the book up to the middle somewhere, reads something to himself, murmuring. I can see yellow snaggleteeth in his wrinkly lipless mouth. Then he suddenly snaps the book shut. "That'll be a dollar."

I gasp, and hand over all my change, weak with relief. When he hands me the book and I am able to hug it to my chest again, it's like it helps free up my words. "Please, sir," I say, "did you maybe notice some ten-year-old twin boys around here?"

His mouth is a squirmy line. "I happened to, yes. I kicked them out for knocking over a display about ten minutes ago." He drops my coins, one by one, into an ancient cash register. "You just missed them."

I leave, clutching the journal. Tiberius Shaw actually wrote the words inside this book! Just like I have my Bird Book, Tiberius Shaw, when he was young, had this green journal with the gold feather that he, himself, probably painted on the front! This very one! His private book! How could they sell this thing? Where did they get it? Well, I can hardly believe it.

I know I still have to find my brothers. But I can't help stopping to sit on the bench outside the shop to just flip quickly through a few pages.

> *My heart's home in Sanctuary Marsh is precisely two miles north of the old visitor center, beyond water inlets that stretch fingerlike into the sanctuary. . . . It is on a knoll, a small hill covered in old-growth pine, oak, and maple, and from that vantage point I look out over the purity of Nature. You'd never know you were so near the corruptions of the capital, mere miles away. . . .*

First I found Shaw's statues at the gift shop.

Then Dad got moved to a hospital that's super-close to Shaw's sanctuary.

Now I am holding Shaw's old journal. His personal journal.

I can't believe in all these coincidences. If I didn't know better, I'd say that it's almost like Shaw's been trying to reach out to me or something. But of course, that's just crazy-weird.

I flip a few more pages, and notice a little pencil sketch of a shorebird. It's very similar to a sketch I did once, of a sandpiper. But this bird's bigger, with a longer beak. It's a beautiful sketch, better than I can do. And underneath, in his careful lettering, it says:

> The little bar-tailed godwit, without breaking for food or drink, will fly seven thousand miles in nine days, from Alaska to New Zealand, as if it is nothing. What stunt of bird bravery is this? His tremendous urge to join family and flock is stronger than any wind or current. It is stronger than anything. And so we should ask ourselves: What can the godwit teach us about our own connection to home?

12

I finally found them. It took me ten more minutes of frantic shouting down every single side street, to locate Joel and Jake, but I did it. Then, we all went to find our social worker lady in the clinic, but she was still gone on her big emergency. The nurse in charge didn't even care. She just told us to "take that mangy beast outside."

More on the mangy beast in a minute.

So now, we're all of us piled on a bench outside the clinic, waiting. Davis has just broken up with Jonathan Dylan Daniels, so she is either sobbing into her hands or staring into space. She seems too upset right now to keep us safe, or deal with hard reality at all. She just stares, and cries.

And about that mangy beast. Apparently, while I was in the Twa Corbies and Davis was breaking up with Jonathan Dylan Daniels, the twins found a little black and white pup tied to a rope in someone's weedy, overgrown lot. There was a sign, written on a piece of scrap cardboard in thick black marker: *Free to good owner.* It looked like both the sign, and the dog, had been there a long time.

There was a metal bowl with an inch of warm water, and ants swimming in it.

A scruffy old guy came out of the house. He told the boys how it had been his nephew's dog, and they could just untie and take him, "If it was okay with their mama." The twins said it sure definitely was.

The old guy gave them a bag of stale kibble, and the leash, and the metal bowl. Joel and Jake washed the ants out with a hose, and gave the dog fresh water right then and there. "You should've seen him. He drank and drank and drank," Jake said.

The dog is white, with cow-patches of wiry black and brown fur. He's got a snub nose and warm brown eyes. He seems glad to be with us. His tail is wagging like mad as he leans against the twins' knees. Also, he may be leaning against them for support, because he only has three legs. The back left one is missing from clear up by the hip bone. Whatever caused it must have happened long ago. It's all healed up. Or maybe he was born that way. He doesn't seem to mind having three legs, anyway. He seems totally used to it, like it's no problem whatsoever.

The dog twitches an ear, then bares his teeth at me in this weird grimace, while wagging his tail. He wags so hard, he throws himself off balance and almost falls over.

"That's a smile!" shouts Jake. "He's smiling at Charlie!"

"No accounting for taste," says Joel.

We have all wanted a puppy for years. But especially Joel and Jake. They spend hours watching dog videos all the time. Joel likes big dogs; Jake likes small dogs. They love to argue about what kind of dog they'd get, if they could get one. It's one of their favorite twin-conversations.

They have some dog-care experience, too. The Blanco family, down the street, started asking them to dog-sit their two black poodles, Punch and Judy, this year. The Blancos skipped right over asking me to dog-sit. They went right from asking Davis, to asking the twins. I don't know why they thought I couldn't take care of Punch and Judy. I would have done a great job. I love dogs, too. I would have been a very careful dog-sitter.

"Hey, Davis," the twins say. "He's smiling at you now!"

"Uh-huh," Davis mumbles, stares off into the

distance. Her eyes have black-mask smears of mascara around them. I remember early this morning at the gas station, when she had that sparkly lip-gloss smile. Nothing's very glossy about Davis anymore.

The dog shows his tiny little teeth and lolling pink tongue, waiting for Davis to get happy. Wag. Wag wag. But Davis keeps staring at nothing.

"The dog can be in the car with us; no problem, right?" says Joel.

"God, it smells," says Davis, waving her hand back and forth.

"It's not an it," says Jake. "It's a him."

"What are we gonna name him? How about Dr. Who?" says Joel.

"That's stupid," says Jake.

"You're stupid," says Joel.

"Shut up," says Jake, tightening his grip on the leash.

Davis slumps over on the bench and puts her head back in her hands for some more quiet sobbing.

I don't say anything. I just hold on to Shaw's green journal, tracing the gold feather on the cover with my finger, over and over and over.

A long time goes by before finally, down the road at the far traffic light, we see a small gray car appear. It looms up and lurches to a stop right in front of us. The door flings open, and a red-eyed, messy-haired Ludmila stumbles out.

"Well. So here are the runaways."

She puts her hands on her hips and looks at Davis. "Very smart, young lady. You take your brothers for little trip?"

Davis just turns her head away.

Joel speaks up. "We were going to go see Dad. Jon said he'd take us," he says in a higher, whinier voice than usual. Joel is sitting on the pile of our backpacks, the dirty three-legged dog snuggled in his lap. "Davis and Jon. They said they'd take us on an adventure, to go be with Dad. That everything would be fine. But then? Well, then . . ."

Ludmila stares at the dog like she's not sure what it is. "I know what happened after that. You all okay? You? You? You?" She points at each of us in turn, and we nod, to answer her, one by one.

"Okay, then," Ludmila says. "You're safe and ready for your grandmother to KILL YOU!"

There's total silence. The dog whines, but Ludmila ignores it. She grabs her phone out of her jeans pocket and jabs a number in with her finger. Then she thrusts the phone out to Davis. We can hear Gram's tiny, faraway voice already shouting through it. She sounds like an angry bee, buzzing and fussing. Davis fits in quicks uh-huhs, yesses, and sorry, Grams. The whole time, tears are sliding out of her eyes.

Meanwhile, Ludmila goes back around to her little car and opens her trunk. She crams as many of our bags in there as she can fit.

"How long will it take us to get home?" I ask. I can't wait to be in my safe, clean room again. To fall asleep for a long, long time and forget about all this.

Ludmila turns, a backpack in each hand. "We are not going home, Charlie," she says, and juts her chin toward Davis, crying on the phone to Gram.

"Then where are we going?" I say, panic starting to squeeze in my throat.

Ludmila doesn't answer. Davis has come to hand back her phone. "I'm—I'm sorry, okay?" Davis hiccups, staring at the sidewalk. "I'm supposed to say I'm sorry for the trouble. And that we'll be good. And thanks for taking us." She sniffs at every other word.

"Wait. Taking us where?" I ask. My stomach is suddenly cold with doubt. I am shaking my hands. I realize I am jumping up and down, up and down.

"To Virginia." Ludmila points to some huge duffel bags strapped to the little gray car's roof. "See? Supplies. More clothes, camping gear. Your grandmother, such a nice lady, good person. She asked me to help, so I help. I bring you all to her. Even though I am not, what you say, a kids' person."

Wait. This is wrong. I've been waiting all this time to go *home*, to my safe, clean room, where I can finally breathe. This can't be happening! This can't be the plan!

My stomach goes into washing machine mode.

"In a few more days, you will be there with your dad. To face whatever comes next, good or bad, like a family together." Ludmila's eyes look like they are trying to lock a tractor beam onto my eyes from behind her smudgy glasses.

But I break that tractor beam. I burst out: "*NO! I want to go home!* I NEED to go home!"

Davis and the twins stare at me. The dog whines.

But Ludmila just opens the side door of the little gray car. "Sorry, kid. It's all decided. No more protests. No more crying. Just driving. Everyone in. It's a long trip and I want to get us somewhere special by midnight. Um . . . Do we have to take that dog? *Really?*"

And like it or not, off we go.

· GREAT HORNED OWL ·

GHOs

13

We have been driving forever in the smallest car in the world. I am next to Ludmila, and Davis is behind me. The twins are behind Ludmila, sharing one seat belt, and the dog is at the half-open window, half on Joel's lap, filling the whole car up with his stinky fish breath. We've just passed Salt Lake City. All our stomachs are growling. We're sleepy, but it's so cramped, our knees in our chests and our bags everywhere—no one could possibly conk out in here.

Jake keeps poking my shoulder, over and over, just to be annoying. I jerk forward, cross my arms, and stare at the ceiling of Ludmila's tiny car. It has beige fabric with this little pattern of three diagonal pinpricks, over and over, pingpingping, pingpingping, pingpingping. I stare at the pinpricks and think of the three stars in Orion's Belt, in the nighttime sky. Besides the Big Dipper, Orion's Belt is the only thing I can ever pick out, because the pingpingping is really bright.

I stare at those beige pinpricks and try to drown out everything else, until my eyes go blurry, or maybe even a little teary.

I think of home. I want to go home.

My room at home has a knotty pinewood ceiling. It's the color of warm honey, with swirls and lines in the grainy wood. Ever since I was a little kid, I've been staring up at that ceiling, and I can sort of make out things in it. I see silhouettes of people's faces. Images. I know that sounds weird.

The main one I look for, the one I greet on my ceiling every morning, is of my mom. I don't remember her personally, of course. But there's this ceiling swirl that looks just like her profile in Dad's favorite photo. It was taken in Mexico City, and she's wearing a doctor's white lab coat. She's got her dark brown hair combed back from her face. Her dark eyes are set kind of wide apart, and her nose is long and straight. She has a wide smile. My dad's in that photo, too, looking so different from her—tall and blond, with those smile-wrinkles around his eyes called crow's-feet that look nothing like crow's-feet.

Anyhow, if you look closely at this one spot on my ceiling, you'll see two pine knots like Mom's wide dark eyes, and between them brown wavy lines in the wood that resemble her nose, and the exact curve of her smile. That's what I look for, when I wake up in the morning.

Who knows when I'll ever get to see that ceiling again.

Ludmila said Gram told her the experts at the new hospital in Virginia are running many high-tech tests. That Dad's intracranial pressure is good. Things look good.

Davis is glad about things looking good. The twins are glad. The dog must be glad because his tail is always wagging; everyone seems glad.

How can they all just accept the word *good*? *Good* is a very vague word like *fine*. Basically meaningless.

Also, it seems like I'm the only one who wants to talk about Jonathan Dylan Daniels's car accident. Davis says not to ever mention his name again. The twins, it's like they've put it behind them. Not me. I can still feel the horrible, floating feeling of Jonathan Dylan Daniels's car spinning. Still hear the *BAM!* The crunch. When I close my eyes, I can still feel it happening, over and over. Each time, I flinch. Each time, I gasp.

"Don't you still hear it in your head?" I ask Davis. "The crunch? The *BAM?*"

"Shut up, Charlie," Davis mutters.

I look over at Ludmila. "Are you a safe driver?" I ask for the fifth time.

"Yes, Charlie," she says. "For the millionth time."

I don't like exaggerators.

We keep driving northeast, through most of Utah. I've never been to Utah. We pass the Great Salt Lake and Ludmila won't let us out of the car, because she keeps saying we are too much in a hurry to get to this mysterious place we have to stop at tonight.

But now, finally, we are all starving. We see a bunch of lit-up fast-food logos by an exit ramp, and that does it.

"FOOD! YES!" shout Joel and Jake at the top of their lungs, making the dog bark. "FOOD! NOW!!"

We pull off at a burger place that's super-bright, with overhead lights that chitter and flitter and hurt my eyes. Hideous pop music blares through the speakers. "I'm going to wash my hands," I tell Davis. "Get me the usual."

"Charlie," Davis says, sighing. "Order your own." She points to the order-taker people in their paper hats behind the counter. "They won't bite."

"Just order for me. Please?"

She shrugs her shoulders in defeat and goes to stand in line.

Yay!

I check out the window to make sure the dog is okay in the car. I can just see his nose sniffing at the inch of cranked-open window we gave him. "Sorry, dog," I whisper to him. "We won't be long. Promise. And I'll bring you a chicken nugget."

The restroom reeks of fake-flowery deodorizing spray. My eyes tear and my nostrils sting, but I get through twelve rounds of *soap-rinse-one-soap-rinse-two-soap-rinse-three* . . .

When I come back, the four of them are already munching, taking up a whole booth.

"I got your usual. Sit there, Charlie." Davis points to the booth behind them.

No problem. From here, I can see out the window better, to check on the dog. Plus, I like my own personal space.

I think about pulling out Tiberius's little green journal, but this is not a sacred enough place. I pull out my Bird Book instead, and start writing in it.

WHY WE SHOULD TURN AROUND AND GO HOME.
DAD WON'T KNOW THE DIFFERENCE.
LUDMILA'S CAR IS WAY TOO SMALL.

Dogs need yards to play in.
It's going to take forever.
Gas is expensive.
The Ludmila problem. (What if Davis is right? Why does she care so much about Dad? Why does she dress so strange?

This gives me an even worse thought, and my stomach churns. I nibble a nugget to calm myself, and write it down:

What if Ludmila is not to be trusted? What if she's fooled Gram into believing she's harmless, but really, deep inside, she has some kind of secret, underhanded plan?)

I scare myself so much with this shocking thought, I can't breathe for a minute. I slam my Bird Book shut and choke on my lemonade. We absolutely have to talk to Gram, so that we can ask her to explain why she thinks this total stranger's trustworthy and okay. Just like something Dad talked about once: "Trust, but verify."

My heart pounds. I lean over the seat and tap Davis on the shoulder.

"What is it, Charlie?" Davis has a little blob of white sauce stuck to her lip.

"We need to talk to Gram again, soon," I tell her. "Also, you need a napkin."

"We'll call her," says Davis. "Put away that book and eat."

The twins inspect my food arrangement. I always lay my chicken nuggets out in a neat horizontal row on my napkin. I like to see them displayed properly, waiting to be slowly consumed or rejected in order from largest to smallest.

I usually do quality control first. Flick off any overly brown or unacceptable bits. Then, if there's an even number of nuggets, I'll start eating left to right. If there's an odd number, I start in the middle, then work my way through, middle-left-right-left-right.

The twins tell Ludmila, "Look at what Charlie does."

Davis says, "And he's always writing in that notebook of his. I guess now, it's like his travel journal. He should probably call it 'Chicken Nuggets Across America.' Because that's all he ever eats." Everyone laughs. It's like they are trying to impress Ludmila by making fun of me.

Joel chimes in, trying hard to do a fake British accent. "The chicken nuggets of Las Vegas vary from the chicken nuggets of San Diego in a slight saltiness of breading," and Davis adds in, "There's a certain *je ne sais quoi* of crisp in the Nevada desert variety."

Ludmila's visual cue is unreadable.

"When can we talk to Gram?" I ask.

"In the morning, Charlie," Ludmila says.

"What's this burning desire to call Gram all of a sudden?" Davis asks.

(Because this lady could be taking us anywhere! Maybe you were right about her to begin with, Davis!) I can't say that out loud, but I try to beam it to Davis telepathically.

I inspect a nugget. There are too many little black flecks in this one, so I put it in the reject pile.

Ludmila is still staring at me with no facial expression. "Everything okay?"

I take a long slow sip of lemonade to try and un-lump my closed-up throat.

"The car's too small. The drive is too long. We should turn back." I am starting to feel like I can't breathe. Brain pressure. Maybe intracranial. My heart is pounding like a rabbit thumping in my chest, bursting to get out. My hands itch.

Davis scrambles out of her red plastic seat and comes over to sit next to me. "Charlie, come on," she says in her kindergarten-teacher, "let's calm Charlie" voice. "We've all been bending over backward for you, so come on now. Think of Dad. He's waiting for us there, in Virginia!"

"Yeah, Charlie," says Joel, his eyes wide.

I can tell the twins really want to believe everything is going to be okay. But when did Davis change from doubting everything about Ludmila, Intruder Gorilla, to trusting her?

I want to go home.

Ludmila is quietly collecting up all our paper garbage. "Well, Charlie's right about my car. It *is* too small for five people and a dog, for a cross-country drive. But don't worry—that's why we need to get to Wyoming."

Maybe she is going to kill us off, or sell us into slavery. We're pretty much at her mercy. Anything could happen. We are not safe anymore. And all I can do is keep my fears to myself, and wait and see.

14

Supposedly, in England, they have this expression: "Don't get your knickers in a twist." It's just a weird way of saying, don't get upset. *Knickers* is a British word for underwear.

Well, right now, my actual underwear is actually twisted, *and* I'm upset. Both of those things. "It's almost midnight!" I moan. "And my butt hurts! When are we going to stop?"

The twins are sleeping in back, curled up with Dog. He started out smelling like rotting fish. Now he smells like rotting fish someone left in a public porta potty overnight. I am gagging so bad, I'm riding with my head out the window.

"For crying out loud, the dog smells fine, Charlie," explodes Davis. "Shut the window!"

We keep on. My knees ache and the seat belt's dug a permanent rut into my neck and my back is screaming to be stretched. We've gone from sunny palm-tree San Diego, to flat, beige Nevada, to rocky red Utah, and now, in the growing dark, we're heading through low, rolling hills in Wyoming. Big herds of cattle graze just off the road. We come on a whole ton of them in a huge fenced enclosure that stretches at least half a mile. I didn't think this was humanly possible, but they maybe stink worse than the dog. I roll up the window fast.

"Phew! Ick! I can't believe that's how those poor things have to live," says Davis.

The disgusting, stinky cow prisons whizz past. Scrub pasture turns to rolling hills. It gets wilder, really big and empty, like the open space is just going to swallow up our car. The sun set behind us hours ago, but the moon's so bright, we can see silhouettes of pretty much everything.

And ahead looms the silhouette of a mountain, jutting up out of the darkening sky. Ludmila exits the highway and angles us toward it.

"Is that where we're going?" I wheeze. I am sick from all the bad smells and the disturbing cow prison.

She nods.

"I don't see why we couldn't just go home."

"I know, kid. Sometimes you don't get a choice."

We drive some more. The mountain doesn't seem any closer.

"Where is *your* home?" I ask her.

"San Diego, like you."

"No, I mean, like, where were you born? You talk with an accent. You were born somewhere else, right? Like, Russia?"

She snorts. "Russia, *kako glupo*!"

"What?"

She doesn't answer. A big bug splatters on the windshield. Ick.

"Okay, not Russia, so where?"

"I was born in a place that doesn't really exist anymore," she says as she tries to spray wiper fluid on the windshield to clean off the bug guts, but we're out. We watch them turn into big bug-gut window-smears. She curses, then starts to laugh.

"Okay, I'll tell you this. My brother was notorious for wasting windshield-wiper fluid. One teeny speck on the windshield, and he'd press the button and hold it down until blue liquid streamed all over the car. I hated this! So wasteful! He did it just to hear me yell. And he could never remember the English word for this windshield liquid, so he used to call it the *psssssht psssssht* fluid, you know, like the noise it makes when it comes up out of the dispenser. 'What do you know, we're out of *pssssssht pssssssht* again,' he'd say, and I'd say 'Well of course we are!' and it totally infuriated me. Amar loved infuriating me." She glances at Davis. "Maybe this is a brother thing."

"Well, we don't infuriate Davis," I say.

"No?"

I don't say anything for a while. The mountain looks a little bit closer. Then a lightbulb goes off in my head. I point at the tattoo on her right hand. "Did you get that because of your brother?" I ask.

She nods. "When things got bad, he always told me: 'Don't worry Mila, I'm your right-hand man, I'm always here for you." She shakes out her fingers and wrist, then puts her hand back on the steering wheel. "So this is where I put his name. On my right hand. My Amar."

I want to ask her if he's alive or dead. But something about her face makes the words stop in my throat.

15

*Each time a birder spots and identifies a bird, a
small connection is made between the two of them.
A new relationship is kindled—not just with the bird,
but with the whole natural world.*
—Tiberius Shaw, PhD

Finally, we're crunching over a gravel drive at the base of the dark Wyoming mountain. My bones feel numb, except for in my butt, which I can't feel at all. Crickets are chirping everywhere around us, and there's a misty chill sifting through my half-open car window.

Our headlights flash over a flat parking area to the right; we see a few other cars, an old RV, and a big machine called a Sno-Cat on giant caterpillar treads, half covered with a tarp.

"That's how they get up the mountain in the winter," she says, pointing to it. "In the warm weather, they use a four-by-four."

"Who's *they*?" asks Joel.

"Yeah," says Jake, yawning. "Where are we?"

Maybe she's bringing us to some scary cult headquarters or something. That's where cults are usually located: mountains. Kids at school were talking about this mountaintop cult near us in San Diego. It was a long time ago. The cult members wanted to hitch a ride on a comet, and they thought they had to kill themselves to do it.

Maybe this is some other type of horrible mountaintop cult she's bringing us to.

Boom, boom, boom, goes my heart. Chirp, chirp, go crickets. It is black-dark out.

Ludmila doesn't answer Joel's question. She walks away from us, pulls out her phone, and talks into it for a few minutes. Then, with her phone flashlight, she walks over to an old RV camper parked near the bushes, and shines her light along a faded-looking orange stripe on its side. She taps her fingers along the stripe, smiling, still talking.

The twins have tumbled out of the car with Dog on his leash. He limps around in circles, then starts sniffing under rocks. We're all glad to get out and stretch.

"Don't lose track of that dog in the dark," Davis says. "Hold on to that leash nice and tight."

"And don't let him sniff around too much," I add. "He could get ticks."

"And by the way," says Davis, "I'm sick of calling him

'that dog.' When are you going to name him already?"

Jake says "Popeye" and Joel says "Limbo" at exactly the same time. Then they start arguing. The dog barks.

"I give up," says Davis.

I'm glad they're making a lot of noise. Maybe it'll scare away any wild animals that might be lurking nearby. I bet there's bears. We're in the pitch-black, in the middle of nowhere. There must be bears. Or, at least, ticks.

"She'll be right down to get us," says Ludmila. We are standing in blackness, lit only by two light blue rectangles: Ludmila's phone, and Davis's. I shiver.

"*Who'll* be right down?" I ask.

Ludmila's voice says, out of the blackness, "It's a fun surprise. Just wait. You'll see."

In my past experience, the word *fun* has never had much to do with the word *surprise*.

Wait—Ludmila just used her cell phone! There's coverage!

"We need to call Gram. NOW."

Davis's voice says, "Charlie, it's two a.m. on the East Coast."

I feel so lost in this dark. Like I don't have a body, just a nervous system that's freaking out. "Then I want to speak to Gram *myself* first thing in the morning. She needs to know where we are."

"Of course," says Ludmila's voice from above one of the blue phone-lights. "There will be a lot to tell her about, once you get to the top."

(Like: We've been abducted into a cult by a Russian spy, and are being forced to catch a ride on a comet.)

The dog starts to growl, then bark. Something's coming. . . .

In a moment, we hear the low roar of an engine. Then, high-beam headlights slant down and around the lot like searchlights, and a big, black, muddy truck bursts into view. The cab door opens, the light goes on inside, and behind the wheel is the tiny head of an old lady. She's got short gray hair tufting out from under an old baseball cap. She puts the truck into park, hops down, and wraps Ludmila in a tight hug.

"I'm so, so, sorry about Amar," I hear the older lady whisper.

The right-hand brother. The tattoo. The *pssssshht pssssshht.*

Ludmila's back goes a little bit stiff at the words.

"Now," says baseball cap lady, turning her flashlight on us. "This gang must be, let's see. Davis, Joel and Jake or Jake and Joel—right? And of course this tall skinny young fellow over here is Charlie. Do I have it right?" We nod. "Well, come on. Time's a-wastin'!"

"Where are we going?" asks Joel, looking at the truck.

She points her finger up in the air. "Straight back up to the top. Assuming I don't drive the damn thing over the edge."

"What's at the top?" asks Jake.

"Didn't Ludmila tell you?"

We hoist ourselves up, and into the blackness we go. We growl around steep curves, so steep that if you look down, you can catch the headlights flitting quickly over tops of pine trees below us that look as small as flimsy green toothpicks.

I don't look down, after that glimpse. I glue my eyes onto the back of that lady's baseball cap.

Joel leans forward and yells out to her, "So . . . who are you?"

"Dr. Joan," she yells back. "Sit back and buckle in!"

"You're Ludmila's friend?" he asks.

"Yup. Long story," she says. Then, suddenly, she points up out the window and shouts, "There he is! That big fella!" I quickly look, follow her finger, but I don't see anything except blackness. "We got GHOs up here," she says. "You better hold on to that little dog of yours."

"What's a GHO?" asks Davis.

But my heart bounces in my chest. I know what it is.

"It's a great horned owl," Dr. Joan says. "Up here, with all the pine forest? We've got 'em up the wazoo."

Someday Birds List:
Bald Eagle
Great Horned Owl
Trumpeter Swan
Sandhill Crane
Turkey Vulture
Emu
Passenger Pigeon
Carolina Parakeet

Dad would be so excited. If I can tell him that I've checked a great horned owl (GHO) off our list of Someday Birds, he would like that. It would make him feel happy. And feeling happy makes you heal quicker. That's what Gram says.

I think about that as the truck shifts gears and roars forward, chugging up and up. What if I tried to spot *all* the birds on our list? Then I could tell Dad I found them all, that I did it for him. It could be like a gift I could give him. A gift to help him get better.

That feels right.

We level off and level off, and now we're driving horizontal instead of vertical. We are at the top of the mountain on a small, flat, dirt-covered area. Next to us is a big silver observatory dome with a house attached to one side. A few other buildings, barely bigger than trailers, are scattered here and there. Some huge generators squat, humming, connected up to the dome. Yellow light pours out of a window on the house part.

"Welcome to WIRO," says Dr. Joan. "It's just me and a couple grad students tonight, so you guys are welcome to the extra bunks. In the morning I'll take you back down to the RV. I checked her over and changed her oil this morning after you called. She's all ready for you."

"WIRO?" Joel asks. "RV?"

"Wyoming Infrared Observatory. And RV, in case you don't know, stands for Recreational Vehicle. Old Bessie, the camper. Ancient but powerful, just like me." Dr. Joan smiles. "Ludmila asked me to lend it to you, and it's damn clear I need to, because you'd never make it all the way back East in that little can opener she drives. Lord knows how you made it *this* far."

"Old Bessie will remind me so much of good times," Ludmila says to Dr. Joan, who smiles and gives her a quick hug.

"So, like, what is this place?" Davis asks. "What's an infrared observatory?"

"Come on inside. We'll be glad to show you!"

We walk over toward the front of the little house that's attached to the big silver dome.

"How do you know each other?" Davis whispers to Ludmila. "What kind of doctor is she?"

"Of astrophysics. It's a long story between us," Ludmila says. "Dr. Joan was my foster mother for little while, when I was about your age. My favorite foster mother, she was. Is."

"Yup," says Dr. Joan, overhearing. "And she wasn't easy. Mila gave me a run for my money, all right." Ludmila and Dr. Joan smile at each other and hug again.

I don't get it. But anyhow. So far, we know:

We're not being forced to join a cult. Probably.

Ludmila's from somewhere in Eastern Europe but doesn't want to talk about it.

She's got a secret involving our dad.

She is a way better driver than Jonathan Dylan Daniels.

She has had a few foster mothers, including Dr. Joan.

She was trouble when she was Davis's age.

Her dead brother's name was Amar.

She doesn't tell us too much. But I don't think she lies.

Well, that's progress. I will have to write all that down in my Bird Book as soon as possible.

The girls go inside the silver-dome house, but I stay out in the dark with Joel and Jake. I want to watch out for GHOs, for Dad's list. And also to help protect the dog, while the twins run around with him and try to get him to pee. They are a little bit careless, and it's dark out here. And I don't want the poor puppy to get picked off the mountain by a hungry owl.

There's also the danger of slipping off the side. The edges of this area slope away fast. And the edge is right where he goes, of course, tottering on his three scrawny little legs.

"Max, come back!" says Joel.

"Leonard, watch out!" says Jake at exactly the same time. Then they glare at each other. But the dog ignores them both—he is busy nosing around in pine needles. Then, his whole little body stiffens. He darts forward, picks up something in his mouth, and starts prancing around with it. "He's got a mouse!" shouts Joel. But that's not what it is.

It's a tight, neat, rectangular brown packet. Joel wedges it out of the dog's mouth. And when he shines his flashlight through it, it looks like someone wrapped the skeleton of some small, delicate animal in a rectangle of brown, fine leaves.

"Ugh! That's disgusting!"

"Whoa! Gross! What is it, do you think?" they ask.

I am so excited, I am jumping up and down. "It's an owl pellet!" I say. "When owls eat mice and stuff, they digest the good parts, and then burp out these neat little packets of all the stuff they don't digest. But I've only read about it in books. I've never seen a real one!"

"Congratulations," says Joel, handing it over to me, wrinkling his nose.

"Gross!" says Jake. "Charlie washes his hands like fifty times a day and won't go near the garbage can because of germs, but he's happy to hold something an owl pooped out. Tell me that makes sense."

"He didn't poop it out," says Joel. "He puked it. Right, Charlie?"

We take the owl pellet and the dog inside. Coming in out of the dark, it's all homey and brightly lit in there, with a living room and kitchen. It's like a weird smashup of a giant high-tech telescope and a small cozy house.

Dr. Joan and Ludmila are in the kitchen, putting together a midnight supper. They are laughing and talking. The air smells like onions and peppers and garlic sautéed in olive oil, which makes my eyes sting. It smells both good and bad—way too intense—and my sinuses start panging and throbbing. Nobody believes me when I try to describe this, so I've stopped even bothering to mention it, but overwhelming cooking smells are just another of my tragic burdens.

We sit at a table—Dr. Joan, us, and two sleepy students in rumpled sweatshirts. Dr. Joan throws all kinds of food at us. Sausages, toast, omelets. I sit on the far edge of the bench and nibble around the raisins in a cookie.

"Why don't you show these kids how the telescope works?" Dr. Joan asks the college students, after we eat. So they bring us through a door into a big, domed space. It's cold in here, and in the middle of the room, there's this enormous yellow and black piece of machinery that bends at right angles up to the domed roof. It's the telescope itself! They show us the computer system with a keyboard control panel that lets them control it. They show us how they adjust two big mirrors, one concave and one convex. Once they're in front of the keyboards, they wake up a bit.

"So. We can adjust the accuracy within one-tenth of an arc second, which is 1/36,000 of a degree," says one of the students. "Pretty damned precise for a heap of junk built back in the 1970s."

I can't even imagine numbers that small. Not to mention looking through a telescope that powerful at a universe that big.

"Yeah," says the second student. "This place isn't even set up for remote viewing. You know, I'd guess probably most astrophysicists have never even looked through a real telescope like this. They do all their viewing remotely online."

"Way easier," says the first student. "But truly, way less fun."

After we've had our tour of the telescope, the twins go into the bathroom and try their best to wash Dog in the shower, with dish soap and warm water, because Davis insists. But he still smells awful, if you ask me. Then, pale and tired, they go in to sleep. Davis is also so tired, she can barely talk. She just waves goodnight.

Meanwhile, Ludmila and Dr. Joan are talking quietly together in a back office. I've been trying to listen really hard, but I can't tell what they're saying.

I decide to draw Dad a drawing of a great horned owl on Jelm Mountain, Wyoming. Maybe that's enough, along with having found the owl pellet.

I get to work. The eyes are the most important— they have to seem like they're glowing, and that's a hard effect to get right with these particular colored pencils. I am just starting to write in some owl facts when I realize Dr. Joan is looking over my shoulder.

"Hey! That's good!"

I snap the Bird Book closed. I don't like to share my artwork. It makes my stomach feel weird.

"Very realistic. Have you spent a lot of time birding? Spotting them in the field?"

"I don't really 'bird,' so much," I say. "I just copy facts and pictures out of other books."

"Why don't you?"

"Because I don't like to go outside unless I have to."

"Oh now. You got to get out in the *field*. Secondhand information in this world only takes you so far."

"Well, I think inside is cleaner and safer."

"That so?" Dr. Joan folds her arms and frowns at me. Then she crosses the room, grabs a jacket off a hook, and throws it at my face. "Come on. We're going out, and that's an order."

I already washed up for bed. If I go out, then I'll have to wash my hands all over again, twelve times. And this jacket smells funny, and it has buttons; I don't wear buttons, and I don't want to put it on.

But then I think about the list. Maybe I'll see that owl for the Someday Birds List. So I do the only thing I can: swallow hard, accept the grimy jacket, and follow her.

It feels like it's dropped ten degrees since we first drove up. It doesn't feel like a summer night anymore. Dr. Joan herds me into the center of this midnight clearing on top of this steep Wyoming mountain, takes my chin in her hand, and before I can reel back in shock from having her cold fingers touching my face, she aims my chin up.

Whoa.

The sky above me is like a wheeling slice of thick, black velvet. It's like no sky I have ever seen before. It's like I can reach my hand out and touch the stars, *they are that close.* As close and sparkling as diamonds. So close I feel like I could almost taste them in my mouth. So beautiful, I don't ever want to stop looking at them. But I am so dizzy, with my head up, that I feel like passing out. I close my eyes, hold my breath, and wait for it to pass.

"Young scientist, observe. What do you see?" asks Dr. Joan.

"Um, over there? The Big Dipper?"

"Yup. What else?"

"That's all I see. Sorry."

"Don't be sorry. Be glad!" Joan says. "Think of all you have to look forward to! *So much good stuff still to learn!*"

We stare up at the sky in stillness. Then Joan starts teaching me more constellations. She shows me a bright star called Deneb, part of Cygnus the Swan, and Altair, part of Aquila the Eagle. Who knew so many constellations were named after birds? She is just pointing out the three bright stars of something called the Summer Triangle, when a whooshing noise cuts through the air in the trees right behind our heads.

Joan whispers, "*There's* that big old devil!"

We turn quickly, and her flashlight catches a brown and white flutter disappearing into pine branches.

"That's our Mr. GHO," whispers Joan. "He's always around. He's pretty bold, and used to us. Don't make a sound, and he might make another pass. Oh—and put up your hood. Don't want him going after your hair."

The jacket hood smells sort of smoky, but I put it up, quick.

We creep on tiptoe toward the pines, and wait. And wait. My heart is knocking against my chest. My fingers are stiff with the cold. And just when I think the wind has got me chilled through to the bone, and I can't take it anymore:

Whoosh!

A great ghostly shape sails up and across the night sky overhead. I can see white and brown feathers, and giant, black-tipped wings. I see talons, pulled in tight. I swear I can even feel the rush of air on my cheeks as he swoops past. My heart is racing a million beats a second.

Mr. GHO is gone as quickly as he came. I scan the trees, and the sky, but it's just plain black velvet out there again, sprinkled with those piercing-bright diamond-stars. The night seems emptier without the owl. The amazing owl. The big old devil. A Someday Bird, the very first check mark I can make off Dad's list. I can tell Dad this. I can say now that I have seen a great horned owl out in the wild.

What would Gram say to that? What would Dad say,

if he could see me here, on top of this mountain, with stars and birds, and talking to a new person I'd never even met before?

What would Tiberius Shaw say? Is this how he feels about birds, too?

We startle when we hear another noise:

The great slotted opening for the telescope is sliding and turning, its big eye looking up at another sector of the universe.

Joan says, "When I get too caught up in our digital work, all our computer measurements and calculations, I like to take a walk outside and just look up. It beats all. Doesn't it?"

As we are walking back to the observatory-house, I see Ludmila in the window. "We don't know Ludmila very well," I tell her. "She just showed up one day. You know her way better. Is she okay? What about her brother?"

Dr. Joan says in a quiet, flat voice, "Amar was just killed recently, in Afghanistan."

We are standing outside, with Joan's hand on the doorknob. I shut my eyes to concentrate, so my words can come out more carefully. "Ludmila kept visiting my dad in the hospital. But none of us know why."

Joan stops and takes her hand off the knob. She

puts her hands on her hips.

"Well. Ludmila has been working on a physical therapy degree, off and on for years. Was she working in the hospital?"

"Ellie and the nurses told us she wasn't."

Dr. Joan shrugs. Then she says, "That poor young woman has had it rough. She and Amar were war orphans, Charlie. They were born in Bosnia, and got caught in the siege of Sarajevo. But don't bring that up with her. Let her decide when and what to tell you. Like I said, she doesn't like to revisit her dark times."

We open the door and go back inside.

Dark times, meaning bad times. And here, we've been out in this beautiful cold blackness, here on top of the mountain, and it's been a *good* dark time. So good that now, when we open the door to the observatory, with Ludmila smiling to greet us, the warm bright artificial brightness hits like a terrible force.

16

The next morning, Ludmila wakes us early. "Time to rock and roll, sleepyheads," she says, and the little dog, curled up on a pillow on the floor near Joel, yips at her. I look out the window at nothing but gray fluff: the whole mountain is covered in mist.

I'm sorry to say good-bye. I would have liked to stay and learn more about the infrared telescope. I'd like to see how they cool it down—the students said they use liquid nitrogen, and that it's both really cold, and really cool. I'd like to spend more time outside with Joan, learning the constellations, and waiting for GHO to swoop by.

The morning mist is like moist cotton pasted onto our faces.

"Never fear! I know this trail like the back of my hand!" Dr. Joan shouts over her shoulder as she revs the truck engine with a roar.

Ludmila is in the back with the twins huddled against either side of her; the dog in her lap. Davis is looking nervously out the far window. I claim "shotgun" because of motion sickness. Also because I think I like Dr. Joan. It seems funny, how I thought we were going to get killed in a cult, but instead it was fine. And the Someday Birds List looks like this, now:

Bald Eagle
Great Horned Owl **(CHECK!)**
Trumpeter Swan
Sandhill Crane
Turkey Vulture
Emu
Passenger Pigeon
Carolina Parakeet

Joan keeps thinking of more things to yell back to Ludmila. I wish she'd keep her eyes on the foggy road. "You'll have to stock up on food," she yells, and the truck goes veering off to the left. "The waste tank should be okay!"—and we skid one tire over the brink into the abyss.

"What's a waste tank?" asks Jake, which makes Ludmila smile in a weird way.

"Old Bessie ain't the Ritz, but it should get you there and back in one piece!" shouts Dr. Joan.

There—and *back*? I've never thought about coming back. Will we have our dad with us?

And what will it be like, once we're there, in Virginia?

An idea occurs to me. In Virginia, I will be pretty close to the Sanctuary Marsh.

To Tiberius Shaw's house.

Maybe there will be a way to go see it.

To go see him.

When we get to the parking area at the base of the mountain, the twins and the dog jump out of the truck and walk over to inspect this thing everyone is calling "Old Bessie."

It's a faded old camper with an orange-brown stripe along the side. It has a bunch of windows with stiff plaid curtains. It looks like the last time someone drove it was a long, long time ago.

Dr. Joan pats the bumper. "Ol' Bessie's up to it. Don't worry."

Ludmila takes the keys, and we pile into the musty narrow interior. There's a rubber mat running down the center. On one side is a small table of glossy honey-colored wood, with built-in benches. On the other, a cooktop, small sink, wooden shelves, and cabinets. A tiny wooden door folds in, airplane-style, to the toilet.

I am afraid to even peek at how bad that toilet is. I have a public bathroom rating system that I keep in my head, and anything that I think rates lower than two stars, I won't even enter. My heart starts thudding; I am getting the cold sweats about this trip.

At the end of the camper are four built-in bunks, with blue mattresses on wooden platforms, two on each side. Dr. Joan hands us pillows and sleeping bags.

"There are five of us and only four bunks," I point out.

"I'll drive while you sleep," says Ludmila. "Or the twins can double up now and then."

The twins have already both crawled into a bunk. "Cool!" they say, sliding around on a disgusting, dusty blue mattress. "It's like being in a submarine! Come check it out!"

It smells like rubber and old rust. I don't know how

I am going to breathe in here, let alone sleep or go to the bathroom. I make my way back to the table-bench, sit, and cup my hands over my nose and mouth, trying to block the rubbery smell. No use. I ratchet down the flimsy window by the table. My hands come away covered with crumbled spiderwebs and dirt. I flap them and start to scream.

"Start 'er up!" shouts Dr. Joan, slapping the wall, then heading down the steps.

Ludmila turns the key: *Grrrr . . . chug chug chug.* A cloud of stinky exhaust curls in through my open window. I jerk it shut again, coughing.

"You're off!" shouts Dr. Joan, standing on the safe, nice ground outside. "You're on your way, sweet ol' girl!" I don't know if she means the camper or Ludmila is a sweet ol' girl. I am going to guess she means the camper.

We wave good-bye as Ludmila maneuvers us onto the bumpy dirt road, and then, eventually, just when I think I'll throw up, the highway.

I just noticed one thing about this vehicle, at least, that's sort of neat. Somebody custom-painted the ceiling. It's all dark blue, with silver constellations. I look for Libra, the scales—that's my sign. Joan showed it to me in the sky last night. I find it over Ludmila's head, toward the front.

Davis is humming along to something in her

earphones. The twins are bunching up a blanket in the bunk to make Dog a safe nest.

Dog is looking happier and happier since his rescue. He's lost that hunched-up look. I think he's given it to me.

How will I stand driving in this stinky, dirty rattle-trap all the way to Virginia?

I'm the only one feeling miserabler and miserabler.

· TRUMPETER SWAN ·

OWL HOLES and RULES of DISTANCE

17

Resilience, Repair, Resurrection. The natural world is capable of all three, if humans would only show a little Redemption.
—Tiberius Shaw, PhD

As we head out of Laramie, Ludmila pulls off the road and looks at her map. "Here is the thing. If we take Interstate 80 we could go straight there, almost," she says, pointing at a horizontal line due east. "But what you think? Look at this." She digs for her phone and hands it to Davis.

"What's it say?" Joel asks.

Davis frowns. "It says: *Tell the kids that all of Robert's initial test results are promising. He's doing great! Dr. Spielman says it's amazing how the brain can learn to rewire itself, after injury. Brain plasticity, I think he called it. Dr. Spielman's an absolute wonder!*"

Davis rolls her eyes and flaps her hand, imitating Gram.

"The tests continue, it's all status quo here, so don't rush. These poor kids have seen nothing but a waiting room all summer. . ." Davis's voice slows down. *". . . So why don't you help them have . . . fun. I'll wire you money. Do some things, find ways to at least enjoy the trip. Lord knows, it'll all still be here when you arrive. Thanks again."* Davis heaves a big sigh and claps the phone shut.

We're all quiet for a little while.

Then Davis says, "Have *fun*? *Do things*? I'd rather just get there already. How's it gonna help Dad if we're just driving aimlessly around the country?" She flops back in her seat.

Ludmila says, "It might make your Gram feel better to know you at least had some good experiences, amid all the worry of this summer."

I have a thought.

"You know what, you guys? Dad and I had this list of birds to see someday. And we've already seen one—the great horned owl. There's seven more on the list. I want to try to find some of the others. For Dad. So . . . maybe, along the way, we could go some places to do that. To find the birds on my list. Dad's Someday Birds."

"Oh, Lord. Not birds!" Davis scrunches up her face. The twins groan even louder.

"If we could check off all of Dad's birds, I think he would really like that. I bet it would make him happy. Which would help him feel better. It's something that we could do."

Ludmila and Davis make eye contact, and then Davis smacks herself in the forehead with the palms of her hands a few times.

Ludmila says, "Charlie, that's sweet, but . . ."

"Yeah, Charlie," says Joel. "Checking birds off some dumb list is not going to help Dad feel better. It's only gonna help *you* feel better."

Silence spreads in the car. A small lump forms in my throat.

Then Ludmila says in a strange voice, "Well, maybe that's a good enough reason."

Two fat raindrops splotch on the windshield. Then more. Ludmila turns on the wipers. "So where do we go, Charlie, to find your Someday Birds? The highway turn-off is coming up. We have to decide which direction."

"Don't worry," I tell them. "I know just the place to start."

18

*Some bird species mate for life and stay together
no matter what. Others seem to go through love
affairs like changes of clothes.*
—Tiberius Shaw, PhD

I start to get excited. We've passed a huge flat grassy field of elk, peacefully grazing. We've seen hillsides of burnt black tree-skeletons, land that was once covered with trees. We've traveled along a dark forest road. Now we spy a wooden sign up ahead that announces the wondrous news:

WELCOME TO YELLOWSTONE

We're there!

Tall evergreens make a canopy over us as we bump along another few miles. It's way different from San Diego's palm trees and beaches. Darker, more mysterious. Cooler.

"Hey!" says Joel, perking up and pointing out the window. "Buffalo!"

Sure enough, off to the right, through the trees, there's an open field full of shaggy brown monsters.

"I want to pet one!" Jake says in the same lovey-singsong voice he uses with the dog.

"Very funny," says Davis. "Those things are really dangerous. You can't get too close."

"And besides," I say, "we're only here to find Dad's trumpeter swan."

No one answers me.

The RV campground is strewn with shiny silver bullet-shaped trailers, tiny pop-up tent trailers, giant black monster buses, all kinds of things. Folks have laundry lines with wet towels and underwear and hiking socks and stuff strung across them in the wan sunlight.

"There are bears here, right?" Joel says.

"Yup," says Ludmila.

I think we were all hoping she would say "nope."

We pull into a spot and Ludmila puts on the brake with a squeak. The twins spill out the door, chanting, "Buffalo! Buffalo!"

"Great," moans Davis, covering her eyes with her hands.

"It's 'bison,'" I explain.

I take Dog down the steps on his leash. He limps over to pee on a brown log. The nice thing about having only three legs is he never has to lift that other back leg out of the way when he wants to pee. He just twists his hip and lets it go.

"What are we going to name this poor dog?" I ask, but Joel and Jake are already racing around the campground. "Come on, Charlie! Run to the field and back with us!"

"First we buy food and supplies," Ludmila says.

Yes! I'm hoping they have a nice clean bathroom so I can wash the rubbery Aroma of Camper out of my nose. I refuse to use Old Bessie's one-star toilet, so I really have to pee. And rinse my itchy, crawly hands.

The convenience store is so far away from the campground, they should call it the *in*convenience store. By the time we get there, my bladder is ready to burst. Ludmila browses the aisles, muttering to herself in a language which I guess, according to what Dr. Joan told me, is Bosnian. While I fidget, holding the dog, she fills her basket with:

Cans of chicken soup (With soggy flecks of green and orange in the broth.) REJECT!

Granny Smith apples (I only do Honeycrisp.) REJECT!

Oranges (Too tangy.) REJECT!

Bananas (Too many brown spots—gagorama.) REJECT!

Paper plates, cups, bowls (Okay, no complaints.)

Cereal (Ugh, raisins.) REJECT!

Skim milk (Tastes like someone poured water over a cow.) REJECT!

Orange juice (Pulp! Help!) REJECT!

Bread (With seeds!) REJECT!

Peanut butter (Not my brand.) REJECT!

Strawberry jam (More seeds.) REJECT!

And popcorn (Which only gets stuck between your teeth. Who can eat this stuff?) *REJECT!*

I make her buy me a box of frozen chicken nuggets. It's kind of expensive, and the box has that slick ice film, like it's been in the freezer too long. But I've gotta eat *something*.

Ludmila's still wandering aisles, and I can't hold it in anymore. I head for the restroom behind the building. Plus, my hands are desperate with the need to be washed. I still feel unsteady on my feet from the long drive, and my head is wobbly-spinny. That's what travel does to me. No one else realizes how hard it is. My dumb body gets pummeled by all this stuff that no one else even guesses at.

The minute I open the door to the bathroom, I know

I'm in trouble. It's a concrete cinder block with no toilet paper, and the soap dispenser is empty.

Disappointing, to say the least. Half star. One star, at best.

But still, I pee. And I totally, absolutely, critically, urgently *have to wash my hands.* Not soap-rinse-once, not soap-rinse-twice, but soap-rinse-a-million-times.

But I can't, so there's nothing to do but take the dog and go back in the store. I am feeling so bad, so desperate, I blurt out to the clerk without even thinking it through—without even worrying about my words, or how he'll react, or anything:

"Please tell me where the best, cleanest bathroom in Yellowstone is. One you'd rate at least three stars. It's urgent."

The clerk pulls at his beard and peers at me. "Urgent? Well . . . The restrooms are probably better in the lodges. Old Faithful Lodge?" He slides a brochure over the counter. "It's worth checking out, anyway. About ten minutes by car."

I turn to Ludmila, desperate. "Can we drive down to the Old Faithful Lodge? *Right now?*"

She squints at me from behind her thick black glasses. "Later, Charlie."

No! Now! I can feel the germs actually crawling around on my hands. If I don't get a chance to wash,

I'll—I don't know! I squinch up my eyes. Breathe in. Breathe out. I try to remember what Dad used to tell me. *Drop your shoulders. Take a deep breathe. Imagine a calm forest.* . . .

Grrr.

We walk back to the RV area along a grassy field with bison grazing. They are woolly brown monstrous beasts all right. I notice how the big ones keep the baby bison protected in the center of the herd.

"After we put away this stuff, can we come back out to see the buffalo? I mean bison?" the twins ask. "Are they tame?"

I say, "No. We don't have time for bison. I need to wash my hands at the Old Faithful Lodge restroom, and then we need to go find Dad's trumpeter swan."

But it's like I didn't even talk. Everyone's paying attention to the bison, not me. I sigh. You can smell their funky bison-poop smell even way over here. What's so great about them?

Davis says to Joel and Jake, "What do you mean, are they tame—are you kidding? Of course they're not tame! Look at this brochure." She flips it at us. "It says you have to stay at least twenty-five feet away. So be careful. Give me your grocery bags," she says. "Go on. Charlie, you go with them to see the bison, and make sure they stay at least twenty-five feet back."

We cross the road. The bison are behind a low split-rail fence. They could jump it if they wanted to, or merely bulldoze it over. Instead, they're calmly grazing. Cars go right by them, slowing to watch, people craning their heads and arms out of the windows, snapping photos. The bison seem unbothered by everything. I wish I had that skill.

I hold Dog tightly in my arms, which keeps him safe, and also helps me forget about my dirty hands. Something about holding him makes other stuff tolerable.

The twins duck under the fence toward the herd. It smells so overpowering, I think I might faint.

"Let's pretend we're ancient Sioux trackers!" Joel says. "We're closing in for the kill!"

My silly brothers tiptoe in closer, circling around the herd of woolly brown giants. A grizzled bison at the edge of the herd looks out at them from one wild black eye, and snorts.

"Remember what Davis said, you guys. The twenty-five-foot rule!" I shout.

Something about the look in the eye of that big fellow is bothering me.

I shift the dog to one hip, loop his leash around my arm, and dig Davis's brochure out of my pocket.

"Come check 'em out, Charlie!" says Joel. "Don't be such a wuss. One just pooped!"

"Yeah, rank!" says Jake. "Can you smell it?"

"Are you just gonna stay there and read a brochure?" says Jake. "You dork."

I notice something. The old bison behind them, at the edge of the herd, has lowered its head and taken a step toward the twins. Then it stops, snorts, paws the ground, and goes back to grazing.

Something doesn't seem right about this twenty-five-foot rule of Davis's. I quickly skim the brochure to make sure:

Big as they are, bison can sprint three times faster than humans can run. They are unpredictable and dangerous. No vacation picture is worth personal injury. If any wild animal changes its behavior due to your presence, you are too close. Do not approach wildlife, no matter how tame or calm they may appear to you in the moment. Always obey instructions from park staff on scene. You must stay at least 100 yards (91 meters) away from bears and wolves and at least 25 yards (22.8 meters) away from all other large animals—bison, elk, bighorn sheep, deer, moose, and coyotes. Consider it the Rule of Distance.

I read it again to make sure. Why was Davis saying twenty-five feet? It's twenty-five *yards*.

Not feet.

I look up just in time to see that big old bison start to lope toward the twins.

I yell, louder than I've ever yelled before, *"Joel! Jake! RUN!"*

They turn, see the beast, and jump straight up in the air. Then they each take off in a different direction. This is probably good, because the bison doesn't know which twin to pursue. Finally, it chooses Jake. He is sprinting at a good clip toward the split-rail fence by the road, his face white, his little legs pumping like pistons, and the bison is bearing down on him at a slow trot. But Jake is fast. He is almost there.

Please, God, I pray. Let Jake make the hurdle. Let this bison not be in the mood for fence-jumping today!

Joel is safe down the other end of the pasture, shouting and waving his arms, but the bison is starting to lower its head. Like a bull in the ring, it gains speed, loping after my little brother. I hold my breath and pray: let Jake make the hurdle let Jake make the hurdle let Jake make it—and I'm jumping up and down, my hands flapping, and the dog is barking, and the bison is gaining ground on Jake—

When suddenly this teenage guy with a blond ponytail comes up out of nowhere, running into the field to the left of Jake, blowing a whistle and waving a big red Yellowstone sweatshirt around. He catches the bison's eye. The big brown grizzled old thing slows, and turns its giant head. Now it seems confused. It considers the sweatshirt. It pauses, then stops a moment. Finally, it decides to veer back toward the herd.

Meanwhile, Jake jumps over that fence quicker than I've ever seen him move in his life.

I stare at the ponytail guy, who's standing there, holding the red shirt, panting hard.

"You guys!" I say to my little brothers. "You guys!" I can't think of anything else to say to them. I am in brain-shock, my heart still pounding.

Ponytail guy has something to say, though. He has a lot to say. "Are you two trying to get yourselves killed?" he yells. "Don't you know these are *wild animals*? You don't mess with the bison, man!"

"But we stayed twenty-five feet, pretty much," Joel panted out.

I stab my finger at the brochure that, just a few minutes ago, they had called me a dork for reading. "It's not twenty-five feet. It's *YARDS*!"

"Whoa," says Joel. "That's more, right? That's like, what, seventy-five feet!"

Jake just shakes his head. "Great. Davis, the math genius."

"Who's Davis?" asks blond guy.

On cue, here she comes, running down the road with her long brown hair flying, sneakers flapping, face red. "You guys!" she shouts, but she's not looking at the twins.

Blond ponytail guy stares at her like a deer in the headlights. "Are these two maniacs your brothers?" he says, grinning. His teeth are that weird blue-white, too-bleached color. "I saw them and came out running, and you're lucky I did. You know how dangerous that is, what they did? They were way too close. My older brother's a park ranger—if he'd seen this, he'd be reaming us all out big-time."

He holds out his hand to Davis. "I'm Tony."

Davis's face is flushing really red.

No one is remembering it was me, not Tony, who warned the twins to run. We didn't even need this guy with his stupid red sweatshirt. Probably. And didn't Davis just break up with Jonathan Dylan Daniels like two days ago? Why is she all red in the face, smiling and talking to a different boy already?

"Oh my gosh, I am so sorry," she says, flipping her hair. "We just literally rolled into Dodge. Haven't even had time to set up camp, when these little guys ran off."

"We didn't run off," I start to protest, but Tony cuts me off like I don't exist. He has a dimple in the direct center of his chin.

"Oh, you just got here? If you want, I could show you around. I work right there, at the information center." He flashes his blinding blue-white teeth.

Good griefus, as Gram would say.

19

*The grooming habits of certain birds serve for far
more than just hygienic purposes.*
—Tiberius Shaw, PhD

Davis has always been my guide. She's always
decoded stuff for me. Mysteries like why Ashley Gallagher pushed me down into the mud at recess back in
fourth grade. ("You can't just corner her all the time and
talk her ear off about birds, Charlie.") Why counting is
bad. ("You think it calms you, but Charlie, it's impris-
oning you because *you can't not do it!*") What visual cues
mean in the mirror. ("Frowny face equals get the heck
out of my room, dork.")

"Charlie," Davis used to tell me, back when she mainly
acted like she still loved me, "you are a great kid. You're
thoughtful. And kind. And you care about people. And
if people don't get you, if they don't want to take the time

to look beyond the little quirks that make you special, well, then that's their loss, and don't you worry about it, because I love you, and you always have *me*."

But I don't think I have Davis anymore.

Instead, she always gets just as frustrated with me as Ashley Gallagher used to. Like Gram sometimes does.

Because here we are at the Old Faithful Lodge, and this is what she says:

"*Charlie, come out of that bathroom right now!*" Davis is knocking on the door hard, and yelling like she's really angry. "When are you gonna stop this ridiculous habit? You're the only one who didn't get to see the geyser, and now it's too late. We have to go!"

Soap-rinse-one-soap-rinse-two-soap-rinse-three-soap-rinse-four-soap-rinse-five-soap-rinse-six-soap-rinse-seven-soap-rinse-eight-soap-rinse-nine-soap-rinse-ten-soap-rinse-eleven-soap-rinse . . .

Sometimes it takes a longer chain of washes to get calm.

"The geyser will blow again, right?" I ask.

"Yeah, in half an hour," says Davis. "So you have to choose. Old Faithful, or your old swan. Because we can't do both before it gets dark."

Well, of course we have to go look for Dad's trumpeter. Who cares about a bunch of spraying water?

We head to Yellowstone Lake.

In Tony's car, Joel (who hates to read) is actually quoting from the Old Faithful brochure, his dirty finger pointing at each word. "What's a hydrothermal feature? It says that half of the whole world's hydrothermal features are in Yellowstone," he reads. "Like, about ten thousand."

"They're things like hot springs," says Tony. "And mud pots, or paint pots, which are big puddles of bubbling, boiling mud, sometimes in really bright colors due to the minerals and stuff in them. And there are steam vents, and of course the geysers."

Joel says, "Cool! Let's go see—"

"Trumpeters," I say.

"Okay, Charlie," says Davis. "Sheesh! We're going!"

The sun is starting to dip behind the trees, and the surface of the lake water twinkles silver-black as I crane my head out the window, hoping for a good view.

"We can't stay here long," Tony says, pulling up onto the grass to park. "My brother will be wondering where I took his car."

"Oh, no worries," says Davis. "Our friend's probably wondering the same."

"Our babysitter, she means," Joel adds, and Davis coughs.

"Well, she's more like a family friend," Davis says quickly. "She's this weird person who we met in my dad's old hospital. . . ."

As Tony parks, I take off out of the car, running toward the lake.

I can see small dabs of white, a far distance out on the darkening water. They are probably swans. Yes, definitely swans! But at this distance, I can't tell if I am seeing trumpeters or mute swans. Mutes have orange beaks, while trumpeters have black. Mutes are a total nuisance intruder bird, destroying local habitats, while poor, beautiful native trumpeters have to struggle really hard to survive.

I hate to admit it, but as I stare harder at this group, it seems to me that their beaks look orange. My heart sinks. It's just a group of mutes, three or four of them, gliding together near some tall lake weeds.

But wait. Farther down the lake, another swan emerges from an underwater dive. It holds its long neck up, high and proud, and I see the lump as it swallows something. It skims along, and I realize it is bigger, slightly, than the mutes. And it has—does it?—maybe. Maybe it has a black beak. I just can't tell in this light. It could be either.

If only I had binoculars!

The bigger swan swims toward the small group of

mutes, one of which flaps its giant white wings in warning, ruffling the water. They are not allowing this big guy to join them. It stays alone by itself, serene, like it knows very well that it doesn't belong with the others. Is this because it's a trumpeter? I squeeze my eyelids with my fingers, anything to see better.

The sun is almost down. It's useless. The car horn honks behind me. "Did you see them, Charlie?" Davis yells. "Did you find them?"

I don't have the heart to yell anything back to her.

I just don't know. There is no way to tell.

Someday Birds List:
Bald Eagle
Great Horned Owl **(CHECK!)**
Trumpeter Swan **(Undecided. HALF CHECK.)**
Sandhill Crane
Turkey Vulture
Emu **(not unless we go to Virginia by way of Australia)**
Passenger Pigeon **(as if!)**
Carolina Parakeet **(Dad being ridiculous)**

20

Birds are usually quite cooperative among members of their own family—but as with any generalization, there are always exceptions.

—Tiberius Shaw, PhD

It's night now, and I lift the window curtain in the camper to peer out at the group around the campfire outside. The twins, Ludmila, Davis, and Tony. They are having a grand old time, roasting hot dogs in the dark around the cheery blaze.

Dog is here in the dark, in my bunk with me. He sniffs the air hungrily.

"How can you stand the smell of hot dogs?" I ask Dog. "Or the stinky smell of that campfire? Trust me, it's not worth it."

He licks the back of my hand. This dog may have three legs, bulgy eyes, and funny teeth. He may snore, and his breath may stink like fish. But I totally love him.

He's my friend. He's great company. And he loves me back. I really think he does. The twins are too wild and rambunctious for his unsteady legs. They don't pay him enough attention. And Davis also ignores him. So it's become him and me. I'm the one who feeds and walks him. And when I hold him and pet him, somehow I forget all about the fact that my hands are itching and throbbing to be washed.

"Joel and Jake haven't even bothered to give you a name yet," I tell poor Dog. "That's not right."

He sneezes, and clear, watery dog snot shoots out of his nostrils onto my blanket. But that's no problem. I just trade blankets with Davis.

"Hmmm . . . What should we call you?"

The dog looks up at me with his warm, slightly bulgy brown eyes. He licks the back of my hand. His whiskers tickle.

"Whiskers?"

He sneezes again and shakes his snout. No. Not Whiskers. That's more of a cat name, anyway.

"How about . . . Spot?" He has a bunch of brown and black patches, like a little cow-dog. But he doesn't look too happy about Spot.

"How about . . . Cow-Dog?" That's just dumb.

The dog sniffs around my blankets, then nudges Tiberius Shaw's green journal with his wet nose. He licks at the gold-embossed feather. He tries to nibble on the corner of the cover.

"You like that book?" I ask him. I open up to the photo card of Tiberius Shaw, staring out at us with his dark eyes and wiry white eyebrows. Come to think of it, this dog has almost the same-looking wiry white eyebrows.

"Ruff!" says the dog, sniffing at the photo of Tiberius Shaw, PhD. "Ruff! Ruff!" He is getting all excited for some reason.

"You like that guy?" I ask. "That's Tiberius. He's—"

Then I know what the dog's name should be.

"Come on, Tiberius," I tell him, clipping on his leash. "Let's go outside and tell everyone what your name is. And maybe get you a small piece of hot dog."

Much later, after everyone's asleep, I click on my small flashlight and open Dr. Tiberius Shaw's green journal, flipping to see if maybe he wrote something about trumpeter swans. Instead, I come across a hand-done sketch. I bet Tiberius Shaw drew it himself! Beneath the picture, it says: *Swallows on the move, in the evening air. These birds live and die for the flock, remaining within touching distance of each other for their entire lives. Deriving meaning from the flock,*

from each other, these birds move as one through the world.

And it makes me wonder. Are *we* moving together as one through the world? Are we a flock?

Dad had said to me, all those months ago, *are you a flocker or a loner, Charlie?*

I used to think my family was my flock, but really, not anymore. All they do is yell at me because I slow them down. Because I am always complaining. Because I am always washing.

Well, so what?

I click off the flashlight. I lie back on the musty blue mattress, and Tiberius snuggles into me. I pet him gently, straight down his old spotted back, and he looks at me with pure love. I know it is pure love. I can read the visual cue in his bulgy brown dog-eyes. *Tiberius* is my flock.

"Good boy," I whisper. "Good, good boy."

He sighs and squirms, and soon, despite the awful mattress and his hideous fish breath, I miraculously manage to fall asleep.

The next thing I know, birds are tweeting and the sun's beaming in. Everyone's up already, clunking around, packing stuff. Ludmila is nagging the twins to help her stash the folding chairs and secure stuff in the little kitchen so it doesn't roll and clank around once she starts driving.

Almost time to leave Yellowstone.

I stumble down the steps with Tiberius and around the corner of the camper, to find a spot for us both to pee. There's that guy Tony and Davis, standing way too close to each other.

"Get out of here," Davis says.

"Come on, Tiberius," I say, and I glare at them. "Let's leave these obnoxious people alone."

I walk Tiberius on his leash toward a patch of trees, and we do our business. I sit on a log, looking in through the leafy branches. Tiberius sniffs around. I pick a maple leaf and twirl it around in my fingers while he meanders. Millions of these leaves all around, so many you don't even really think of them as leaves, until you pick one single leaf, and it comes into focus. It's got veins running through it, and it's soft, with a dark green summer color, and it's got this amazing symmetrical beauty. And then, you think: wow.

I crouch down and spread the leaf over my knee, feeling its rough backside. I don't want to think about anything right now except this leaf. Can't I just stay here and be a hermit, and live in a hut in the woods? A very hygienic hut. Hidden, so no one can find me.

Tiberius whines, as if he knows my thoughts and doesn't agree with them one bit.

Suddenly, by my left ear, away from where he's sniffing and turning in circles, I hear a loud *scrrrrritch*. Like scraping metal.

I peer over at a big oak tree, and I have to let my eyes adjust before I see it. There's a little screech owl, no bigger than my hand, fluffing up its feathers, peeping out of a hole in the trunk. It looks at me from its round black doorway, and I look at it, and it blinks its yellow eyes once, twice. Tiberius barks, and in a flash, the owl's gone, back inside that snug hole.

My heart is pounding. How can such a little cute bird make such a huge, obnoxious noise? Amazing.

"Why'd you scare it, Tiberius?" I scold him, but he doesn't care. Well, at least now I can add a screech owl onto the Someday Birds List, as a bonus prize for Dad.

I like the screech owl. I like to think of it living here in the woods, hidden away all snug in its tree trunk among the big soft maple leaves, all alone, the whole world leaving it alone and in peace.

I am starting to deeply hate riding in that crowded camper. I wish *I* had a hole.

PRAIRIE CHICKEN

FOSSILS and FIRE BIRDS

21

The gears of Old Bessie grind and growl as Davis
reads from yet another of her thick stack of brochures.
She took pretty much every free pamphlet and map
the Yellowstone Area visitor center had to offer, while
we were out with Tony yesterday, and they're in a stack
on our little wood table. She's got us cutting northeast
through Montana now, just because she's always wanted
to see it. Plus, she wrote a history paper on Little Bighorn, so apparently now we have to go there.

Davis puts on a loud, TV announcer's voice and leans
forward.

"The historic Beartooth Highway has been called the most beautiful drive in America! It was first traveled by Civil War General Sheridan in 1882."

"Really? Something tells me that Native Americans probably traveled it before that old general did," says Ludmila.

We are powering through switchbacks to make it up and over a super-steep mountain pass. Switchbacks are when you change directions with 180-degree turns. It feels like you're going to roll right out of your seat. Switchback is a good word to describe what it's like, too, when you think your life is going one way (peaceful summer at home), but instead, it slides off in a whole other direction (crazy drive across country), one way (Dad working from home and healthy), and then a whole other way (Dad going to Afghanistan and getting hurt).

Back and forth, up and up, this way and that, lurch and slosh. Tiberius whimpers in his sleep, in his blanket-nest between the seats.

A few feet from my window, the road drops off into nothing but air. A rocky abyss waits below. It's terrifying. We pass snow—snow!—on a cliff ledge that juts out into sky. I close my eyes to keep from fainting.

"Charlie," says Ludmila, sneaking a glance at me. "Why don't you close that book if you feel so sick?"

"I wasn't reading it," I say, gulping air. "I was just looking at this picture of the archaeopteryx."

"The what?"

"Archaeopteryx. The very first bird that evolved from dinosaurs." I look down at the yellowed photo that Shaw had taped into the book: a very delicate skeleton of a tiny, pterodactyl-like thing, wings akimbo, pressed into rock. One day, this little guy fell back into the mud, and one hundred million years later, people found him. They even found a preserved feather.

We swerve around another cliff face. The rock's so close, I could put my arm out Old Bessie's window and touch it. The brochures say Montana has over a hundred fossil sites, and some of the oldest rocks on the earth. They've found lots of dinosaurs, even prehistoric crocodiles here. I wonder what mystery could be behind this very rock we're passing. Who knows? We could be like ten feet away from dinosaur-birds that no human's ever seen.

A snowflake swirls down onto the windshield; I watch it melt.

"You're crazy," Joel says, resting his chin on the back of my seat. "How could a dinosaur turn into a bird?"

I sigh. This is hard to explain. "The theory is that the reptile scales sort of turned into quills. Which eventually spread into feathers."

Ludmila says, "I can't believe so much change could happen."

"That's genetics. It didn't happen overnight. It was after millions of years living in treetops and lots of generations," I say.

A few more minutes go by, then Davis says, "That archaeopteryx thing is cool. I wonder if people could ever do that. Physically evolve, I mean."

"To get wings?" I ask.

"No," says Davis. "In other ways. Wouldn't it be cool if we evolved to be smarter? And more peaceful? Like, our bodies would just *not be able* to be violent?"

Ludmila snorts loudly. "That will never happen," she scoffs. "In fact, sometimes I think we are evolving in the reverse. Too much insane fighting, with the whole of this crazy human race." She glares straight ahead, past the rock face, and guns the engine a little too wildly.

I close my eyes while my head and stomach lurch, and the engine keeps complaining, grinding hard as we head even farther up and up and up, switchback and switchback, switchback and switchback, until it feels like we're heading into everywhere and nowhere at once.

22

*Real Bird behavior can differ from our assumptions.
I have witnessed bloody battles between Jays
and Crows that have filled the air with the
squawking black chaos of war.*
—Tiberius Shaw, PhD

"Okay, we're nearing Little Bighorn," says Davis, reading from one of her many brochures. "Site of the great battle. Two thousand Lakota Sioux and Cheyenne, peacefully hanging out. Along comes General Custer with well under a thousand men, trying to slaughter them. He screwed up his information, messed up the odds. And in self-defense, they had no choice but to destroy Custer. And afterward, the US government retaliated by destroying their whole way of life. It's all so, well, awful. But there's a museum. Should we?"

Ludmila clears her throat. "I don't like war monuments," she says.

"And we want to get to Wall Drug and check out the

free ice water!" says Joel. "That looks funner."

We're not exactly sure what Wall Drug is, but there have been tons of road signs advertising "free ice water," which the twins think is incredibly fun and mysterious, like maybe that means there's a magic well there, or something.

"But I wrote that whole report on Little Bighorn. I had to read books and books about it!" says Davis. "Can't we just check it out super quickly? It'll earn me some great brownnoser points if I actually go. Plus, I have to pee."

So we follow the signs to the Little Bighorn Battlefield National Monument. Everything seems really peaceful, with hills of prairie grasses waving this way and that.

"You'd never know that once upon a time, these peaceful hills ran with blood," says Davis in a scary Halloween voice.

"*Ne budi glup*—don't be stupid," says Ludmila.

We park in a lot that's already almost full. People are milling about, unloading cars. The air smells like cigarette smoke and barbecues and dust and pollen, and I get one of my major sneeze fests. My record is fifty-one sneezes in a row. I think I may surpass it today. Tiberius looks up at me from the end of his leash, waiting for the onslaught of spray to stop.

"Gesundheit!" says a deep voice.

A man with a giant beer belly and sweat dripping from his eyebrows is standing by a huge truck parked next to us. He reaches in and pulls out a rifle with a red, white, and blue strap. I think for a minute he is going to shoot me for sneezing.

"Here for the reenactment?" he says. "Might be *my* last stand, wearing all this gear in today's heat." He puts a Civil War–style cap on his head. He looks straight at me, expects me to answer him. I just look down and shake my head around in a yes-no ambiguous fashion, because I have no idea what he is talking about.

Behind Beer Belly man, a tall, thin boy about Davis's age appears. He's got broad shoulders and scruffy brown hair. He scratches his head and looks around, and when he sees my sister, he blushes. She sees him, too, and they sort of smile at each other in this goofy, familiar kind of way, even though they clearly have never seen each other before.

Davis grabs my hand and says "Come on!" and before I can complain about how I hate holding hands, she pulls me and Tiberius up the hill where Ludmila and the twins are already walking toward the museum building.

"That boy and you were looking at each other funny," I tell Davis, shaking out my fingers.

"Shush," Davis says, glancing back. "God, Charlie. Do you have to notice *everything*?" The boy, with his

Beer Belly dad and mom, is heading off to where folks in old-fashioned clothes are setting up under a big tent. When I look back, he's still staring over here at Davis.

We catch up to the twins and Ludmila by the museum entrance, where a big sign says:

Battle Reenactment Today!

"YES!" shouts Jake. The twins jump up and high-five each other.

"I hope the guns are real!" says Jake.

"Stupid, why would they shoot real guns at each other?" says Joel.

"Stupid, they'd be blanks," says Jake.

I pick up Tiberius and hold him close to my chest.

The little museum's practically empty. There are glass cases full of old uniforms, maps, swords, guns. At the far end, they've opened a set of double doors through which you can see a bright green hillside, with gray stone markers scattered in the grass.

"Ludmila, can we go see the people in the tents? Please, please?" says Joel. He clasps his hands together and tries to look cute.

"I'll keep an eye on them," Davis quickly offers.

"Well," says Ludmila.

After they leave, I tell her, "I think she just wants to

keep an eye on that tall boy she was looking at in the parking lot."

Ludmila smiles.

I wonder how Jonathan Dylan Daniels's arm is healing. Does Davis even remember him? I thought they were going to get married or something. Now it's like he never existed.

The twins are already running past Davis up the hill. They spy the Beer Belly couple at a picnic table, and go right up to them. Davis is standing with the tall scruffy boy, her hands clasped behind her back, in her pink top and white shorts, her long brown hair tied back in a ponytail. The tall boy kicks at a rock with his toe.

How do they do that? Just go up to strangers and talk to them, and then suddenly they know them?

It is so hot! My shirt is sticking to my underarms and my head is pounding. How can they stand it on that hillside? My body is twitching and buzzing, my hands crawling with grime. I squinch my eyes. *No washing. I don't need to wash. I can handle this,* I tell myself.

No, I can't.

I give Tiberius's leash to Ludmila, and head to the bathroom.

Soap-rinse-one-soap-rinse-two-soap-rinse-three-soap-rinse-four-soap-rinse-five . . .

And when I come out, I notice that Ludmila has

taken Tiberius back out to the entry, to stare at some strange words that are displayed on the wall there. I can't tell what language they are in. They look as mysterious as the Bosnian words that Ludmila mutters sometimes.

But underneath the strange words, there is an English translation. It says:

Know the Power that Is Peace. —Black Elk

Ludmila's eyes are kind of heavy-looking. Her eyebrows are scrunched. Her mouth is turned down and kind of twisted. If I were to read her visual cue, I'd say she looked . . . sad? Mad?

"Hi," I say.

She doesn't turn. She keeps staring at the wall. "I hate this whole idea of reenactment," she says. "Because too many people just think of it as a celebration. Imagine. In a hundred years, what if they reenacted the Sarajevo siege?" she asks the wall. "What if a bunch of people in the future think it would be fun to dress up in clothes like my family wore in the 1990s, and have a celebration picnic? And pretend to kill each other?"

I don't understand what she's talking about. "What was the siege?" I ask.

"*What was the siege?*" She blinks hard at me. "What do they teach you in those schools?"

"We did up to the Industrial Revolution."

She stamps her foot. "There was terrible war in my

country!" She is almost shouting. Tiberius stops nosing around, looks up and stares at her. So do some other people. "Thousands of innocent people killed! My whole country, bombed! Destroyed! Innocent families, women, and children."

I do not know what to say. I do not know if she is mad at me, or at the war, or both. I say, "I am so sorry to hear that." Of course I am. I truly, really am. I can't even imagine that.

Ludmila stands so close to me, I can see a half inch of blondish-brown hair roots starting to grow out under all that pink. She stares through the thick dirty lenses of her glasses right at me, and says, in her deep voice, "We were murdered, in the middle of Europe, in the 1990s, and the whole world, they just watched and did nothing."

Ludmila hands me the leash and turns away. "I'm sorry," she whispers, and sort of clomps off in her heavy black platform shoes, white knee socks, and flowery sundress.

There are some older ladies near us who have been looking at her. People do look at Ludmila. People look at me, sometimes, too—but not usually until after I start talking.

"It's not nice to stare," I say to them in a loud, flat voice, and they quickly turn away.

Tiberius and I find Ludmila back near the parking lot. She is sitting on a bench in the shade, staring at the stack of brochures. I loop the dog's leash under the leg of the bench so he can mosey around if he wants. But he just decides to sit down right on top of my feet. His butt warms my toes. I keep my feet still so as not to disturb him.

I take out Shaw's green journal and flip through the pages, making the words fly past like birds. I like to see what my eye will suddenly catch, see what turns up. You never know.

I notice a colorful sketch of two ruby-throated hummingbirds doing battle. Beneath it is written: *The hummingbird will fight his own brother to the death.* I show it to Ludmila. She is just about to say something when the loudspeaker crackles and beeps.

"Howdy, folks!" says a monster-truck-commercial voice. "Just a reminder that we're two hours away from the annual Battle of the Little Bighorn reenactment, hosted, as always, by the Real Bird Family. If you're interested in sticking around, it'll be down at Medicine Tail Coulee."

I look down at the page in Tiberius's green journal, where his handwriting says: *Real Bird behavior.* "Did that guy just say something about a REAL BIRD family?" I ask Ludmila.

She nods, and points to the brochure in her lap. "I guess it's the last name of the Crow Indian family that organizes the show. See? It says it right here. Real Bird."

That's another kind of a weird coincidence, I think. I note it in my own Bird Book. I'm starting a list of things that I want to ask Tiberius Shaw when I find his house in the Sanctuary Marsh in Virginia. Most of the questions I have written down are about real bird behavior, and real people behavior. And then, some of them are more personal, and kind of about Dad.

We are not going to hang around for the reenactment—we are getting right back on the road. So Davis and the twins are hugging their new friends, the Beer Belly family, good-bye. Mrs. Beer Belly turns to the twins and smiles. "Now you two behave yourselves and have a super-duper fun rest of your trip, okay?" she says, bending down to embrace both of them at once.

They hug her back.

"And know for sure that I'll be praying for your poor daddy. Praying hard. He's just bound to be all right. I know it," she says.

"*How* do you know it?" I say to her.

Davis suddenly appears out of nowhere to stand next

to me. "Don't mind Charlie," she says to the lady. "We're sorry."

What is there to be sorry for?

Ludmila is thanking Mr. and Mrs. Beer Belly for their kindness while Tiberius barks. Davis's new boyfriend is on the other side of the pickup truck. He blows Davis a slow kiss when he thinks no one sees.

Ick.

That night, at our campsite in the RV park, we're all tired. The twins smell like sweat and dirt—it's been a long day. Davis is not saying much, just sitting at the little table, staring out the dark window with her earphones in, smiling to herself at something. I don't even want to think about what. Or who.

"Come on, Charlie," says Ludmila to me, clicking on a flashlight and grabbing the leash. "Time to walk the what-you-call-him-now, Tiberius."

"Tiberius," Davis says, rolling her eyes. "All my life, I've wanted a golden retriever named Honey, so of course we end up with a scrawny three-legged mutt named Tiberius." But she pets him gently all along his back, down to the end of his long thin tail, as he limps past her.

"Dunno why he sticks with Charlie so much," says Joel, without even looking up from his handheld game.

"'Cause you already stepped on his tail like four times," says Jake.

"Did not!"

"Because you boys are too rough," Ludmila says. "Tiberius likes things calm, same as Charlie."

They are still bickering over that as Ludmila, Tiberius, and I make our way along a wide, mowed path through fields of tall prairie grass.

We are quiet as we walk. I think about that hillside today, with all the stones and crosses on it. I wonder who died there, what their stories were. Stories of people from one hundred and forty years ago. When they were fighting, did they think they were doing the right thing?

Were they?

I think of Dad. What stories did he want to tell about his soldier friends?

Tiberius pokes around. Ludmila has been very quiet all day, but now she says to me, "When I was little, you know, I wanted a dog, too. My brother, Amar, and I, we begged our parents all the time. But then the war came, and it was no time for dogs."

We follow Tiberius down a little side trail through the tall grass. He limps around, sniffing the ground.

"There was a park near our apartment in Sarajevo, a nice place where people walked their dogs. Then, later, it was a place where many people were shot and killed."

I almost can't believe she just said that. I have no idea what to say back.

Suddenly, Tiberius stiffens and barks. An odd noise, a garbled chirp, comes from the grass. I move the flashlight, and right there, caught in the light, is a brown-speckled bird! It scurries in front of a cuplike nest, stamping and scolding Tiberius, who leaps back in surprise. I tighten up on the leash, and feel a flash of joy. I know what this is.

"That's a bird from Tiberius Shaw's book!" I tell Ludmila. "It's called a prairie chicken! They stamp their feet around in a sort of mating dance. They look like chickens with this orange balloon thing on their necks. And when the prairie burns, they can survive it. So the Native Americans call them 'fire birds.'"

Ludmila stares into the brush, where the little fire bird has quickly disappeared. "That's a good thing," she says. "Being able to survive."

Back at the camper, Ludmila doesn't go in. She sits in one of the two folding chairs and stares. I sit in the other chair and wait. Something's been itching at her all day, like there are words that she's got to wash her hands clean of.

"Ludmila," I say. "Davis says you were snooping, when you first came to our house. Snooping in Dad's office."

She jerks her head back. "What? Oh. Well. I didn't mean to seem so nosy. It's just—I was looking around. I wanted—I wanted to see if maybe your father had a photograph lying around or something. Photos of the soldiers, and maybe of my brother. Of Amar."

She is looping and unlooping Tiberius's leash around and around her hand.

I feel a strange shock in my stomach. "Why would my dad have a photo of him?"

Then, I think I understand. They must have known each other in Afghanistan. Of course they must have. Gram knew there was some kind of connection. She would say it to Ellie at the gift shop all the time. She just didn't want to rush Ludmila into having to talk about it.

"Did you find one? A photo, I mean?" I ask, trying to remember all the shots my dad had displayed on his bulletin boards and shelves. There were tons of them. He was a good photographer.

"No." Ludmila clicks off our little lantern.

In the dark, amid the chirping insects and the rustling tall grass, she's quiet for what seems like a really long time.

I figure she couldn't possibly want to talk to me about it, but I ask anyway. "Will you tell us your story, some time, Ludmila?"

Nothing but crickets.

So I stand up, and I'm just about to take Tiberius back inside, when Ludmila's voice finally comes out of the darkness, soft and low.

23

"Okay. Imagine us young, like you and the twins. I was nine, Amar, twelve. We lived in a big old apartment building. It was full of houseplants and bright table-cloths and people stopping by all the time, and lovely cooking smells and cheerful voices and fiddle music. We lived on fourth floor. It was an old stone building, with all kinds of what-you-call, carving-stone decorations on the front, in the beautiful old European city of Sarajevo, in what was, is, was, known as Bosnia."

"This sort of sounds like the beginning of a fairy tale," I tell her.

"You think?" She snorts. "It won't end like one, so be warned."

The camper door opens; the light makes us squint. It's Davis. She comes slowly down the steps to join us.

"You too?" Ludmila says. "Is this children's story hour?"

Davis sits down silently on the last step, in the dark with us, and waits.

"Okay. Let's see . . . Our father, by now, was gone a long time. More than one year, since he put on his old uniform, kissed us good-bye, left us crying. Going to some place called 'the front.' No one wanted to explain what that meant, to me. I remember wondering: the front of where?

"My mother was going to have a baby. Amar wanted brother, I wanted a new sister, we spent much time fighting over that.

"'All we need is for baby to be safe and healthy,' my mother would say. But she was very worried, with all the madness and craziness in the streets, with us, stuck in our half-deserted apartment building, without our father around to help. Our grandfather, he lived with us, but he was very old and couldn't do much. And many of the neighbors were gone by now.

"Anyhow. Our father used to take us to the park and teach us to throw and catch. How to run very fast. How to climb a tree. My father believed girls should learn to do everything, same as boys. He was a doctor. He had gone to medical school at Washington University, in the state of Missouri, and he loved to talk about America. He wanted his children to see it someday. But he also loved Sarajevo, loved it enough to leave his family to fight to try to protect it.

"'This is a bunch of nonsense,' he'd said to us before he left. 'We live in modern, civilized world. No one will let this craziness happen. These lunatics in the hills, they will be stopped soon. Things will blow right over. I give it a month, then I will be back, and all will be well!'"

Ludmila makes a kind of snort-laugh, there, in the dark. "Such faith in the world!"

Then she goes on:

"A month went by. Two months. Then three. Our beautiful town of Sarajevo was under siege. The thugs surrounding us, in the hills, were sniping at innocent people, gunning us down in the streets. You never knew when or where there might be shooting. There was less and less food available. Our stomachs growled all the time. Mother and Grandfather would hurry back from market with nothing more than old, moldy vegetables. Each time Mother made it home safely from scavenging food, running with one hand on bag, one hand on belly, we all would be crying with our relief.

"We had taken the geraniums out of our pretty planters and planted carrots and lettuce. We shared seeds with neighbors. We uprooted all the potted plants and window boxes. We planted the cut-up eyes of our very last potatoes and put them in the window boxes.

"When Mother grew too big with baby, Grandfather took over all the going out. He would take a knapsack with bottles of homemade brandy for the black market, to trade for food. 'Don't worry,' Grandpa told us. 'I can run faster than wind,' he joked, because we all knew how painfully slowly he walked with his cane. He was old, but brave. He pretended to be brave, for us.

"One night, one hungry, hard night, he went out with his very last three bottles of homemade liquor tucked in his knapsack, to trade for milk and bread. We wait. Midnight. One. Two. Three . . . Dawn came. Still, my grandfather never came back," Ludmila says in her low, husky whisper. "Later, the neighbor found out he was shot in a raid at black market."

We sit for a while in the dark.

"I'm sorry, Ludmila. So sorry. And what about your father?" Davis finally whispers.

"He didn't make it either. Not a very good fairy-tale story. Sorry!"

"It sounds horrible," I say to Ludmila. "Like, medieval times."

"Yes. But it feels like only yesterday, when my world went up in smoke and fire."

I try hard to think about what to say next. "But, after the smoke and fire, you survived," I tell her. "You survived, Ludmila. Just like the fire bird."

Later, in bed, I think about the last time I saw Dad. He hadn't put on an old uniform, like Ludmila's dad had. No. He was just wearing a gray T-shirt from the school Fun Run, and a pair of his regular jeans when he left. But something was still different about him. All his bags were piled up in the hall. I hate him leaving, so I ran upstairs to my room to lie on my bed, stare at my mom's profile on the pine-knot ceiling, and wait for the sound of the front door closing.

But Dad followed me. "Charlie?"

He leaned into my doorway, holding on to the frame, so that I could only see his upper half, slanted diagonally. Like he already was aiming himself downstairs, out and away from us.

"Love you, buddy." Dad slapped the doorframe with his hand. "Be good. Listen to Gram. She means well. And email me!" he said. "Tell me what's going on."

"What's so great there," I said, "that you have to go?"

He straightened up so I could see all of him in the doorway. "I'm not going because I think it's going to be great."

"Then why?"

He thought for a minute. "I'm going because it's the opposite of great. Because it's terrible."

"Yeah?"

"It's important to tell the stories of the people that get caught up in war and violence. We can't pretend it isn't happening. So I'll be over there, writing it down, for them. To save their stories. And why don't you write something, too? We can message back and forth."

"What the heck do *I* have to write about?"

Dad had smiled. "Birds," he'd said.

Then he was gone.

That night in the camper, I dream about fire. Old-fashioned General Custer on his horse, on a grassy hillside, yelling "Fire!" A desert jeep exploding in flames. Ludmila's grandfather and mother, weighed down with bags, running in a fog of fiery smoke.

Prairie grass, ablaze.

Then, a little brown speckled bird struts into my dream. That's what I focus on, behind my closed eyelids: a bird, pecking around despite the flaming prairie grass. A bird, finding a way to survive.

GREEN PARROT

PARROT, RESCUE

24

Someday Birds List:
Bald Eagle
Great Horned Owl **(CHECK!)**
Trumpeter Swan **(HALF CHECK!)**
Sandhill Crane
Turkey Vulture
Emu (in Australia)
Passenger Pigeon **(extinct)**
Carolina Parakeet **(also extinct)**
Screech Owl **(bonus bird from Yellowstone)**
Prairie Chicken **(bonus bird from Montana)**

I stare at the list. It's tough, but not hopeless. Since we'll be driving through Minnesota and Wisconsin in a few days, we'll be passing through bald eagle nesting areas. And it's still feasible that while we're in the Midwest, by fields and lakes, that we could come across a sandhill crane.

Joel is hanging over the seat, trying to read over my shoulder. "Dad doesn't care about those dumb birds, Charlie," he says.

Davis turns around and slaps at him. "Shut up, Joel." Then she says to me, "Dad is going to be really happy to know you're trying to see the birds on that list. As long as your bird-watching doesn't slow down our progress. Right, Ludmila?"

"It's birding," I tell her. "Not bird-watching." Why is that so hard for people to remember?

We've left Montana behind, and we're finally on our way to Wall Drug, South Dakota, and its magical, mysterious offer of "free ice water" that the twins can't seem to shut up about.

"Hey," says Davis. "We're passing right by Mount Rushmore. Isn't that kind of a cross-country road trip must-see?"

Joel and Jake groan. "But the ice water!"

We turn off I-90 and curl back down southwest a bit to Rapid City and Keystone. I don't mind. Anytime we stop, I can scout for birds.

Mount Rushmore looks smaller than I thought it was going to be. I'd always imagined those heads to be enormous, something you could see from space, but they're more the size of something on the Las Vegas strip.

I watch the trees. I think I see a Steller's jay, up high in a pine. His coarse rusty-hinge call was the first clue; then I swear I saw a flash of blue among the pine needles. I find a bench, take out my Bird Book, and make a sketch. Then I try to sketch the presidents' heads. But it comes out all cartoony. I'm way better at birds than people.

After an hour at Rushmore, we're back on the road. And as we head east, more and more of those strange road signs start looming up.

"What do you think 'free ice water' actually means? There's got to be something more to it . . . ," Joel says.

"Yeah," says Jake. "It's got to be code for some kind of secret drink, or something."

Davis just rolls her eyes.

Soon, we're crunching into the gravel drive of Wall Drug. It's like an old-style, western-themed, touristy mall. The twins are squirming out of their seats.

It seems bigger inside than outside, with storefront boutiques in long hallways that branch off in various confusing directions. Everyone in here looks sweaty and dazed, like they just rolled out of their cars. Which they have, just like us.

"Hey, mister, where's the ice water?" Joel tugs on a man's green apron, standing outside a western bookstore.

"Where's the special ice water?" Jake adds. The man waves them vaguely toward the left.

I smell coffee and French-fry grease and candles and potpourri, hear the clink of dishes and the shrieks of annoyed little kids. There's too much noise, and light, and action. Too many people in here.

I need to wash my hands.

I do like I do in the halls at school: keep my eyes down and walk like I know exactly where I'm going, even if I don't. I keep turning down different hallways filled with weird tourist shops, until eventually I find a men's room.

The soap here comes out of a huge brown bottle with a sticker on it that says, "For Sale in Our Own Apothecary Shoppe!"

Soap-rinse-one-soap-rinse-two-soap-rinse-three-soap-rinse-four-soap-rinse-five . . .

Then, breathing deeply, I step back out—and my stomach squirms. I've lost them! I'm all turned around. On the alert for familiar voices or a tuft of pink hair, I wander the maze of boutiques and hallways and people. I try to remember what they were all wearing. Davis has this T-shirt that says "The Sports Team from My Area Is Superior to the Sports Team from Your Area," which she says is to make fun of sports fans. But she also wears a blue Chargers shirt sometimes, so I don't get it. Anyhow,

I don't think she has either of them on today. And of all the crazy outfits Ludmila owns, I can't remember what she had on this morning. I speed up, darting around corners and down halls, looking everywhere for that flash of her pink hair. Nothing.

I wander out to a courtyard, and suddenly, a blood-curdling shriek assaults my ears. Then a shrill, garbled, inhuman voice behind me says, "Step up, step up!"

There's a flash of green wings, and before I can put up my arm to protect myself, I feel a whoosh of air—then, daggers dig into my scalp.

Oh my gosh. There's a parrot on my head.

I look around in a panic, and realize I'm standing by a bunch of parrots—I see a grey and cockatiels and even some macaws—on tall wooden perches, bobbing their heads this way and that. Parrots! In a semicircle, in a small alcove in the courtyard.

The bird on my head feels like he's scratching some of my hair completely out. I might end up being the only kid to start school this fall with an actual bald spot.

"Doodie! *Doodie*, you naughty fellow! Get off!" A smiling, plump lady waddles up to me like a flustery hen. She has a bun of frizzy red hair, and she's wearing a green sweatshirt that says "Parrot Rescue."

"Step up!" she sings to the bird on my head, high and loud, flapping her elbows up and down and almost smacking me in the nose. Her voice makes my ears hurt almost as much as the parrot. "*Step up, Doodie!* There's a pretty bird! Who's a pretty bird?" she shrieks.

With one last sickening scrunch of claws down into my scalp, Doodie pushes off and flutters onto the lady's arm to calmly preen his feathers. He's the biggest, brightest macaw parrot I've ever seen.

His face is white marked with black, and he has a great, curved golden beak. His eye is purplish, ringed with white, then black. He only has the one eye. Where the other eye should be there's only scarred-up bird skin, like a patch of black leather.

"Let's just straighten your hair back, there: oops!" she says, bending my head down with her non-parrot-holding hand. "He pooped on you! Naughty Doodie! Stay right where you are!"

I'm not sure if she's talking to me or the parrot, but I don't move. I am paralyzed, anyway, with parrot-poop-horror.

She puts big green Doodie back on his perch, and reattaches his leg leash. The bird tilts his head and winks his one eye.

Then, the lady waddles toward a giant "Parrot Rescue" tote bag, and fishes out some wet wipes and paper towels.

"Stay still," she orders. I feel like if I don't obey her,

I may end up on a perch with a leg leash myself. This thought makes me switch from parrot-poop-horror, to parrot-poop-hysteria.

"Stop giggling or I'll have to leave the bird poop where it is. And believe me, you don't want that." She frowns, concentrating, reaching up with her big arm. As she pulls bird poop out of my hair, her arm jiggles an inch from my nose. This makes me want to laugh even more. I think I am going to have a laughter meltdown.

I am lost in Wall Drug and held captive by an arm-jiggling lady and my head is covered with parrot poop. I shake, that's how hard I'm laughing to myself.

"What's so funny?" she asks.

"I'm not sure!" I squeak.

"Okay. That should just about do it." She takes one last wet wipe from the box and cleans off her thick pink fingers. "Sorry about that. I don't know why that leg leash keeps coming undone. It's never usually an issue—Doodie never leaves his perch. He must have really liked you." She smiles. "He must have sensed something about you. Doodie's a very good judge of character."

I don't look at her. I look around at Doodie and company. "Are these birds all rescues?"

"Yes. We're a traveling exhibit, of sorts. To raise awareness, maybe get some folks interested in adopting. Parrots live a very, very long time, and sometimes they get abandoned, or their owners' circumstances change, they move or can't keep 'em, or pass away. Doodie's owner was a sweet old lady, but she passed on, and the daughter travels for work and couldn't take care of him."

"What happened to his eye?"

"No one knows. Poor sweetums. But it doesn't seem to bother him none."

This lady is talking to me like we are old friends. Like we actually know each other.

"Can I hold him the way you did?" I ask her, putting my elbow up.

"Of course!" the lady says, cracking a big smile. "Walk right up to him with your arm out. Just like that. You're a natural. Just tell him: 'Step up!'"

I do, and his scaly orange-brown claws clasp tightly around my forearm. I gasp. It's a weird feeling. I could think of it as a really bad feeling, but I try not to. I stay focused on Doodie, not my arm. He tilts his one, shiny, blue-black eye at me, and it's like he really sees me. Like he's trying to tell me something, but I can't quite read his visual cue. He has a bright yellow forehead, and his feathers lock together so seamlessly they look like velvet. He starts to gently pull at the neck of my T-shirt with his big yellow beak.

"See that?" the lady exclaims. "He's showing you love, by grooming your feathers, preening, only you don't have any feathers, so he's—oops, sorry—he's tearing the heck out of your collar—sorry about that."

She laughs, and I am laughing again, too. It's funny. When people touch me, it makes my skin crawl. But this parrot? Just like with Tiberius, I don't seem to mind it as much. Still, I move so I'm lined up right by the stand, and let Doodie hop back onto his wooden dowel.

That was fun.

"I have to say, young man, you are a bird natural! Do you want to meet a few more new friends?" the lady asks. She is nice. I like her.

We go from perch to perch. She introduces me, and a few of the other birds "step up" on my arm. The gray parrot can sing "You're a Grand Old Flag." There are a few cockatiels, and another macaw that she says is over forty years old and can swear in Spanish, French, and English. "He's got a strange accent when he speaks English," she says. And that reminds me of Ludmila.

I am starting to worry about the others. I say thank you to the frizzy-red-haired lady.

"Anytime, sweetie," she says. "Say good-bye to our new friend, Doodie!"

And Doodie says, "Anytime, sweetie!"

I am smiling. I feel braver, and still full of excitement from the parrots. I am smiling as I head past the Wall Drug gift shop, the Wall Drug bookshop, the Wall Drug apothecary, and the Wall Drug jewelry emporium.

But my smile slowly fades as I still can't find Davis, the twins, or Ludmila.

Finally, I push open the swinging screen door and look around the parking lot. There they all are, already waiting by Old Bessie!

"Finally!" shouts Ludmila. Her arms are folded; her eyebrows scrunched. Visual cue: mad.

"Oh, for Pete's sake, finally is right!" says Davis, sounding just like Gram.

"Ruff!" says Tiberius, jumping in the air for joy. I run to him, and he sniffs me madly up and down. He must smell the birds.

The twins are silent, kicking their toes in the dirt and gravel. Davis says they are disappointed. They had been really looking forward to the ice water, but it turned out to be just a regular water dispenser, like at the dentist. All those road signs for a little cone-shaped paper cup of water that disintegrated in their hands.

"Stupid water," says Jake.

"Yeah," says Joel. "They could've built a magical fountain for the price of their stupid road signs."

Davis and Ludmila think this is really funny for some reason. They are still laughing quietly to themselves as we drive away.

25

Birds can and do experience behavioral illnesses,
typically due to problems when they are deprived
of the flock. They have been known to screech,
to confine themselves to small spaces, to turn
in circles for hours. They have been known to
obsessively pluck their own feathers out. A very
sorry state of affairs for a bird indeed.
—Tiberius Shaw, PhD

We hit the eastern part of South Dakota, and we all decide we can't stand another night in the camper.

Hallelujah!

We are treating ourselves to a motel. It's right next door to the biggest Walmart I've ever seen. We went to stock up on toilet paper, snacks, and stuff. All the workers were old, and I started noticing their skin. Pinkish whitish beige, and hairy, with moles and pimples and growths and bumps and freckles and stuff. Davis and the twins and I, we have smooth light brown skin, and straight brown hair like our mom. Davis's skin is especially smooth. It's weird to say, because she's my sister, but I guess it's true that she is kind of pretty.

Despite our splurge on a motel room, I sleep badly. This trip has been hard. My hands are raw and chapped from all the washing. I am tired of bad nights' sleep. I am tired, even—and I do not say this lightly—of always eating chicken nuggets. I am tired of the unending highway noise and the vibration of the camper rattling, of the bad moldy sweaty smell of the blue mattresses, of everything changing all the time. I just want to get there already. Get to Dad and Gram. See Dad get better with the expert doctor Gram likes. Show him how much progress I've made on his Someday Birds List. Have him get better, and then: GO HOME.

The twins are jumping on the motel bed and watching an old Superman movie. Ludmila turns it off. "I want you to pay attention, okay? I have a question for you all." She lays a paper road map out on the bed.

"Okay, so you all can see. Geography lesson. We are here"—she points with a chipped, black-polished nail—"in Sioux Falls. And here"—she points with a chipped, silver-polished nail—"is where your dad and Gram are, this hospital, outside of Washington, DC. You see?" The space on the map between her silver-and-black fingernails is about eight inches, a blue line curving down from

I-90 East, to I-76 around Ohio moving through Pennsylvania, to I-95 South. "It's about 1,200 miles. That's about twenty hours of driving. And we have a few days to do it. So, where do you want to stop along the way?"

The twins go back to jumping, but more softly now. I fish out Tiberius Shaw's green journal, and flip the pages.

"Oh no," Davis groans.

"Yes—I knew it. We're going to pass right through the bald eagle breeding grounds around the Mississippi River," I tell them. "And Dad likes bald eagles. It's on the list. So we have to stop there, for starters."

Ludmila sighs, and Davis falls back flat on the other double bed.

"The only good thing about this whole dumb trip is that it gives us a chance to look for Dad's Someday Birds. We *have* to find Dad's birds."

Ludmila pats me on the shoulder and I try not to flinch. "Okay, Charlie. First stop, Charlie's bald eagle hunt. Then where?"

"We-ell," says Davis, "you know Josh? That boy I met from the Little Bighorn? He said I could come visit him in Chicago anytime. Let's stop in Chicago!"

The twins bat their eyelashes and fan their faces with their hands and croon in a fake Southern accent, "Oh Joshie! Joshie, give us a little kissie!"

"Yes, I think we *should* stop in Chicago," says Ludmila, ignoring them. "My friend Mariana works at the Field Museum. Where they have lots of cool things. Stuffed birds for Charlie. Dinosaurs. Mummies."

Joel and Jake are jumping full force on the bed again, shouting "MUMMIES!"

"Then where?" asks Davis.

"Then where?" ask the twins.

"Well . . . ," I say. "Then there's the most important place of all." I find the page in Shaw's green journal where he talks about his home.

> My secret home sits amid a stand of pine
> on a mound overlooking the silver fingers
> of Sanctuary Marsh. You will find me there,
> surrounded by birds of all flocks, miraculous
> birds that soar and wing and explain to me
> the workings of the world in ways I crave to
> express, to share, someday, with a like-minded
> friend. . . .

I say, "There is a special bird sanctuary in Virginia. It's really close to Dad's hospital. We need to go. I need to try to find Tiberius Shaw there."

Joel flops back on the bed and groans. "Charlie and his birds. Why is it always his way or the highway?"

Everyone is looking at each other, but not at me.

"You mean that guy that did the little bird statues, back at the old hospital gift shop?" Davis asks. "You want to visit him in person? Just go knock on his door?"

Joel and Jake laugh.

I take a deep breath and try to explain. "Davis. He's the biggest bird-behavior expert there is. And think about it. First I found his bird statues in the gift shop. Then I basically stumbled across his very own private journal. And now his actual home turns out to be right near where we are going."

"It's destiny!" Jake yells, flapping his arms as he jumps on the bed, and Tiberius, the dog, starts barking madly.

"Well, Charlie," says Ludmila, scooping up the dog to shush him. "We certainly can try to visit the sanctuary." I see her and Davis exchange a look. "But no promises about visiting anybody's private house. That's taking things a little far, don't you think?"

I don't answer. I just nod. That's enough for me, for now.

We load back into the camper, and we head east on I-90 into a foggy summer rain. The sky looks like cement, and the air smells like rain sizzling on hot pavement.

178

South Dakota is green and straight, so different from the beige desert of Las Vegas, the purple mountains of Wyoming, or the grassy plains of Montana.

I am in the front so I don't get carsick, as usual. Ludmila flicks on the wipers and pumps the *pssssht, pssssht*. As the windshield clears, I think about her brother, making up that funny word for windshield-wiper fluid. What would it be like, to be plunged into a whole new world and have to learn a strange language? To not know how to say stuff?

Then, I think: that's kind of like Dad. He is in a whole new world where he doesn't know how to say stuff.

I shake that thought away.

"Ludmila," I ask, "what happened next? Back in Sarajevo, when you were a kid?"

She brushes the electric-blue bangs of her wig out of her eyes. "What do you mean?"

Swish, swish go the wipers. *Swish, swish.*

"I think you should tell us more of the story."

Behind me, sitting at the little camper table, Davis takes her earphones out of her ears. The twins are back in the bunks, curled up with Tiberius, playing some handheld game.

Ludmila taps her fingers on the wheel, thinking. "Where did I leave off?"

"With your mother about to have a baby, pretty much."

179

"You really want this? It is not a pretty story."

"You know all about *us*," says Davis. "And we don't know *anything* about you."

Ludmila looks straight out at the rain for a really long time, then she starts speaking.

26

"So, things were getting worse," Ludmila tells us. "Me and Amar and very pregnant mother. Hungry. Worried. Living in no-longer-sunny apartment, with shelling all the time, boom boom. No father, no grandfather, both gone. Amar is the only man. He tries to act all big and important, like he can take care of us. He always did."

Ludmila's eyes are bleary, but she shakes her head so hard, her blue wig gets a little out of place.

"My mother tried to tell us stories and invent funny games for us to play. But underneath it all, we were very afraid. The days, all too often, were filled with whistles and explosions and broken glass. The lights would flicker and go out. The heat stopped working, and we would put on two, three, four sweaters, one on top of the other, to stay warm. I could hear people crying and wailing in the streets. Even though my mother had covered the windows with paper and pushed all the furniture up against them, so we couldn't look out, I could still hear things. Very bad things.

"'Don't worry,' she would whisper to us. "'We will find a way to leave Sarajevo soon.'

"'And how are we gonna do that? And when? Before the baby, or after?' Amar would ask. Amar was always very direct, practical, and to the point. 'Look at you, Mama,' Amar said. 'You can barely climb up and down the stairs to the cellar. How are you going to get us out of here?' She had no answer to that one. No answer at all.

"Anyhow. The more scary noises there were outside in the street, the more time we spent down in the cellar of the apartment house, huddled with our neighbors. There was Mrs. Zelinka, who unraveled her sweater to knit us each a cap and scarf to help stay warm. And Mr. Szabo, who told us wild and crazy fairy tales.

"We would hide down in that cellar with the neighbors for hours when we heard the shelling, all the cries and booms and crashes and whistles. Over the months we all watched my mother's belly grow.

"Mrs. Zelinka, Mr. Szabo, and the other grown-ups knew the baby coming would not be an easy or a good time for Mama. They did not believe her when she said she was going to find us a way out. They watched her belly with worry and with fear."

Ludmila stops her story just as we reach a bridge going over a river. She says, "Enough of this. We are free and happy in this country, today. So let's look around. It's not every day you cross the mighty Mississippi."

It's just a normal river—gray and choppy, this rainy day, and not extra wide.

"I thought the Mississippi was huge," Davis says from her seat behind us. "With riverboats and Mark Twain and all that."

"Yeah," says Joel, who's just made his way out to the camper table, too. "I thought this river was famous."

"It *is* famous," I tell him. "It's famous for bald eagles. And we need to find one for Dad's bird list. So look sharp, people."

Davis and Joel groan, but I pay no attention. "We've only found two off the list, the great horned owl and the trumpeter swan. That's a pathetic track record, and we're more than halfway across the country."

Davis and the twins are grumpy, but Ludmila smiles at me. As usual, I cannot tell at all what she is thinking.

But maybe some bald-eagle-spotting will help her forget about Sarajevo for a while.

We drive across the bridge—across the mighty Mississippi—with our eyes peeled.

Nope. No eagles. At least, not yet.

27

On the other side, it's Wisconsin—which pretty much looks just like Minnesota.

"I went to college here," says Ludmila. "UW–Madison."

"Do all the students there have pink hair like you?" asks Joel.

"No. Some have purple. Some red," says Ludmila, giving him a funny dead-eye stare. "I studied physical therapy. Prosthetics, artificial limbs. I wanted to work for the Red Cross, help people recover after wars. But I dropped out."

"Oh, that's too bad," says Davis. "Why?"

Ludmila shrugs. "I don't know. Maybe I got too sad," she says.

"You know," she adds, a minute later, changing the subject, "sometimes people call this area 'Minnesconsin,' little towns and lakes, fishing and ice fishing in winter. And dairy farms, of course. But there's a spot around here that's kind of unique. It's called the Dells. That's where we're stopping tonight. Tomorrow, we're doing something in the morning for Charlie, and in the afternoon we're doing something for Joel and Jake."

"What? What are we doing?" Joel asks, jumping up and down in his seat, and causing Tiberius to bark.

Ludmila says what she always does. "Wait and find out."

· BALD EAGLE ·

DUCKS and EAGLES

28

The early years of a bald eagle's life is spent in free and glorious exploration, winging its way across vast swaths of greater North America. Indeed, it is my belief that "free and glorious exploration" should be key components of all young creatures' lives, avian and human alike.
—Tiberius Shaw, PhD

Early the next morning, we are all sitting in something called a Wisconsin Duck. It's this weird vehicle that's open on the sides and painted army green. The point is, it can go on land, and then drive right into the water and float. That's what we're about to do.

Ludmila says the main reason people used to come to the Wisconsin Dells was because of the Wisconsin River, which flows through a gorge near here, past some narrow cliffs. It was a good fishing and camping spot, so it got famous. The town grew and got really touristy. Nowadays, she says, most people don't come for the river. They come for cotton candy, the Ripley's Believe

It or Not! Museum, saltwater taffy, and especially for the waterparks, where you can get soaking wet, indoor and out, summer and winter, in every possible way.

I don't like getting wet in *any* possible way. But later, after this Duck ride, which is for me (because they say that sometimes there are eagles on the river!), we are going to a waterpark for Joel and Jake. I'm trying not to think about it. I'm too busy trying not to feel sick from the smells of exhaust, along with a stinky rubbery poncho the lady next to me is wearing, on this hard bench seat.

The Duck rumbles along some bumpy side roads while the guide, who is also the driver, shouts stuff. I'm kind of excited, because I've never driven into a river before. And maybe, just maybe, I'll see that eagle for Dad. I have my eyes peeled. I'm hyper-alert. I'm ready.

"Stop looking like such a dork," says Joel.

I ignore him.

Our guide's a big, solid old lady with short gray hair and lots of small earrings up and down her ears. She puts the engine in neutral, then shouts over the noise about what's going to happen. Like we can't already figure that out. "This boat you are sitting in," she yells, "is an original amphibious unit from World War II. Prepare to be amazed, as this incredible vehicle is about to drive into the water!"

We've barely prepared our amazement when we lurch

forward and *kersplash,* we're floating, and the sound of the motor in the back goes from a *grrrrr* to *bloop-bloop-bloop.* I look at Davis and she looks at me. The lady in the stinky rubber poncho smiles—I quickly look down. She takes out her phone and twists this way and that to snap photos of the water. Some people are halfheartedly clapping. Why? The boat just did what it was supposed to do.

"Now, ladies and gentlemen," says the tour guide, "we will head upriver for a leisurely ride."

There are about twenty passengers, silent in the morning fog. Everyone's eyes are on the tour guide.

"Folks, you are riding in a very special vehicle, created in 1942 by General Motors to navigate the harbors of European cities that had been totally obliterated, turned into rubble, in World War II. They needed a way for supplies to be brought from land to boat, and boat to land."

"Thank goodness things like that don't happen anymore, eh?" says the rubbery-smelling lady next to me.

I tell her, "But they do. A European city was obliterated in the 1990s. It was Sarajevo. I don't know about whether they needed boats, though."

"The vehicle you're riding in today has a 115-horsepower Cummings diesel engine. The six-wheel drive, ten-speed transmission has a power transfer for water propulsion, and a tiller line connected to the rudder. In fact, if you would all turn around, you will notice that the construction of the Duck's very special amphibious motor has been raised several inches to accommodate the new higher caliber . . ."

Yada yada yada. Everyone twists around obediently to look behind them at the motor—

Except me. I don't turn around. My eyes are riveted dead straight ahead.

Right behind the tour guide's left shoulder where no one else can notice it—because they're all turned around looking at the engine—is a real, live, bald eagle. I am not kidding. I do not kid. He is there like a sign. Like a symbol. That symbol that he is. He is there for me, and for Dad.

I whisper to Dad, even though I know he can't hear it: "*He's here! The eagle from our list! He came!*"

He is perched on a pine branch overhanging the murky green water, a postage stamp come to life. He cocks his head, showing off his powerful golden beak and a piercing eye. He is a thousand times more fabulous-looking than any photo or drawing. I can see each individual feather overlapping down his velvety brown body. He bends to preen a feather on his shoulder. He looks like the Master of the Universe.

And still, no one sees. Because they are all too busy being interested in the horsepower of the gas engine from 1940 something whatever transmission speed whatever at the back of the boat. Unbelievable.

"The Duck can go fifty miles per hour on land, and six knots on water!" the tour guide exclaims.

"Ooh, uh-huh! Ah!" people say to the cloud of blue motor-smoke back there.

I try to get Jake's attention, but I don't want to unlock my eyes from the eagle. And Jake's looking the other way. I am still the only one who has noticed.

Bald Eagle. **CHECK!!!!**

You know, it has to be said: bald eagles are not as noble as some people think. They're kind of lazy and nasty, and would rather steal a fish than catch one themselves. They'll eat carrion—that means dead animal meat, like roadkill. And they'll even snack on garbage. They cheat and trick and bully other birds—so in the "appropriate US symbol" department, they come up dubious. In the "cool-looking" department, of course, they score big.

In the "Dad's Someday Birds List" department, they're a home run.

The eagle turns his head and glares right at me. Then, he lifts off the branch and disappears back into the woods. There is only the slight sound his wings make:

Luff.

And he is gone.

I would have thought I had dreamed it, if I didn't see the heavy branch still bobbing up and down from where he was perched. I close my eyes and try to imprint his image on my brain, those thick yellow talons, that head! I want to sketch him later. What is it like to be as strong as that?

"You missed it! There was a bald eagle, *right there*!" I lean over and tell Davis when the tour lady stops talking.

"Uh-huh," says Davis. She smiles at me like I just said "Nice weather we're having."

"No, really," I try again. "He was right there! You were all turned around to see the motor."

"As long as you're happy, Charlie," she says.

Sometimes my sister is infuriating.

29

The search for love is mysterious in every species.
The thrill of spying a potential mate across either a
crowded forest floor—or dance floor—amounts to
the same thing: a frisson, the thrill of the approach.
The glory, of the possibility of love.
—Tiberius Shaw, PhD

By the time the Duck puts us back on dry land, the sun is coming out, and there are prickles of real heat on our shoulders.

"It's turning into a scorcher. Real waterpark weather," says Davis, and the twins jump up and down. I don't know how they can think about more rides. I've had enough movement for a lifetime.

But every time I think about the bald eagle, I get the feeling like I have this thrilling secret. Only I saw him. He saw only me. That was pretty much worth the whole seasick, carsick Duck trip. It was worth it for Dad's list— and for me, too. Dad would be proud, I think. I can't wait to sketch him. And to check Shaw's journal, too, to see if he wrote about eagles.

But first, the waterpark.

It's gotten really hot. The sky's a hazy kind of pale blue. This morning's early mist is history. The sun glares down full force.

Davis is wearing a white bikini top and a pair of really short shorts. Ludmila says, "Why don't you wear the one-piece I packed for you?" Davis rolls her eyes.

Ludmila is wearing a long black sundress, black high-tops with the toes cut out, a floppy black hat, and dark black sunglasses. She has smeared thick white sunscreen all over her shoulders—and mine, and the twins—so we all smell like coconut custard. The sunscreen feels so sticky and gross, even the twins complain. "It's better than burning," Ludmila scolds. Every day, it's like she acts a little more like Gram.

Davis still doesn't trust her completely. Last night, after dinner, she opened a zipper compartment in her purse and showed me the flash drive with Dad's computer files, the one she made when she caught Ludmila snooping in Dad's office before we left. "I think somebody else in the family should know that I'm holding on to this," she whispered to me. "Just in case."

"In case of what?" I asked.

"Of whatever. I mean, just know that they're here. She's been acting really nice with us, but what's her ultimate goal? Why does she care so much about Dad? I still think it was the right thing to do—for me to keep his files safe, I mean. Until we know for sure what her deal is. Because we don't know what Dad was writing when he got injured! What if it's supposed to be something secret? Even something secret, about Amar? And she's snooping around? We have to protect Dad."

I don't think she's right about this. But Davis doesn't listen to what I think.

That was last night. Now, outside the waterpark, I watch Davis swing her purse up on her bare shoulder, and I think about the flash drive in the secret inside pocket. Ludmila puts the bottle of sunscreen away in *her* purse, and we all walk to the entrance, except the twins, who've broken into a run up ahead.

Behind us, in the camper, poor Tiberius is left behind. But he's parked in the shade, with lots of fresh water. And we plan to take turns on coming back to check on him, every hour.

Up ahead, I see a huge tangle of bright-colored tube slides, and a pool where people are getting hit by a mechanical tidal wave. Joel and Jake head straight for it. Ludmila, her sun hat flopping, follows with our tickets.

Davis has noticed a group of teenagers hanging out at the snack bar. A couple of girls in bathing suits and T-shirts, and some guys, bare-chested and tan, with long shaggy hair. They are sitting on top of a picnic table.

"I'm going to the snack bar," Davis says.

She goes up and orders, and while she's waiting, she smiles over at the group. I watch as one of the guys slowly gets up and goes over to talk to her. He puts one hand up on the wall, right above her head and slightly to the right, and leans over her, and they keep talking and smiling. It looks like he's probably giving her a good view of his armpit hair, but she doesn't seem to mind it.

I'm thinking of those prairie chicken fire birds. Males go at dawn to a clearing in the prairie grass, something called a *lek*, and stomp their feet around really loudly. A lot of birds have singing or dancing contests like that. And bower birds in Australia, they actually build whole big houses of woven straw in order to impress their mates. They even decorate the front lawns with shiny, colorful bits of this and that. There's a picture of that in Shaw's journal, too.

But all it seems to take for Davis to feel flirty is the sight of muscles and a smile. And maybe armpit hair. Gross.

Meanwhile, Ludmila and the twins are almost at the front of the line.

"Are you coming on the ride, Charlie?" the twins ask me.

"No."

"Oh really," says Joel.

"What a shock," says Jake.

Those guys know how much I hate rides. Then I realize they are being sarcastic. And this makes something flip in my stomach. I am kind of mad. I want to prove to them I can do it. I think about the eagle, about being strong.

"On second thought I've changed my mind. I'll go."

Jake and Joel just look at me. Ludmila doesn't say anything; she just rips off another ticket and hands it to me.

I gulp. I've gone and done it now. But with one twin behind me and one ahead of me, there's no way out. With shaky legs, I climb the ladder. It's as tall as a three-story building. "Come on, Charlie," my brothers say. "One step at a time!"

Yes—step by step, getting closer to doom.

The attendant hands me a big, slippery rectangle of blue plastic. I am confused. He says, "Look!" and points to Jake, ahead of me, sitting on the plastic, already at the top of the slide with his legs stretched straight ahead of him. How does he just automatically know how to do these kinds of things?

The waterslide is a pitch-black tube that plunges down, twisting and turning, and ends in some kind of abyss where, at the last second, a tidal wave is supposed to knock you over.

And this is considered fun.

My heart is hammering, but I catch Jake looking at me—he gives me a thumbs-up. And Joel, holding his own piece of blue plastic, says, "Hey, Charlie, this is awesome!"

The attendant says, "One, two, THREE!" and pushes Jake into the dark void of the tube. I hear an echo of his scream die away. I am frozen, stuck at the top.

The attendant pushes Joel down the next hole. He is gone. Ludmila is waiting down below. I can see her black floppy hat tilted up at us, tiny as my thumbnail.

The attendant peels my hands away from the sides of the tube. "Sit down *here*! No, put your legs *out*. Not that way," he commands. I'm about to ask where to keep my arms when he counts "ONE-TWO-THREE" really fast and before I can catch a breath, he pushes me. And I am flying down . . . down . . . down . . . into the black mouth of the abyss.

I am going to die.

I slip up onto the curved sides of the tube and back to the center again, in total darkness, careening around and up and down in bewildering directions. I can feel each riveted section under my butt, *kathump-kathump-kathump*. I am half on, half off the piece of blue plastic. I am in total darkness with no control! No control! I just have to ride this out. My heart is still pounding like a hammer. My breathing is shallow. I am hyperventilating.

Then something catches on the side of my leg. It's like a hot poker just burned a line along it.

I remember the attendant telling me to keep my feet straight ahead and together, so I do. I concentrate on doing just that, and on breathing. I can't tell whether my eyes are open or closed; there's basically no difference.

After an eternity of blind terror, the tube spits me out in a waist-high pool of water. It's like being thrown out of nothingness and back into the real live world.

Other people are scrambling out of the chutes on either side of me, laughing and screaming. Joel and Jake are screaming, too, laughing and high-fiving each other. They see me and wade over, hopping forward through the choppy water lapping around their board shorts, which are knocked half off them, and they each hold up a hand to slap.

My brothers have never wanted to high-five me before.

Never once that I've ever remembered, not once in my whole, entire life.

I put up both my palms, and we slap, make contact—just as a tidal wave hits and crashes us all to bits. It's like being knocked inside a washing machine. I flounder for a while, and choke and snort water, then I feel a small hand yank me up—it's Joel. The three of us are back standing up in the water again, and now we are laughing, all three of us together. And my brothers are pushing me out of the wading pool toward the exit.

"Did you see Charlie?" Jake shouts to Ludmila, who is waiting with towels. She is smiling so wide, I can see all of her straight, white teeth. It's so easy to read her visual cue!

"Charlie did it! He did it!"

Joel and Jake are smiling and laughing. They are happy for me. It's like they are proud of me! I feel like one of them! I am happy in a way that makes my stomach scrunch, that makes me want to jump up in the air.

Then Ludmila points to my leg. "You're bleeding, Charlie!"

It's true. I look down, and there's a line of blood all along the side of my right leg.

"Jeez, it figures," says Jake.

And this is a weird thing: before I noticed the cut, it didn't hurt at all. But the minute I see it, it starts to sting. Bad.

"I thought there was something sharp that poked me

when I was going down inside the slide." I feel myself go pale and wobbly.

"It just figures," says Jake. "We finally get him to do something fun, and then *this* happens."

Blood is starting to run down my leg into my Croc shoe. I start to feel like I am going to faint.

Ludmila roots around in her purse, finds paper napkins, and wraps them tightly on my leg. "Keep pressing. We go find the first aid."

The twins groan and look around. "Where's Davis? Can she take us on some more rides while you get Charlie fixed?"

Davis is nowhere in sight. I'm bleeding through the napkins already. My head feels funny and far away. "Sorry, kids," says Ludmila. "Right now, please, to stay together."

The little first-aid trailer is not much bigger than Old Bessie. A lady cleans out my cut, and it stings like crazy. I yelp and yowl a little bit. She asks about the location of the metal screw that scratched me, but I am deep inside myself and can't talk, so Ludmila and the twins have to answer for me.

After they patch me up, the nurse says, "When was your last tetanus shot? You might need one."

Great. More good news.

But they are worried that we will complain or sue them, I guess, so they give us all kinds of free coupons. Free passes to the park, free food vouchers, free admission to Ripley's Believe It or Not! Museum, and last but not least, a free night's stay at someplace called the Coyote Holler Lodge. It is the hotel that's attached to the waterpark.

My leg doesn't feel too terribly horrible. It's tingly and stiff, but I guess I'll live. I think back to the bald eagle, on the water this morning. Maybe he really did transfer some strength to me.

I wait on a lounge chair by the pool, while Ludmila checks on Tiberius, and Davis takes the twins on a few other rides.

You know, it's weird. Before I got pushed down into that black hole of a ride, I was scared to death I would get hurt. And then: I *did* get hurt. But getting hurt wasn't as bad as *being afraid of getting hurt*. If I had to say what the very worst part of that ride was? I'd say it was the few seconds *before* I got pushed down the hole.

Weird.

30

*As words spill forth from our lips, it is said we
murmur. Starlings, those throngs of European
immigrants, spill forth across the lip of the sky in
their own murmurations, and so they speak to us. A
complex system, a grand family of interconnection,
they dive and swoop and weave. What are they
trying to murmur to us—and each other—as they
move across the empty page of the sky?*
—Tiberius Shaw, PhD

If you are offered a coupon for a free night's stay at
the Coyote Holler Lodge in compensation for being horribly wounded by a faulty screw in their waterpark slide,
it would be crazy not to accept. So after the park, we
head right over.

In addition to the outdoor waterpark, the Coyote
Holler Lodge also has an indoor waterpark attached to
it. I limp on my cut leg through a lobby lined with big
fake cactuses sporting cowboy hats, and crack open the

door just to take a look. Then I close it fast. It's a chaos of shrieking kids and steamy chlorine.

Joel says, "This place has a three-story spiral slide! You go into it through a giant toilet seat! It's awesome! You climb in and get flushed down."

Davis says, "I think I already have that 'flushed-down-the-toilet' kind of feeling."

After we check into our super-air-conditioned room, we head to the hotel restaurant, which is called the Road-runner Roadhouse. We scramble into a big deep booth with red leathery seats, and order right away, because we're starving. And I make the amazing discovery that the Roadrunner Roadhouse in the Wisconsin Dells makes the *best chicken nuggets in the universe.*

Tender, totally-white-meat chicken with perfectly crispy coating, not too spicy, not too bland, and a side of golden fries that are the perfect combination of crispy outside, soft, golden, buttery almost-mashed-consistency potato inside. It all comes in a giant red plastic basket lined with a red-and-white-checked paper napkin. I eat every last crumb and wish there were more, more, more.

The twins gobble down theirs, too. Although they ruin it with disgusting ketchup and dipping sauces.

As we munch, Davis shifts around in her seat. She clears her throat a few times. Finally, she asks Ludmila, "So, um. I was just wondering. When your brother was in the army, what did he do there, anyway?"

Ludmila frowns. But then her face kind of recovers its normal straight-staring look, and she sighs.

"He was an attaché, like, sort of a community reaching-out person for his unit. He was very friendly, very open, my brother. Not like me. Amar talked to everybody, loved everybody, so it was a good fit."

Ludmila is playing with the saltshaker. She cups her hand and spills a little salt out into it. She stares at the salt as she talks. "He loved everybody, but especially your father. They were friends, you know. It was part of Amar's job to drive the visitors around, so. He was your father's driver."

We are all quiet as this sinks in.

"In the jeep?" Davis whispers, her face pale.

Ludmila flings the salt from her hand over her left shoulder. "Amar was the driver. He was the one who drove your father around. Until that day. And now I drive you around. Funny world."

All four of us, our eyes just go big. It suddenly seems unbelievable that we didn't know this all along.

That Amar and Dad were friends.

That they were in the same jeep.

How could we not have known this?

Davis and the twins all reach out at the same time to

put their hands on top of Ludmila's, on top of the pile of salt she's made on the table.

I hate the feeling of gritty salt, so I don't put out my hand. But: "I'm sorry to hear that, Ludmila," I say.

"I know, Charlie," she says. She is both teary, and smiling.

At just about sunset, Davis and I take Tiberius out to pee behind the hotel. The front of this place is super-fancy, with columns and a waterfall and everything, but the back is just plain gray cement block. It's kind of funny.

"Yeah, it is," says Davis. "Some things in this world are just not what they seem."

We're not talking much. We are thinking through what Ludmila told us about Amar and Dad.

"If Amar died in the jeep accident, then shouldn't that make Ludmila feel mad at Dad—and us?" says Davis.

"I don't know," I say.

"God, I feel so stupid," Davis says. "Here I thought she was some kind of spy, or after some information of Dad's. But she probably just wants to feel close to Dad because he was with her brother when he died. Right? That's it, right? And that's only natural." Davis sighs.

I shrug, and we keep walking. Or rather Davis walks; Tiberius and I both limp. The cut on my leg is stiff and sore.

We cross the lot and head into a field of tall grass. Tiberius skitters this way and that, zigzagging like crazy after mice. There's probably a whole little mouse universe out of our sight here. There is so much in the world that you can't see.

Suddenly Davis stops walking. She points toward the pale purple horizon. "What's that?"

At first I think they are bats, but then I know. Tiny pinpricks of black, thousands of them, dot the sky over the distant fields, flying in close formation. The black dots swoop one way, then another, swirling and changing shapes, from a big oval, to a fast-twisting figure eight, to a great sail, floating over the fields.

They are starlings. A murmuration of starlings, to be precise. We watch them dive and flip, crossing over each other in all kinds of twisting, tugging, stretching shapes. There must be thousands. Or are they just one thing? The shape of something bigger?

Davis holds up her phone to take a video. "We can show Dad. Hey. How do they keep from smacking into each other? It's a miracle!"

She's never been interested in birds before. I'm excited to tell her. "They get strategic information from seven points around them. From seven birds flying nearest them. It tells them how far or how close they can get."

"Huh. That's wild. Wow. I mean, imagine if people had that," says Davis to herself. She thinks a minute. "Are the seven touching-distance birds all members of the same family?"

I shrug. "I don't know. They could be. Because you'd really have to trust those birds."

Davis asks, "What if you were a starling? Who would your seven touching-distance birds be?"

"That's a pretty weird question, Davis. But I guess they would be Dad, Gram, Joel, Jake, you. That's five. And maybe Ludmila . . ."

"Okay. And?"

"Tiberius Shaw."

Davis laughs. "Charlie, you talk about Tiberius Shaw even more than you talk about Dad, these days."

I think about this. Tiberius Shaw is my bird guru idol. I need him to help me learn more about birds, because facts about birds help me calm down. Facts about birds turn mysteries—like murmurations—into something knowable and real. And finding birds in the wild, to cross off Dad's list, well, that's like a calm blanket settling down on me, soothing all my nerves. It's better than a hundred hand-washings.

I wonder what it will be like when I finally meet Tiberius Shaw. I have so many questions. What is he working on now? How much time does he spend out in the wild? How did he lose the little green book? Or did he give it away? I know I would feel terrible if I lost my Bird Book. Does he miss it, or was it so long ago that he's forgotten about it? Does he want it back? And does he remember putting in all those hints, about where to find him in the Sanctuary Marsh, in the place on the island with the best view? Has anybody else ever tried to find him there?

That's what I think about while Davis and I watch the starling flock dive and swoop, doubling back on itself, changing and morphing into one eerie shape after another. They become smaller and smaller, high and far away in the dusky Wisconsin air, until they finally disappear.

The next morning, we have a quick breakfast in the Roadrunner Roadhouse, which smells like coffee and bacon and warm cinnamon rolls. And Ludmila makes our daily call to Gram. She puts the phone on speaker and sets it faceup on the table.

It's always hard at first, to hear Gram's tough gruff voice. But then we get over it.

"So, tell me what you did yesterday."

Ludmila says, "Charlie went down a waterslide!"

"You gotta be joshin' me. Charlie? Went on a ride? Well, what a little daredevil! Hey, Charlie, I'm proud of you! And I bet it was fun, right? I bet you loved it. Right?"

"I cut my leg and I probably need a tetanus shot," I inform her.

Ludmila says, "Unfortunately, yes, he got this big long scratch from a loose screw."

Joel jumps in. "Charlie *is* a loose screw." He and Jake laugh.

"But they didn't want Charlie to sue them, so we got a free night at a hotel," says Joel.

"Come again?" says Gram over the crackly connection. "What's that?"

"How's Dad?" Davis asks.

"Oh honey, they're still testing and scanning. Just in case he needs to go into more surgery, they want to make sure they know every single little thing they could possibly want to know."

"Surgery?" Davis's eyes pop. We all freeze and hold our breath.

"Oh, don't you worry," Gram says. "Don't you worry one bit. He won't need more surgery; Dr. Spielman's just taking precautions. Everything's fine! Your job right now is to have some fun. You haven't had much of a summer, so I want you to live it up."

Live it up. Ha.

We go back to the chilly room and pack up. No one speaks. I think we are all still imagining Dad, in that new hospital. Why did Gram have to say the words "more surgery"?

I don't want to think about it.

I imagine what it'll be like to tell Dad: "Remember how I hate the outdoors? Well, I've come all the way across the country to you, and I've seen all the birds on our Someday list, Dad."

It will be like a hundred hand-washings of calm.

· TURKEY VULTURE ·

HALL of BIRDS

31

*The Hall of Birds at the Field Museum is a Hall for
the Ages. Every human should visit it at least once,
to garner a sense of the diversity in the natural
world, of live and let live. And of what we've let die.*
—Tiberius Shaw, PhD

I am trying to find images of the Hall of Birds on Ludmila's phone as she circles the Field Museum parking lot. It is pounding rain, but I don't even mind. I am so excited I can't stop scrolling, even though the motion sickness makes me want to puke.

"Charlie's gonna make us spend the whole time in the stupid bird place. I want to see the mummies," says Joel.

He has on Ludmila's electric-blue wig. Ludmila is just letting him wear it. He reaches up to adjust it.

Sometimes Joel likes to make himself look different from Jake. Once, when they were about five, he went into the bathroom and cut off most of his hair. Another time he wore one of Dad's ties like a headband around his head for a week. Now, I guess, it's Ludmila's electric-blue wig. He says he does it because he gets tired of everyone thinking he's not him.

"You can go see the mummies, Joel," says Ludmila, craning her neck to look for parking spots. Rain is sloshing down hard on the windshield. Old Bessie smells even mustier when it rains. "Mummies, birds, yes. But first we find Mariana."

That's the name of her friend from Sarajevo. She works in the offices here.

We park so far away we're soaked when we finally make it up the big, wide, stone steps. This place is like an enormous palace, with columns and giant colorful pennants above the entry, flapping in the rain. I hear echoing voices of crowds of people and footsteps and talking and laughter and people putting umbrellas away and buying tickets.

"Hall of Birds," I say. "Hall of Birds Hall of Birds Hall of Birds." My heart is pumping with joy.

"We get it, Charlie." Davis pokes me in the ribs.

Just then, Ludmila shrieks. A slim, dark-haired lady, waiting by the ticket booth, also shrieks and runs over to her. They hug, smiling, and blabber in what I guess is Bosnian. Everyone filing through the entry stares at them a little bit.

Ludmila introduces us to Mariana, who nods at each of us and pats Joel gently on his electric-blue head.

Ludmila and Mariana keep hugging each other in sudden bursts. Their eyes look glassy. They blabber some more. Then Mariana digs in her wallet and pulls out a photo of three little kids. "My boys," she says, handing it to Ludmila.

"My God," says Ludmila. "And I only ever met Luka. Two more boys, you've had! What is Luka, like five, six, now? You've been busy."

"It is insanity, yes. Going to college at night. Working here days. And the boys. The good thing is Karim got promoted at the hotel—he is really working his way up."

"So, you two have known each other a long time?" Davis asks.

"We went to the same school, lived on the same street," Mariana says. Then she turns and puts a hand on Ludmila's arm. "I'm so sorry about Amar, Mila. I'm so sorry." That strange, glassy look in both their eyes gets worse. Ludmila's eyes get red, and she looks down.

"Why did he keep going back there, over and over, all those tours?" Mariana asks Ludmila. She sounds almost mad about it.

Ludmila's mouth goes into a straight line. She shakes her head, but doesn't answer.

We are still standing in the entrance, dripping. I

can see Sue, the world's largest and most complete T. rex skeleton, rising up above everything, back along the main floor. A pterodactyl hovers over her, wings outspread, hanging by some invisible wire. Joel and Jake are jumping up and down. We are all impatient to get going.

While Mariana and Ludmila are jabbering and talking, Davis hands me a brochure with the picture of a big pelican on the cover:

The bird collection of the Field Museum is one of the largest in the world, with more than 500,000 specimens representing almost all bird families in the world. We have 90% of the world's genera and species here, and specimens include study skins, eggs, nests, and skeletons. We also have a tremendous database, and we stand at the forefront of research, both in the field and in the lab . . .

I have my backpack with my Bird Book and colored pencils. I hope they will let me set up shop somewhere and do some sketching.

Finally, Ludmila and Mariana run out of Bosnian things to say. Ludmila turns to us. "Davis, you want to take the twins to the mummies?" Ludmila says. "Mariana has arranged something for Charlie."

We cut across the main floor where a big crowd mills around that famous T. rex dinosaur, Sue. Her skeleton tilts forward and her little arms dangle in front of her. She's hovering like some sort of museum party hostess.

Sue is smaller than I thought a T. rex would be. Those *Jurassic Park* movies made them look tall as skyscrapers. But in any case, with that set of teeth, it's nice to know they're extinct. Although dinosaurs do still exist in a way, because birds, starting with that little archaeopteryx I showed Ludmila back in Montana, are direct dinosaur descendants. Birds go way back. Further than us.

Joel, Jake, and Davis have joined the big, buzzing, milling crowd, which is like a murmuration of people, slowly circling, shifting shapes, orbiting the skeleton. But Mariana, Ludmila, and I, we turn past the dino-murmuration, and find ourselves face-to-face with a glass case of puffins.

I breathe in sharply. I stand still. The puffins are only the start. There are more cases. Other cases. Big, shining, glass cases everywhere, stretching across a whole Hall of Birds. There are cases with raptors, shorebirds, songbirds, ocean birds. They stand on perfect legs, or sit on nests, or hang from wire as if in flight, against backdrops of snow, of marsh, ocean, or forest. These stuffed birds are so lifelike, so lit up with beautiful light in their fake glass wildernesses.

I don't know where to go, what to look at first.

"I'll be right back, bird boy," says Mariana, smiling. "I'm going to see if my friend Helen can let you into the lab."

Ludmila tousles my hair, which she should know I hate, and then goes to join the twins and Davis at the mummies.

Who could possibly care about mummies?

Perfectly still shorebirds stand on real sand with painted water behind them. There's a white pelican, wings outspread, frozen in time. Caught in a moment, trapped in suspended animation, just so that people like me can get up close, put our noses against the glass, and imagine we're right there with him, in flight.

These birds are not quite alive, but they are also not quite dead. It's a hard thing to explain. It gives me a funny feeling in my stomach.

I take out my Bird Book. This is going to be way better than drawing even from Audubon's bird plates in the baby elephant book. I can see each individual feather. I start penciling the outlines of the pelican's wings, his flattened head and his plunging, pointed beak that stretches back up and surrounds his tiny eye. All I concentrate on is that one pinprick pupil of eye.

Mariana comes and taps me on the shoulder. I jump.

"Hey!" she says. Then she bends over my sketchbook and peers at my pelican. "Did you draw all that just now? That's amazing!"

I slam the book shut. I never let anyone see my work.

"Do you want to see what goes on in the back, and

talk to a real ornithologist? I told Helen I had a budding pupil out here."

I think: budding trees. Pelican-eye pupil. Student. I am a growing student.

We go through a door marked *private* to where a blond lady in a lab coat is waiting. "You must be our young scientist," she says, putting out her hand.

I am too shy to take it, so I tell the floor: "My name is Charlie."

"Nice to meet you, Charlie. I'm Helen. If you want to see our lab, I can show you how we prepare 'study skins' of the birds, for research purposes."

She leads us through a door to a room with a bunch of desks, cubicles, and sturdy tables, where a couple of wrinkly retired-age people in Field Museum T-shirts sit. They have special magnifying desk lamps, and little tweezers and tool-things. They are each working with what looks like lumps of feathers.

"These birds were brought to us after they flew into buildings nearby. We have a program where we preserve them," says Helen.

An old lady looks up from her pile of feathers and smiles. "See?" she says to me. "I cut open the bird, remove the insides, restuff it with cotton, and sew it back up. That's how we make a study skin."

My stomach feels quirky.

Helen says, "Any bird you're particularly interested in? For instance, do you like owls?"

I think about the little screech owl in the tree at Yellowstone. I think about the rush of air on my cheek at the top of Jelm Mountain, that starry night when the GHO swept across the black sky. It was like he had announced with a cry, "Make way—I am the first Someday bird to be found! Now you must go forth, and find the rest!"

"Yes," I tell her. "I like owls."

Helen brings me to a wall of long, wide drawers, and slides the first one open. It's filled with dead screech owls, their little heads laid out in careful order, row by row. I gulp. I'm afraid I will breathe in what they smell like. I don't want to get close, yet I do. It's sort of like they're zombie birds—dead, yet also, alive. Sleeping in drawers, biding their time.

There are many, many drawers in this room.

"I know it does seem very strange at first, doesn't it?" says Helen. "To see them preserved like this. Everyone feels weird, the first time they open a specimen drawer."

"Yes."

"But scientists need access to specimens like this for study. For instance, we've had amazing advances in our DNA lab—they've been able to sequence the genome of bird samples that are over a hundred years old. They've been able to compare that bird DNA with the genetic makeup of modern birds. Someday, we hope to strengthen the genetic code of modern birds that are in danger by using bits of extinct code to reinforce the health of the species. Wouldn't that be amazing?"

I nod.

"And we need these samples in order to do that kind of research. Who knows how these specimens could be of use, even in the very near future? Things may be possible that we can't even imagine today."

"Like bringing birds back to life?" I ask.

"You mean like they do in the dinosaur movies?" Helen smiles. "Maybe." Helen walks farther down, to a different set of drawers. "Look here," she says.

She opens the drawer, and I take a deep breath. There, lying head to toe, are the inert, almost fake-looking bodies of dovelike gray birds.

I know them. I know what they are.

"Passenger pigeons," Helen says. "It's been over one hundred years now since the passenger pigeon went extinct. Once it was the most abundant bird in all of North America. Flocks of passenger pigeons would darken the sky for miles as flocks flew past. Can you imagine what that sight must have been like?

"And they performed an important ecological function, spreading seeds and fruits along a wild path across the country. But now they are all gone. The last passenger pigeon died at the Cincinnati Zoo in 1914. Her name was Martha."

I stare at the puppet-like gray birds, so carefully laid out head to toe, each with a little tag tied to it.

"So do you think scientists could bring them back?" I ask. "Do you think that someday we could ever see them flying in the sky again? Would that be the right thing to do? Bring them back to life?"

Helen raises her eyebrows and smiles and shrugs, all at the same time. It's hard to read that visual cue.

We walk together back through the lab, past the old people with their tweezers and piles of feathers. She hands me a brochure about DNA research. "This will tell you more, if you're interested. It's amazing what we can do, genetically, these days, to help birds and other endangered species."

This time I let her shake my hand. And I say thank you very, very much.

I go back to the hall and wander around in a daze. Ludmila said to stay there till they come back for me. Well, I don't think I ever want to leave. There is so much to think about, my head is spinning.

I open my Bird Book, and find the page for Dad's Someday Birds List.

Bald Eagle **(CHECK!)**
Great Horned Owl **(CHECK!)**
Trumpeter Swan **(HALF CHECK!)**
Sandhill Crane **(still looking)**
Turkey Vulture **(still looking)**
Emu **(maybe in Australia)**
Passenger Pigeon **(CHECK!)**
Carolina Parakeet
Screech Owl **(bonus bird from Yellowstone)**
Prairie Chicken **(bonus bird from Montana)**
Starling Murmuration **(bonus from Wisconsin)**

Oh! I should have asked Helen if she had a drawer back there that was full of Carolina parakeets! I probably could have crossed them off the list, too! But I was so caught up in her talk about genetics and birds, I forgot about everything else in my head.

I am really mad at myself for being too shy and scattered to ask her.

Still. There's been progress. I touch the names on the list, touch the checkmarks with the tip of my finger, and a feeling of satisfaction washes over me. Definitely: progress.

It suddenly occurs to me that there might be an emu in the Hall of Birds. I run from case to case, through a maze of bird cases in alcoves and halls, until there, in a tall display, is a kind of fluffy brown-and-gray bird that's almost as big as an ostrich.

CHECK!

I sit down and start sketching him so I can show Dad. I've got the emu!

Now it's just the turkey vultures—and the sandhill cranes. Well, and that poor old Carolina parakeet, who's probably in one of Helen's drawers. I am so close. But I'm not going knocking on that *private* lab door again by myself. Too scared.

I think about the pretty green and yellow parakeet. I sketched it once, from Audubon's book. I think about how Dad used to like local stories about them, when he was a kid. How he liked to imagine them flocking by the thousands. And, just like the passenger pigeons, how they got hunted into oblivion. How they went from being everywhere, to being nowhere.

It makes me shiver, to think how quickly life can stop. Like putting out a light.

The twins come to find me. I slam my notebook shut so they don't see my emu sketch. It turned out pretty good.

"Guess what, Charlie?" they say. "We found something else in this museum you're gonna love. Come with us!"

Joel pulls and Jake pushes. I think it's going to be a mummy or dinosaur or something.

"Where are we going?" I'm getting grouchy.

"Just wait—you'll love it."

We go down a flight of stairs, and suddenly I am standing in front of a restroom door.

"Check it out!" Joel shouts. "Charlie's dream come true!"

There is a big sign by the door that reads: *America's Best Restroom Award, 2011.*

I laugh, and so do the twins. They usually make fun of my public-bathroom rating system. But it looks like I'm not the only one who does it.

All three of us go in, and I gasp in amazement. The sinks are sparkling. The soap dispensers are all nicely filled. Everything is blue and white. The ceiling is painted like a blue sky with fluffy clouds, and the whole place is lit up like heaven itself.

"Five stars," I tell Joel and Jake. "Definitely. Top of the list."

That night, we stay with Mariana at her house. She lives downtown underneath an L train—which is what they call an elevated train track—in a tiny old house with a dirty carpet covered in Lego pieces. As always, they hurt like crazy when you step on them. Joel and Jake are cross-legged on the floor with two of Mariana's kids, building robots. Well, Joel and Jake are building robots; the little boys, who are maybe five and three, are just throwing the pieces around.

"Why you wearing that?" the older kid asks Joel, who still has on Ludmila's blue wig.

Joel just shrugs. The little boys pulls it off and puts it on his own head.

Mariana comes into the room with a baby on her hip. "Niko, Luka, pick up those Legos right now; dinner's in ten minutes!"

"Joel, Jake, help," says Ludmila, from behind Mariana. "Charlie, you too."

Why me? I didn't make this mess. The Legos are grimy, and there are crumbs in the carpet. I see tumbleweeds of dust under the couch. And two of the kids have green gunk running out of their nose. We could get infected with some dangerous microbes in this place.

My head starts to hurt and my hands itch and crawl. I ask Mariana where to wash, and she shows me the bathroom.

In less than an hour, I've gone from the best bathroom in America to the worst. There's smeared toothpaste and a few long black hairs stuck to the rim of the old white sink. The faucet is covered with something chalky and white, and around the handles, there's green mold and reddish brown rust. The mirror is smeared with dots and spots.

One star. Half a star.

I try not to panic, but my heart is pumping. I tiptoe out to the kitchen, which is cleaner, flapping my hands the whole time. "I need to use this sink *right now*," I say to Ludmila, louder than I meant to.

Mariana stops stirring the steaming pot on her stove and looks up. "Okay."

I wash.

"Yeah, so we forgot to mention my brother is a clean freak. And he's got some OCD action going on," Davis says from her chair at the little kitchen table. She's sitting with the grown-up women so she feels like a big shot.

"But we love him anyway."

I ignore them.

Soap-rinse-one-soap-rinse-two-soap-rinse-three-soap-rinse-four . . . I mumble to myself, grumpy. This is the first time I have ever done my routine directly in front of anyone else, but here in this tiny house where we are all on top of each other, there's no choice. So to heck with it. I turn off the faucet with a piece of paper towel to protect my fingers.

Mariana raises one eyebrow, but keeps stirring her

pot of rice. "Do you always count when you wash, Charlie? To twelve, like that?"

I don't say anything.

"Yes, he does," says Davis. "He thinks he's doing it secretly, but we all know. He used to count to eleven. Now it's twelve."

I shrug and look down.

Mariana seems interested in all this. "Why twelve, Charlie?"

"I'm twelve," I say to the floor.

"Ah," says Mariana. "Is that so? Well, tell me this. Do you plan to still be washing like this all your life? So, have you thought about how much time it will take to wash up when you are twenty? When you're forty?"

My cheeks suddenly feel burning hot. I am confused. I don't know what to say.

"Don't worry; it's okay. I know how you feel," she says. "I used to count in the shower, too, Charlie. It's nothing to be ashamed of. And it took me forever to learn to drive, because I used to get panic attacks in cars. I couldn't drive for years. So I understand what you are feeling about all this. I was just telling Ludmila how I am going to college to learn to be a therapist, now, to help other people deal with these things."

Ludmila nods. "I remember when you were afraid to drive."

"I had to counteract it, little by little." Mariana keeps stirring her pot. "That's the trick. Fight it, bit by bit. Next time, Charlie, you should try washing only eleven times. Force yourself. Then ten times, then nine, eight, you know? That's how you can do it—little bit by little bit."

I say, "But that's like counting back in time to when I was little. That's not progressing."

Mariana and Ludmila and Davis look at each other in a funny way.

"But it is progressing," says Ludmila. "Counting backward, but moving forward, growing out of something that's holding you back."

For dinner, Mariana serves a spicy-sauced sort of lamb stew over rice. I can't try it, even though everyone is urging me to. I just stare at the bowl. The whole table of people is saying, "Come on, come on, Charlie, you can do it!" They are rooting like it's a sports match or something.

But I can't. I can barely stand the sharp nostril-panging smell of it. So Mariana finally breaks down and gives me plain rice, and microwaves some old chicken nuggets from the freezer she says she feeds the baby now and then. They are shaped liked alphabet letters. I eat a *D*, a *U*, and an *M*, and realize my dinner almost spells

DUMB. Which is how I feel, because even the baby is eating the spicy lamb stew.

After bedtime, I lie in a pile of blankets on Mariana's floor together with Joel. Jake and Davis are on the couch; everyone is softly snoring. I can't sleep. There are too many dust bunnies tumbleweeding around under that couch.

I can hear Mariana and Ludmila talking softly in the kitchen. The light over the kitchen table is spilling across the doorway and casting a soft glow across my backpack, right here by my arm.

Mariana's kids are asleep in their room. Karim, Mariana's husband, works the night shift, so we might not meet him. I'm kind of relieved. There are enough people stuffed in this tiny house already.

I think about the Field Museum, Helen the ornithologist, and the drawers full of birds. The museum is closed now, the rooms dark. The lights in the beautiful glass displays of birds are turned off. I think about all the birds in the cases, always in flight, or standing in sand, or eating fake fish. In the middle of a motion, posed like that, forever and ever, night and day. And I think about the research lab.

I haven't looked at the brochure Helen gave me yet. I slip it softly out of my pack and hold it up to the slant of yellow light coming in from the kitchen.

It says "DNA Research." There are all kinds of photos and explanations about the genome, the code of life, the arrangement of genes based on combinations of four different molecular building blocks named A, C, G, and T that determine everything about you, sort of like People-Legos. Like whether you'll have blue eyes or brown, blond hair or red. Whether you're prone to cavities, or to baldness. Whether you're anxious or easygoing. Whether you have a disposition for certain diseases or conditions. It's this last one that interests the biologists. They want to help wild species be more resilient in fighting disease and endangerment.

I look at the back of the brochure. It's hard to read in the flickering shadow of the kitchen light. But it's a list of contributing research scientists. And there, at the bottom of the middle row, slightly set off from the rest, one name jumps out at me and makes my stomach flip:

Tiberius Shaw, PhD

In the early morning, while we're still laid out on the floor and mostly asleep, I start to smell coffee. Davis is still there on the couch, her eyes open. We hear the clinking of spoons, whispers, voices: Mariana and Ludmila are in the kitchen. Davis puts her fingers to her lips to tell me to shush. We both stay silent and listen to them talk.

". . . So you still were not on speaking terms?"

"I hadn't talked to Amar in two years. I was so angry at him, Mariana! Why did he want the army? Why? After all we had been through? Hadn't he seen enough fighting, enough war?"

"Maybe he felt like that is what he knew," says Mariana's low voice. "All he knew how to do, in life."

"But he could have gone to university! He had a scholarship! And instead, he chose to fight. To put himself back into harm's way, into violence. I was so furious at him. I am still so furious at him."

There's a pause. I think Ludmila is crying, and Mariana is murmuring things to her. Then Ludmila's voice comes softer, in lurches, and we have to strain to hear her words. "One of the last things Amar said was about Robert, their father . . . Amar thought of him like a father, an uncle . . . was driving him when the IED went off."

Mariana makes a shocked, murmuring noise.

". . . When I learned they'd brought Robert back here alive, I started visiting him. I wanted to help, yes. But I guess I was really hoping Robert would wake up and tell me something about Amar. Did he miss me? Did he ever talk about me, about our old life? Was he happy being a soldier? What was he thinking, feeling? Only this, this poor Robert, these children's father, only he knew."

Mariana says something I can't understand.

Ludmila says something about surgery.

Davis and I are straining our ears so hard, we jump when the front door suddenly rattles open, disturbing everything. It's Mariana's husband, Karim. He is wearing a suit and tie, with a plastic name tag pinned on to his chest. He has to step over our sleeping bags one at a time to get through to the tiny kitchen. "Hell of a night," he says, kissing Mariana. "Double bookings, no one to take graveyard shift, half the staff missed the new training." He is carrying a notebook and laptop.

Davis sits up and looks at me. She and I have heard almost every word Ludmila and Mariana just said. We just look at each other, trying to fully understand.

The twins start to wake up. Davis and I don't say anything. We all struggle and stumble into the kitchen.

Mariana is bouncing the dirty-cheeked baby on her lap now. "Karim, this is Charlie, Davis, Joel, and Jake," she says.

I don't look at him. Davis and the twins shake hands, though. Then Davis, staring at the laptop, asks an odd question. One that makes my heart thump.

"Karim, would it be okay if I showed you guys something important on your computer?"

Davis goes over and paws through her purse, then holds up the little flash drive. She stands in front of Ludmila and says, like she's been rehearsing a speech:

"That night when you first came to our house, I hated you. I didn't know why you insisted on hanging around our dad. And when I saw you snooping through his stuff, in his office? I felt invaded."

Ludmila's mouth makes a round O. She says, "I am sorry, Davis. That is not what I intended."

Davis shrugs. "I'm over it. But now, there's something I think I should show you." She opens the laptop. "I'm sorry I didn't show you before." She plugs in the flash drive. "I saved some of Dad's files onto this, trying to safeguard his stuff, because I thought you were kind of a snoop. He recorded a bunch of things at the military camp before he went. And I think that somewhere in it all, there's an interview with your brother, Amar."

32

Ludmila peers over Davis's shoulder, and everyone else crowds around. Davis scrolls down through files that Dad had marked, "Soldier Interviews," hesitating here and there, like she's not sure what to look for. Finally Ludmila reaches out her tattooed hand and takes the mouse. She scrolls down, down through what looks like a whole bunch of video clips until she finds one that makes her stop.

She takes a deep breath and clicks.

We lean over her shoulder to read some text:

Amar Divjak is thirty-two years old. A Bosnian war orphan who came to the US with his sister, Amar lived with many different foster families, mainly in the St. Louis area, before becoming an American citizen. A brilliant student, he rejected a full scholarship to Washington University in order to join the military. He has requested to be stationed here in order to be near his younger sister, who has had a history of depression and emotional difficulties.

When I first met him, Amar talked about how his sister refuses to see him. After their difficult past, she cannot accept his choice of a military career. He shipped out on his third tour to Afghanistan not long after this interview. And so, after a war-filled childhood, with a troubled sister and so much war in his life, the first question I felt I had to ask Amar was: Why go back? Why keep fighting?

There is an embedded video. Ludmila clicks. Her white knuckles are so close to her lost brother's frozen face on the screen. We strain to look with her.

The video starts with the blurred-out, bad-pixel image of a soldier in fatigues. Then it comes in focus, and we finally get to see Amar's face for the first time. Even though I know, of course, he was real, it's sort of surprising to see the actual person. Something about Ludmila's stories made me think of him as being from long in the past.

He is sitting in a metal folding chair. He's got shaved, stubbly hair, and he's got one of those camouflage shirts with his name embroidered in black on the pocket. He's very thin, with dark, wide eyes.

I startle a little when I hear my dad's voice start up. "Amar, this is going to be, what, your third tour? Just for the record. Why do you keep re-upping?"

It's so weird to hear my dad speak in normal conversation again. It's like someone punched me in the stomach, to hear it.

I look at Davis, the twins. Everyone is just fixated on the laptop. Ludmila looks pale.

On the screen, Amar is silent for a few moments, leaning forward in his chair. Ludmila leans forward to meet him. She quickly fumbles to turn up the volume, her hand shaky. On the screen, Amar crosses his legs and lights a cigarette, like he's waiting for her to do it. Their faces look alike somehow, sister and brother.

It's really weird to watch this and know that Amar, the man on the screen, is dead. Being on the screen like this, it is kind of like being alive-and-dead. Amar makes me think of those extinct birds, preserved in a drawer.

"It's a job I can do," Amar says, his eyes slits against his cigarette smoke. "And I need to put money aside for family reasons."

My dad says, "Tell me about your sister."

"She had a hard time in some of those foster homes. I couldn't take care of her the way I wanted to, the way I promised I would, because after we came to the States, we got split up. I was sent to a military boarding school for only boys. Ludmila got shifted through many different families. Some good. Some not so good. I'd write to her all the time, call her, try to make sure she was doing all right, make sure she was safe.

"But it was hard to keep my promise. I was in military school all the way through high school. I hated it. Bullies. Pranks. I got into a lot of fights. After that, what else was I going to do, if I didn't just keep fighting?

"Mila ran away many times. She dropped out of high school, dropped out of college twice. And she's so smart! She wants to do something to help people, but she can't hold it together. I don't know if she ever will. And she won't talk to me, you see. She won't forgive me for being a soldier. After all we've been through, after the war, she says, why would I keep fighting?" He drags on his cigarette. "Well, why wouldn't I?" Amar shrugs.

There's a small click and pause, but then the camera keeps going.

Amar exhales, leans back, then leans forward again, elbows on knees. "Okay, Robert, so. My sister lives not far from you in San Diego. So I want to ask you a favor." His dark eyes stare wide at the camera, at my dad, when he

239

says this. "We're shipping out together soon, right? But I'll be deployed for nine months, while you're back in two weeks. Would you do me a favor? Would you check on her for me? Call her, like a dad, like an uncle would. Make sure she's okay?"

He stands up and digs a piece of paper out of his pocket. "Her name's Ludmila. We haven't talked in years, but I know she still loves me. If she didn't, she wouldn't be mad. I know that's weird. Anyhow, here's her address." Amar holds out a piece of paper. "She's all alone in the world. Would you reach out?"

The video goes black.

33

Mariana and Karim look at Ludmila. Joel and Jake and Davis and I look at Ludmila. The only sound in the tiny house is of little kids throwing Lego blocks around in the other room, and Tiberius licking Cheerios up off the floor in the corner.

Ludmila sits like a statue with tears streaming down her face.

"Wow," Davis whispers.

"Oh my God, Mila, honey," says Mariana in a very soft voice. "To see his face like that. Wow. I'm so sorry."

Ludmila stands up, sits down, takes off her smudgy glasses, and puts her hands over her eyes.

"Typical Amar. Always such a take-charge big shot,"

says Ludmila. She pushes her wild pink strands of hair up off her forehead with shaky fingers.

"So . . . did our dad ever reach out to you?" Davis asks. Her eyes are very wide.

Ludmila says, "He emailed me only once, just before he left, to introduce himself."

She takes a deep breath. "When I found out what happened, of course I came to the hospital. Robert was my last link to Amar, my last link to family. I was grieving so much; it was all just too hard to explain why I was there."

"But that's why you helped us," Davis says.

Ludmila peers at us through her thick glasses. "That's why I started to help you, yes. Because you connected me to Amar. Because your father had reached out and tried to be kind." She sniffles. "But now? We have spent so much time together now that you feel like my own family. Even this crazy-looking dog." Tiberius is scratching at her knees with his tiny black toenails. He's licked up the last of the Cheerios. She lifts him into her lap, where he scrambles around to face the table and lick more crumbs.

I say, "When we were in Wyoming going up the mountain, I thought the reason you came to help us was because you were going to sell us to a cult."

Everyone laughs way too loud at that. It wasn't really that funny.

242

34

There are things I could show you that would help
you soar through life like a bird on freer wings. If
you could only sit where I sit, you would go forth
renewed, convinced this difficult and often tragic
world holds infinite powers of life regeneration.
—Tiberius Shaw, PhD

There's a lot to think about as we cruise along the highway. Ludmila lost her dad, then her grandfather, then her mom, then her brother, and had to go to a whole other country and learn the language and move around between a whole bunch of foster families. No wonder she had a rough time growing up. And Amar wanted to take care of her, but he got stuck in a tough military school, far away.

Once, Davis told me *amar* meant "to love" in Spanish. Maybe his name should have meant "to fight."

I think about how part of Amar's job was to drive Dad. Does Ludmila blame Dad? Because if Amar hadn't been his driver, maybe he'd be alive.

The car is silent. Even Tiberius is quiet, a warm, sleepy lump in his blanket-nest at my feet. Indiana passes in a blur of cornfields, soy fields, cornfields, soy fields. We are all lost in thought.

Davis breaks our silence.

"I can't stop thinking about it, Ludmila. How lucky you are, that you had a brother like that," she says softly.

Ludmila says, "Look around you, little girl. I had one brother; you have three! Someday you'll realize how lucky *you* are."

Davis rolls her eyes. "*These* three?"

"Hey!" Joel and Jake say at the same time.

Davis turns to them and smiles. "Still," she says, "I can't stop thinking about your story, Ludmila. You know ours. You still haven't finished telling us yours."

Ludmila breathes in, then exhales slowly. "Are you sure you want to hear? It's not pretty."

We are all incredibly quiet. The only sound is the hum of the road, the small rattle of Old Bessie's loose parts, and then, because we've all nodded yes: Ludmila's deep, husky voice, with its strong accent.

"Sarajevo." Ludmila announces quietly. "Imagine us, hungry and tired and fearful, in our apartment building, waiting out the siege. Imagine. This is the moment that my mother goes into labor.

"Her pains started in early morning. I remember

lifting up a corner flap of cardboard, just a small triangle, off the front room window to look out, even though I wasn't allowed to do that; outside the glass, all was black. The city was silent all around us. There was a feeling of being in a giant, dark closet. The trees in the park across the street had been cut down for firewood, so no birds were around to chirp at us, or greet the sun. No songs, that day, not even birdsong.

"Many people already had abandoned the city, gotten out. In our apartment building, only a handful of us were left, including old Mrs. Zelinka, on the floor above.

"My mother, she stood moaning, doubled over, in the cold, dark kitchen. 'Go upstairs,' Mama told us. 'I want you two to go stay with Mrs. Zelinka until I come back. I need to go to the maternity hospital.'

"But Amar held me back. He didn't like old Mrs. Zelinka, who was cranky, and smelled like garlic and cats. So we only pretended to go upstairs. On the landing, Amar said, 'We are going to secretly follow Mama. We are going to protect her.'

"We stayed two blocks back, but there was no fear of being spotted. Mama was too absorbed in her pains, and in waddling as swiftly as she could through the empty, dangerous streets. Every so often she would stop and hold on to the side of the building, to catch her breath. She was so intent, she never looked back to spot us.

"Once, a big, gruff man with a rifle stopped her, and our hearts stopped with her—but Mama said something to him, Lord knows what, and he let her pass. We waited until he turned down a side street, then ran as fast as we could to catch up. I remember the feeling of my feet flying, driven by fear that we'd lose track of her.

"At the maternity hospital, we waited outside as they took Mama in. Amar had it all figured out. 'They'll take Mama upstairs,' he said, 'and then we will sneak into the waiting room.' My heart was pounding like a drum through it all.

"We stayed outside for what felt like hours. We peeped in the clinic doorway once, then leaped away quickly. Mama was still in that waiting room, waiting to sign in! No way we could go in there yet. The room was full of nervous mothers and families. If we kept hanging around, Mama would spot us—and she would be furious. An orderly at the door had already been giving us looks.

"Amar had idea. 'My friend's family runs a café a few streets over. Let's find it, and wait there for a while.' And so we wandered off, a separation we thought would last only a short while.

"But of course, it lasted forever."

Ludmila stops for a moment. We wait. We are all on the edge of our seats. I lift Tiberius onto my lap and start stroking him, soothing him, even though he is perfectly fine and doesn't need it.

"Amar and I, we wandered off, looking for the café, you see," Ludmila goes on. "And that's when the first shell hit. Big explosion. Noise. Heat. Fear. We ran back. Amar pulled me along. From the end of the block, we could see that the hospital was on fire! It was chaos, a nightmare. People screaming for help."

Ludmila's voice cuts out. She takes a giant, deep breath. Then she takes her hands off the steering wheel and shouts, to no one in particular, "Who bombs a maternity hospital?"

We just shake our heads.

"Amar, though, he was strong. He grabbed me and held me back, there on the sidewalk, looking down the street at this disaster. 'Stop crying!' he said. 'We need to go back there and help!'

"And so we did. I don't know how we did it, but we helped people out of the building. Amar carried out a squalling little newborn baby, wrapped in a smoking, scorched blanket. The baby was safe and healthy. A nurse told me to take care of it, in a little garden down the street.

"Ambulances and fire trucks and sirens and noise filled every corner of the air. And still, the sound of snipers, of shots echoing off buildings. Those beautiful, pockmarked, crumbling stone buildings.

"I remember I wanted to just curl in a ball and go to sleep, but I had to hold that little baby. Other people came in and out. People were burned. The nurses worked nonstop. It felt like hours, like days passed, with me standing there, holding that baby.

"And then, Amar came over and yelled at me to run. The fire was spreading; we weren't safe.

"At that point a nurse took the baby from me. We all ran and ran, ran until my side was on fire; my breath fire, everything fire, burning from my insides to the streets themselves, to the whole world."

Ludmila stops talking.

We are seeing signs to Cleveland. The outside, real, normal world comes back into focus. Highway. Greenery. Sunshine. Trees. Calm. The fiery streets of Sarajevo fade. Ludmila's story has seemed so real.

"Go on," Davis whispers. "Go on! What happened next?"

I am not sure I want to know. But Ludmila goes on.

"Well, so. I was running, being dragged along by Amar, when it started to dawn on me, what he already knew, about Mama. Of all the ladies who'd been saved, well. Our mama had never come out the hospital door. She was most certainly gone.

"We ran like crazies. We never stopped. Finally, we spied a rickety old apartment building in a part of town we'd never been, with a half-open alleyway door. We slipped inside—it led down into the cellar. In the dark, quivering and shaking, we thought finally, we could break down and cry; finally, we were alone.

"But strange shadows started moving in the corner of the cellar! I screamed. The shadows got bigger, then changed into the figures of a middle-aged couple. The man wore a clean white shirt and a Jewish yarmulke cap on the back of his head. The woman was shaking almost as much as me, but she had warm, strong arms, and she opened them wide and put them around the two of us, and she hugged us tightly. She put an apple in my hand. I hadn't had an apple in over a year."

Ludmila wipes her eyes. "Thank God for them, this couple. They saved us, the Liebowitzes. We lived with them and shared their food for about a month. They were wonderfully kind, helped us write to find our relatives, but nothing, no one responded. They were journalists, working with the foreign media to cover the war. They wrote a news story that appeared all over Europe, about 'two heroic Muslim kids who helped save babies at the bombed maternity hospital, even after their own mother was killed.' The story got picked up by the international press, and when the UK started taking refugees out, the Liebowitzes made sure we were on one of the first planes out.

"So. There are a few reasons I am here today. Because Mama didn't want us at the maternity hospital. Because Amar had a cool head, and knew what to do," Ludmila says. "And because we chanced upon the door to the Liebowitzes' cellar. They were so kind."

Ludmila stares out at the highway, not seeing it at all. She smiles. "That's what my brother, Amar, said to me, that first night in the cellar, when we knew we'd found safety.

"Amar patted me on the shoulder and he said, 'See, Mila? There is good everywhere. No matter how bad things are, it is always possible to find a bit of good.'"

35

*The beady-eyed black crow drops the oyster he has
stolen on the pavement. It doesn't work, so he tries
something completely different: He puts it on the
road for a car to run over and crack. How smart
he is! How persistent! This bird is strong; he is never
afraid to try new approaches.*
—Tiberius Shaw, PhD

There are only three birds left to find, from Dad's
and my original Someday Birds List:

> Turkey Vulture
> Sandhill Crane
> Carolina Parakeet

The farther we get from the Midwest, the chancier
it is to spot a sandhill crane. If we had driven through
Nebraska, we'd have had a good chance, because they
get something like a half a million cranes through there

every spring—they even have a whole festival about it, from what I've read.

But we're long past Nebraska.

We spent the night at an Ohio campground, and we're already headed to Amish country, in Pennsylvania. I don't care one way or the other about visiting the Amish, but I do know there are lots of woods and fields in Pennsylvania. So I have everyone on the lookout for vultures.

"I don't know, Charlie," says Davis. "Aren't they pretty reclusive? You only see them if there's carrion around. You know, dead meat."

"Hey, I got one. Why do vultures like small suit-cases?" asks Joel. "Because they like carrion. Get it? *Carry-on*."

Davis says, "Tell another joke that bad, and *you'll* be the dead meat."

We're two hours into Pennsylvania, on I-80, bearing down on Virginia and the East Coast soon enough. With no (1) vultures or (2) sandhill cranes spotted so far. Not to mention, no (3) extinct parakeets. The closer we get to the towns, the harder it'll be to find Dad's Someday Birds. And that's where we're headed: a typical Amish town, to stop for the night.

When we pull off the highway, we end up stuck behind a horse and buggy. It's all painted black, and the man driving it has a flat-topped straw hat and a long beard. He's going really slow, and Ludmila is afraid to pass him, so we just crawl along, clippity clop, until we get to the main street. It's interesting, going slow, even though Davis is groaning and smacking her head. I like it. It's more interesting when trees stop being a blur, and turn back into individual trees.

We park, and tumble out of Old Bessie, sighing and stretching. We walk Tiberius up and down a sidewalk, to feel our legs again. We window-shop. There's a display of Pennsylvania Dutch "hexes," round disks of color-ful designs. It says that the hearts in the designs stand for love, the tulips, for faith, and the birds are called *distelfink*, or goldfinches, and they are supposed to bring good luck.

Tiberius is not interested in hexes, distelfink, or stores. Instead, he is fascinated by horse poop. There's a whole disgusting ton of it in the street. I have to keep yanking his leash to get him back up on the curb. I have to yank gently or he'll fall over, due to his one back leg, and the last thing we need is Tiberius falling into a pile of horse poop.

The people walking around here are all either touristy-looking, or Amish-looking. They wear white caps and long dresses, or those flat-topped hats, and beards without mustaches, and plain dark work clothes. Their clothing is simple and functional, which I like, but still, they have too many buttons. Give me stretch-waist shorts and a T-shirt any day of the week, please.

As usual, Joel and Jake are starving—STARVING!—so we turn into the first diner we see. All the waitresses are dressed Amish. Ours has a name tag that says "*Anna*," and she doesn't look any older than Davis. Her hair is all combed tightly back into her white cap and held in place with metal hairpins that look horribly painful. When she turns her head, I see a small pinprick on the side of her nose, like she used to have a nose earring in there. That looks painful, too.

Anna makes a fuss over how cute Tiberius is. "Such an adorable little wee face, yah? But he gets around just fine, now, doesn't he, the poor thing," she says.

For dessert Ludmila orders all of us something called shoofly pie, which Anna reassures me doesn't really have flies in it. Davis forces me to try a crumb. It's kind of brown-sugary. I reject it on principle.

After we eat, Ludmila asks Anna if she knows of a place a small RV could set up for the night.

"Well, we have a campsite at our farm. You'd be welcome, if thou wish. There's a hookup, water pump, and picnic table by our fence. It's not far at'tall," she says, smiling. "But I'll warn you, it may be a bit crazy later on, account of a party we young folk are having."

254

After the food and more walking around, we get back in the camper. We turn off the main road and follow Anna's directions, and about ten minutes out of town, just like she said, a little farm appears. Cornfields, white farmhouse, red barn with one of those hexes on it, with distelfink.

We nervously unhook the gate and drive in. She said to put a few dollars in the mailbox "if thou would be so moved," so we do. Right where she said, by the far fence, is a campsite with a picnic table and water pump—and an old-fashioned wooden outhouse with a small cutout of a star carved into the door. I laugh, because it's so true: This is definitely a one-star operation.

The minute we open the camper door, Tiberius darts right past me! Right into the huge cornfield!

"Get him out of there!" I yell to Joel. "He'll get lost! He'll get ticks!"

"Chill out," says Joel. "There's nothing to hurt him out here. Let him stretch his legs!"

We can hear him yipping happily, barking along the cornrows. He must have disturbed some big black crows—two of them flutter up and circle the air above us, cawing and complaining. Then a third shoots up—it has a long rat tail curling down from its beak! It takes off like a shot toward a distant stand of trees, pumping its wings like crazy. The other crows chase it, squawking protests.

"Ew," Davis says.

"Lots of ew-y things, yes," I say, looking at the outhouse.

Tiberius the dog comes bursting back through the soft green cornstalks, happily panting, and barks at my feet. "I'm not picking you up till somebody checks you over for ticks," I tell him.

"Why don't you do it yourself, Charlie?" Davis asks.

No way. I'm not going near that.

It's dusk when we all sit around eating sandwiches at the splintery picnic table. The twins have a stash of candy they got in one of the shops today, which they're planning to devour for dessert.

"How come the bins said 'penny candy,' but everything cost a dollar?" Joel asks.

"Because it's a cruel, deceptive world," Davis says.

"Well, this is nice," Ludmila says while we munch stale sandwiches and slap mosquitoes. It totally isn't nice.

Finally, we go inside Old Bessie and call it a night. I crawl in my bunk and make a blanket-nest for Tiberius at my feet, as usual. But I am so sick of this thin blue mattress. The top sheet is always slipping off, so my face gets sweaty from sleeping directly on the disgusting, moldy blue plastic, and don't get me wrong, I love Tiberius, but he's giving me cramps in my legs by hogging the whole bottom half of this stupid bed every night.

Davis is across from me, reading with a flashlight. She clicks it off and says goodnight.

I toss and turn.

Toss.

Turn.

It doesn't seem long before the muffled bass thump of a rap song wakes me. I crack open my window. The beat's so low it hurts my ears. Faint laughter floats across the field, and the buzzy sound of lots of people talking— it's that "young folk" party that the waitress Anna was talking about.

Rap music, like nose piercing, doesn't seem very Amish to me.

I slide my legs slowly up away from the dog. Tiberius sighs and twitches one back paw, like's he's dreaming about running. The empty hip joint also moves. It's so funny when he does this. I wonder if he has two legs in his dreams.

(*It's amazing, the things we are capable of, in our dreams. If only we could harness that power when we wake. —Tiberius Shaw*)

More laughter and voices float across the field outside my window. Everyone else is still snoring. But I give up on sleeping. "Come on, beast," I tell Tiberius. He yawns and licks my hand when I clip on his leash, as if to say, "Really? A walk is great, but does it have to be *now*?"

I grab a flashlight, just in case, and together, we creep out the RV door. Slightly uphill, a long distance across the field, a huge crowd of kids is milling around under the light on the big red barn. I can't make out any Amish caps or dresses or suspenders on anyone. No. It's a sort of modern, smoky drinky noisy party that Dad would probably kill Davis for going to. Boys are whooping, and girls are laughing and dancing in small groups.

Just then, as I'm staring across the field, there's a super-loud *CRACK!*

The music suddenly cuts out. There's the sound of commotion, of some people arguing. I walk Tiberius up a little closer, to see what's going on, and then, there's the waitress, Anna, running toward me.

"Ach! Oh my gosh! Are you okay?" she shouts, panting.

"Um, yes?" I say.

"Two stupid boys just shot a rifle right across the field at you. They said they saw a deer. When I told them we had a family in a camper staying right over at the clearing, they nearly—well, they could have killed thee!" She is breathless, her face pale in the darkness. "I'm so sorry! Oh gosh! Well—if you're okay, I have to—"

She turns on her heels and starts running back in the opposite direction to the barn. I watch her rejoin the group and wave her arms around, angry. It looks like Anna is throwing everybody out.

I wonder where her parents are? I hear car doors start to slam, then a line of headlights rove over the field as vehicles turn slowly toward the lane.

And in the flash of one of those headlights, as I'm walking back to the camper, I notice something: an indentation in a cornrow, about ten feet in. Do I dare move closer to see what it is?

Hm. Those boys with the rifle didn't hit me, but they did hit something. The rump of the poor deer twitches, then stills. I freeze, and watch, and wait. It doesn't move. It is dead, but dead. There is nothing I can do to save it, or help it.

I think of Dad, telling us about the circle of life, when I was five and our cat Chigger died. He was trying to make us feel better, but he was more upset than us kids. Chigger was mean, and only ever spat at us from under the couch, so we didn't even like him. But he had been Mom's cat.

I remember, looking at this poor dead deer in the cornstalks, that day Dad had buried Chigger. It was out near the canyon, and he had dug for a long time. He had dug deep. When he came back in, Dad had said, "I just wanted to make sure the coyotes and the big old vultures leave the poor guy alone."

"Come on," I tell Tiberius. "It's almost dawn. Let's go get a sweater and blanket, and then we're coming back here to wait. I have an idea."

I sense dawn before it comes. In a few minutes, a haze of blue-gray hits my eyelids. Things turn from gray shadows into surreal color, lightening by dim degrees. Across the field, a thin yellow lip of sun peeps up, until I can just barely, finally make out the outline of the poor shot-dead deer. It is a lifeless lump, flattening the cornstalks about fifteen feet away from where Tiberius and I are hidden.

Tiberius snuggles in closer. "Just a while longer," I whisper. "It's almost better, sleeping out here in this cozy blanket, than it was in the camper on the sticky blue mattress. Right? It sure smells better."

He turns around three times and heaves into my side to sleep some more. Meanwhile, I scan the sky. And finally, amazingly, two black pinpoints appear against the pre-dawn gray. It must be crows.

I hold my breath. I wait.

And: yes.

The pinpoints grow into two great hulking shapes that pass over, blackening the sky above me. Then they wheel and spiral down just beyond the dead deer.

I want to do silent fist pumps. But I stay tight, frozen, a watching statue.

The birds are ink black, with bright red, bumpy, fleshy heads and tight, spiky neck ruffs. They look around, heads bobbing, checking out the neighborhood.

Tiberius whimpers. I hold his snout shut and hug him tighter to my chest.

I can't see them very well, so I shift just a bit over to the right—and the thicket of cornstalks aligns better, into perfect rows, straight as an arrow. There they are: two turkey vultures, strutting around the dead deer. Or, as they would call it, breakfast.

They arrange themselves behind its belly. The deer's back is to me. Its hind leg is bobbing now from some movement the vultures are making. I definitely don't want to know any more details than that.

Vultures are kind of like nature's trash removal workers. And their digestive tracts actually kill off dangerous bacteria and illness-causing germs, so vulture poop comes out totally sterile. In goes bacteria-filled, stinky dead meat. Out comes completely clean, sterile vulture poop. Talk about efficiency. You have to respect that.

Another fun fact: they poop all over their own legs to cool off.

This Pennsylvania morning's vultures are like a gift. A gross gift. I never thought I'd really get to see them. I never thought I'd be able to cross those birds off my list.

Tiberius and I creep away and head back to the camper, where I brush off all the hay, grass, and dirt, and make extra sure the both of us are tick-free. The others are just waking up. Tiberius scarfs down his kibble breakfast on the picnic table bench. As for me, after seeing those vultures at work, I'm not up for breakfast.

In fact, I think I might go vegetarian.

·MOURNING DOVE·

STRANGE
BIRDS

36

You enter Colonial Williamsburg through this big brick building filled with panels and panels of information. It's very professionally done. I stop and read every panel very carefully, because that's what they are there for, which drives Davis, Ludmila, and the twins crazy, because they just want to get in and get going.

But soon enough, we're through the building and out the other side, like we've passed through a time warp. We're walking the town green in a make-believe world. Men are wandering around in black hats, topcoats and gaiters, ladies stroll in caps and gowns, and everyone's pretending it's the 1700s.

A man is striding along in a brown overcoat, black

hat, and one of those old powdered wigs. I don't know how he can stand it, when it must be ninety-five degrees already.

"Down with British oppression!" he shouts, waving a stick and trying to get a gang of sweaty tourists to join him in an angry mob. But they're more interested in buying T-shirts.

On the other side of the street, a town crier waves a noisy bell while swaggering by in brass-buckled shoes. "Muster on the green in ten minutes!"

"What's a mustard?" Joel asks.

"They shoot off cannons," Davis says.

"Let's GO!" shouts Jake.

I tell Ludmila I don't want to. Stand around for an hour in the heat, hearing ear-pounding cannons and choking on gunpowder smoke? No, thanks.

"Okay, then you just go straight to the tavern, Charlie," Ludmila says, giving me a dead-eye look worthy of Gram. "And don't leave it. Stay there until we come for you. Hear me? Don't leave there. I'm not chasing after you."

Inside the tavern are a bunch of small rooms with bumpy wooden floors where tourists clomp by, sighing happily about the air-conditioning. I find myself jostled off into a room where an old Colonial guy is standing with his arms crossed. He is wearing a homespun white

265

cotton shirt, brown pants, and buckle shoes of black leather. He has gold-framed glasses slipping down his nose, and silver-gray hair in a ponytail tied with black ribbon. When he sees me, he makes a low bow.

"Well, young lad, and what can I do for you?" he asks. Then, suddenly, he lunges forward and squints at me strangely. He makes a big show of polishing his gold-framed glasses and then squinting at me harder. Some of the other tourists in the room start to laugh.

"Why, faith! Ah'n't you the cobbler's boy?" he asks.

"Nnno?" I say. My heart starts pounding.

He raises his hand as if to strike me. "Off with you, back to work, you lazy scalawag!" he shouts.

"Wait! You have the wrong person," I squeak out. I can hear my heartbeat pounding in my ears. What does he want with me? "My name is Charlie."

He brushes my words away with his hand. "Sure and if you're not the apprentice of that Tory scoundrel, Cobbler Smith, then my name's not Marcus McGinty! Away with you now!" He takes a broom from the corner and starts poking and swatting at me as if I'm a cornered rat.

"OW!" I cry, howling, because he's just lifted his broom and pretended to swat me across the rear end. What the heck? I thought he was really going to hit me! What is going on?

266

More people are starting to come into the little room to watch me and McGinty and the broom go at it.

I notice a plump lady in a white cotton cap and a long blue dress and apron. She's watching, too.

People are laughing at us. My face is red, my heart pounding. My brain doesn't have time to figure out what this means because I'm too busy trying to keep one step ahead of McGinty's broom.

The plump lady finally steps forward. "Stay your hand, sirrah," she shouts. "I fear you are terrible mistaken!" She swoops in front of me with a great swish of her skirt. "Sure as I'm the landlady of this fine establishment, I swear it to ye this is not the Tory scoundrel Cobbler Smith's lad!"

I guess this is just some kind of an act they put on. But I can hardly breathe. My heart is pumping. People are looking at me. Staring at me and laughing. They think this is fun, but I don't like being stared at, laughed at. I want these dusty old floorboards to swallow me up.

Mr. McGinty raises his hand as if to strike me over the top of the lady's head. She cries out, throws her arms around me, and hugs me to her big mushy chest of bosom, which is all covered up with some cottony material. "Leave the poor child, will you sirrah!" she shouts. "By heavens, just look at that face!" She takes my chin in her hands. "Just look at the likes of 'im!" She pinches my cheeks. "How dare ye inflict injury on an innocent lad such as this? This, sirrah, is no cobbler's boy!"

I am like a rag doll, no will of my own, as she flops me to her chest again. The audience roars.

This whole thing takes only a few minutes, but it feels like an eternity. When it's finally over and the crowd's moved on, I collapse into a chair.

"Well, young lad," says Mr. McGinty, winking. "You are a good sport, indeed. May I offer you a free lemonade, by way of recompense?" He puts a glass carefully down on a cotton napkin on the table by my hand. It's sweet and tart and cold; I drink it down in big heaving gulps to help wash away the lump in my throat.

"Do you put that act on every day?" I ask him. "With different kids?"

Mr. McGinty steps back, throws his hands up, his mouth a big O. "An act? Never such a thing, sir! Acting is an ignoble career for wayward guttersnipes and immoral tramps. I am no actor, by troth. I am a clean-living barkeep and the faithful resident historian of this fine establishment." He crosses his arms. "Go ahead. Ask me any fact about Colonial times."

"Um, okay. How many American rebels fought in the Revolutionary War?"

He rattles off the answer like a machine. "Over eight years of war, 1775 to 1783, it's estimated that somewhere between two hundred seventeen and two hundred fifty thousand soldiers rallied behind our leader George Washington, whom Congress declared our commander in chief in June 1775. Of those men and boys, it's estimated that a full eight thousand souls may have been killed, and up to twenty-five thousand wounded, in battle. Ask me something harder."

"I can't think of anything right now."

"Then swab down these tables."

Is he for real? McGinty dives behind the bar and comes up with a white rag and an apron. "There's a certain way I want you to do it," he says, putting the cloth rag in my hand. "Are you right-handed? Counterclockwise. A dozen passes, no more, no less."

I look out the window, longing to see Ludmila, Davis, and the twins come up the walk. No such luck.

I wipe down tables.

Tourists wander in now and then. McGinty always challenges them to ask a history question. They usually just ask: "When was the Revolutionary War?" Or "What was the biggest battle?" He'll rattle off long answers, full of battle trivia, while they itch to get going. And every once in a while, if there are a lot of people around, McGinty chases me with the broom again, shouting: "EARN YOUR KEEP, YOU GOOD FOR NOTHING SCALLIWAG!"

I am starting to actually believe I am a lowly servant from the 1770s when that nice, plump lady finally comes back to rescue me. She takes my apron and dishrag and says, "You've been a wonderful sport, kiddo, but I'm springing you now. Marcus means well, but he gets a little carried away. Not many boys your age would have stuck with him for so long."

"About McGinty," I ask. "Does he really think it's the 1770s? He acts like it."

"You know, he gets so into character, I think sometimes he does." She laughs. "But that's because he's, well, kind of a strange bird—you'll have to forgive him. But he knows everything there is to know about Revolutionary history, so this is the perfect place for him, God love him!" She rolls her eyes and shakes her head. "Still, he's not quite right in the head, is he?"

Old McGinty's been driving me crazy, but now I want to defend him. I want to say: "What's wrong with knowing everything about Revolutionary War history?" Or even, "What's wrong with being not quite right in the head?" But I don't say anything.

The landlady gives me a five-dollar gift certificate for the dry goods store. I'm not sure what "dry goods" are, but after saying "Thank you, ma'am" and bowing like I think the cobbler's boy probably would, I leave that place, Ludmila's orders or not.

It must have rained while I was inside the tavern, because everything looks soaking. How did I miss it? Trees are dripping, benches and sidewalks slightly steaming.

And there, down the street, I see Davis, Joel, Jake, and Ludmila. They are walking back from that muster, soaking wet and laughing. Sunlight's glinting on the slick, rainy cobblestones and lighting up their outlines from behind. When Davis smiles at me, her dark brown hair has a glowing copper outline. Ludmila's pink hair is all matted down flat.

I am so glad to see them, I feel all hot and funny inside. And all of a sudden I wonder what they think when they look at me.

Do they look at me the same way that landlady looks at McGinty?

37

Change is possible. It is not to be feared. If only you could sit where I sit, in this secret, green-roofed spot on my small island hill, under the towering pines—this rare hidden jewel, deep within Sanctuary Marsh. From here, one sees how life could be restored. How we can change Nature for the better. And in doing so, change our own, human natures, for the better.
—Tiberius Shaw, PhD

Over dinner that night at Ye Olde Colonial Diner, we have a powwow. It's time to figure out the next day or two of the trip.

I have been thinking for ages about how close we are finally getting to Sanctuary Marsh, so I come prepared with suggestions. I have Shaw's green journal, and a very careful map I've made.

"Good news. The marsh is only an hour or so north. We could get there early and spend the whole day birding," I announce.

I have about 90 percent concluded that I know where

Tiberius Shaw's house is: about a four- or five-mile walk from the visitor center. I have gone over all the parts in Shaw's green journal that mention the area. I have checked it out on Google Earth on the public computer at the RV park office, where we're staying near Williamsburg. There's only one house, according to that map, I think, that could possibly be his.

And although Ludmila and Davis think it's not good manners, I plan to knock on his door anyway. When he sees I am there to give him back his long-lost green journal, it will change everything. He will be so pleased, he will invite me in and tell me all the answers and advice that I need to know.

"But birds are so boring!" Jake moans. "Blah! And there's so much stuff in downtown DC. The spy museum! And that theatre where Lincoln got shot! Don't you want to see that, instead of just bird-watching all day? For crying out loud, Charlie, you can see birds anywhere!"

"This is a special place, Jake. And you should say birding, not bird-watching, just like it's Trekkers, not Trekkies," I inform him. "Bird people are sensitive to that stuff."

Everyone groans. They know not to mess with me when I start to talk fast like this. When I get nervous and my hands get itchy and my feet get rumbly.

Ludmila pulls out her phone. "Well, your

grandmother might have something to say about our schedule. Let's give her a call."

She props her phone up against the big bottle of ketchup on the table, and hits speaker. Outside the window I notice about a dozen little brown finches scrambling for crumbs from an outdoor table. I stare at them while the phone rings. I both want—and don't want—to hear Gram's gruff, familiar voice.

"Hey, Grammy," Davis says.

"Hey, Gram!" say the twins.

"Davis. Joel. Jake. Charlie," Gram says.

She doesn't usually call us by our names. It's always cuties, or honey-bunnies, or cookie pies. Or for me, Lysol Louie.

"Hello. We are in Virginia! We're very close now," says Ludmila in her deep, even voice. "But the boys want to do a few more things. Tomorrow, Charlie very much wants to do the bird-watching in the sanctuary. I mean, the birding. The twins and Davis want to visit DC."

There's silence from Gram's end.

"Or," she says, "we could come check in with you right away, first. We are very close."

More silence.

Then, finally, Gram sighs a long, airy sigh. "Well, I'm very sorry to be the bearer of bad news at the end of your long trip."

I feel like someone just pricked me with an electric shock. We all sit, silent, around the phone, dreading her next words.

"I'm afraid that you'd better come right away, right now. That nice Dr. Spielman was just here—he just left the room, actually. They've scheduled your father for another surgery."

"*What?*"

"They found something and they want to go back in." Gram's voice is tired, flat. Like each word is hard to get out.

Go back in. To my dad's head. To his brain. To what makes him, him.

The chicken nuggets I just ate turn into lead bullets. Panic shoots into my legs, then rebounds like a string of fire back up into my chest. I am not ready to think of Dad having surgery again. The first time was bad enough. No. I don't want it. Not again!

Davis's face looks pale. She is nibbling on a strand of her brown hair from her ponytail—something Gram always yells at her for doing. The twins are sitting very still.

Ludmila says, "We can come to you right now."

"No, don't worry; that's more hullabaloo than I can deal with tonight. Get a good night's sleep and be at the hospital by seven. It's going to be a long day tomorrow."

Ludmila turns off the phone and quietly puts it in her bag. We brush off our hands and scurry and scramble, wordless. The twins pop the last fries in their mouths. They scramble just like those little brown finches, frantic for the last crumbs of a summer day.

Dad was supposed to be getting better at this hospital. Not worse. He is not supposed to go backward, into more problems, into more surgery. It's not supposed to work like this.

It's not until we're back in Old Bessie, chugging toward the motel, that another thought hits me like a punch in the gut:

Tomorrow was going to be the day. My chance with Tiberius Shaw in the sanctuary.

When all my questions about human behavior and bird behavior would get answered.

Sanctuary.

Not surgery.

I am still holding Shaw's green journal in my hands, along with the map I'd made of how to find his house. I've been holding it since Gram's phone call, holding it so tight that the bones in my hand hurt. So tight that my hands need washing, washing, washing.

38

The next morning precisely at six a.m., we moot
Gram in the lobby of the strange new Virginia hospital.
It's odd to see her in this totally out-of-place place.

Gram has one of her sweat suits on. She wears sweat
suits all the time, even though I've never seen her sweat.
Still, today, she looks messy—her short silver hair is sticking out all over, instead of smooth and high, like her
usual hair-helmet. She looks like she's been sleeping on
a couch. Or in a chair by Dad's bed, like she used to in
the early days back in San Diego.

"Hark, the weary travelers," Gram says, opening her
arms. "Where's my hugs? Joel, why on earth are you
wearing that wig? Charlie, did you grow another inch

since I've seen you? Hugs, please!"

The new hospital has dirty smudges from millions of hands around door handles and corners. No potted palm trees, orange couches, or gift shop in sight. No Ellie in her blue vest. No little bird sculptures waiting for me on a shelf.

I think: *This* is where they sent Dad? *This* is where the expert brain surgeons work? But when we get upstairs to the special neurology unit, it's a little more reassuring. It's cleaner and newer, with a modern-looking nurses' station. A bunch of nurses talk on phones and write in charts.

Ludmila is dressed crazier than usual. That green dog collar. The combat boots with the flowery dress. It seems like the more stressed-out things are, the crazier Ludmila dresses.

We all troop and clomp down the hall after Gram. She stops at Dad's door, then turns and looks at us with watery eyes, her hand on the knob. "The timing stinks. As it turns out, we only have a few minutes."

And then, there is Dad, sitting up in his new hospital bed.

There's a little piece of toilet paper stuck to his chin, with a tiny red dot in the center, a shaving nick. He used to let me watch him shave. He'd even spread a layer of his thick, creamy shaving foam along the side of the tub, and tell me to write the alphabet in it, when I was little. I loved the clean smell of it on my hands.

Dad's got a green hospital gown on, his arms at his sides. He looks like he's in the dark and someone's shining a flashlight in his face and he can't figure out where the light is coming from.

"Hi, Daddy-o!" says Davis, real extra loud.

"Hi, Dad," says Joel, knocking gently on his helmet.

"Oh, for crying out loud, don't knock on it, numbskull!" says Gram. "What, did you forget everything already?"

Dad squints at Jake and Joel. He reaches out his hand to them and smiles.

"Don't. Worry about it. Champs," he says. It's the first time we've heard his voice in so long. It only comes out of the right half of his mouth, and it's a little slurred and raspy, but it's definitely Dad.

That's when everyone starts crying.

But I don't cry. I just stand by the door, by the hand-sanitizer pump, breathing hard. Breathe in.

Breathe out.

I need to tell Dad I've found almost all of the birds on our Someday Birds List. But I don't think now is the time. Too much is happening too fast.

A big dark-skinned nurse in a bright pink top comes in and claps her hands. "All right, family," she sings. "It's time!" Gram straggles up from her seat. Davis locks her arms around Dad's neck like she won't let go without a fight, and he smiles at her, pats her hand.

Gram's face looks like a wrinkled-up Kleenex.

The nurse's voice gets softer. "Come on now, folks! Don't you worry, because you've got Dr. Spielman, and he is amazing. Your dad's made so much progress already. And Dr. Spielman is going to fix it to make sure he can keep on making more progress. He'll take very good care of Robert. But we have to stay on schedule here."

Two orderlies come in with a gurney, which is what you call one of those table-beds on wheels. The big nurse keeps clapping her hands, trying to scatter us like pigeons.

They send us to a separate neurology waiting room. It's across a sky bridge in a newer section of the hospital, on the other side of the street. The twins pound across, testing its strength. I tiptoe after them and stop in the middle to look out the window at the traffic below. I am up high like a bird, floating above the street.

"Charlie!" Gram calls. "Move your keester!"

Something gray flutters toward me: a mourning dove lands on the outside ledge. There's only an inch of glass separating her from my hand. She has no idea I am right here, so close to her. She coos, and I can almost feel the vibration on my palm.

I used to think it was *morning dove,* as in time of day, not *mourning dove,* as in grieving.

"CHARLIE!"

The dove spooks, and flies away.

This new waiting room has low green couches, a coffee table, and an annoying news show blaring on a flat-screen TV. It also has a Nintendo 64.

"Mario!" Joel and Jake shout, flopping down together on a floor cushion. Joel flings Ludmila's wig off into a corner and hands his brother a controller. They sit shoulder to shoulder. My two brothers are sticking to each other like glue today.

Davis looks pale. Her mouth is set in a straight line. Visual cue: Fear? Worry? Love?

Gram has dark wedges of purple tiredness underneath her watery blue eyes. She rubs them as the video game theme song starts. It clashes with the sound from the television, where twin blond ladies in red, white, and blue outfits shout at us, while photos of soldiers flash in the background. Gram clicks it off with the remote and says, "Crazy nonsense; you can't hear yourself think."

It's going to be a long surgery. They are going to drill back inside my dad's head and fix another small spot they found that's swollen and bleeding. It's a problem that they think they might have missed the first time around—it was a small thing, but it's gotten worse. So they have to do it. They say they have to fix it.

Dr. Spielman is old and gray-haired like Gram. He looks like he could play a doctor on TV. He spends a lot of time talking to Gram, holding and patting her hand and talking in a soft voice. He says he will come out to give us regular updates.

I keep my backpack right by me, with Shaw's little green journal by my side, as well as my Bird Book. I think about the mourning dove. I close my eyes and remember the feel of her vibration against the glass. The small neat head, the streamlined body. I take my pencil and begin to sketch.

The door back into the surgery area has a long rectangular window. I see a doctor in a blue surgical cap come up to that window, look out at us, and then turn around and go back down the hall.

"What does *that* mean?" Davis nudges Gram, looking at the door.

"Lord knows," says Gram. She is knitting a small round blue wool disk on needles that are connected by some kind of tubing.

"What is that, Gram?" I ask.

"Cap for your father," she says, adjusting the bag of

wool at her feet. I look in. There are at least a dozen caps in there already.

An hour passes. Two. My butt aches, my knees ache, my head aches.

I notice Dr. Spielman, the surgeon, in the window of the surgical area. He has blue scrubs, a blue hat. He peers out at us and motions with his hand for Gram to come forward.

She freezes for a minute, then puts down her knitting needles. The doctor opens the door for her; she slips in, and they stand where we can just barely see them, through the long narrow window that's set in the door. Davis and I watch, frozen. I grip the green plastic armrests of the chair so hard, I have wrist cramps.

We can see part of Gram—her profile—and we can see the doctor's chest and arms. He is gesturing with his hands. He is making a cutting motion. Now his hands are palms up, like he is offering something to Gram, but his hands are empty. He shrugs.

What does it mean?

Now, through the narrow rectangle, we see that Gram is putting her face in her own hands. Her shoulders slump forward, and she starts to shake. The doctor's hands go down to his sides, hanging useless.

What are these visual cues?

In the pit of my stomach a terrible realization starts to form. Then it travels to my feet, and becomes a rumble.

A rumble in my feet is not good.

When I was little and something bad or scary would happen, or just something that confused me so much I got afraid from my own not-knowing-ness, I would start to feel this rumble in my feet. And when the rumble shot up through my body and burst through the top of my head, I would run.

One day in fifth grade, I got called to the principal's office. I didn't know what for. It turned out to be some dumb reason like I was missing a field trip slip, but earlier that day, I had gotten pushed by David Gomez at recess and had pushed him back, so I was scared. The principal was a mean man. I was so scared that my feet wouldn't let me go in his office. I came down the main hall intending to turn right, but at the last minute, my rumble feet changed their mind and ran me out the front door, across the parking lot, and down the street. It was like I had no control at all. My head went blank. I ran blind—I just followed my frantic feet.

I ended up running into the public library next door. I hid in a corner of the children's section. After a while a librarian noticed me huddled there rocking, and got me to confess.

When she took me back to school, Dad was there! All wild-eyed, worried, and upset. They'd even called the police. Dad hugged me tight and made me promise not to ever, ever get rumble feet again. I'd had to stand there and let him hug me for what felt like forever, and I had to promise.

But today, I can't keep that promise. My feet are rumbling now like they rumbled then. I need to go. I watch Gram's shoulders shaking behind the door, and I can't stand it—the rumble is shooting up through my body out of the top of my head—I need to go—

I'm gone.

Across the glass sky bridge, down the stairs, and out on the street, frantic, following my feet, and at the entrance, I see the wide-open yellow door of a taxi, and a person getting out of it with a walker, and I almost knock him over I'm in such a rush to get myself and my backpack and my pounding heart and my rumble feet into that cab.

"Where to?" says the driver in an accent that's kind of like Ludmila's as he pulls away from the curb.

I tell him.

· CAROLINA PARAKEET ·

RARE
BIRDS

39

I take the southern entrance by the visitor center and
wend my way inward, through and across the marsh
for some time north and east. After a while, a stand
of deep, dark pine and cedar appears like a mirage,
shimmering on its own island hill, with no apparent
way to reach it. But there is always an approach
to the unreachable. Persist, move closer, and the
treasure rises up like a gift: my hidden refuge within
this refuge, its roof the greenest of greens.
—Tiberius Shaw

In my backpack is my wallet with practically a year
of allowance money—I don't really need to spend allowance on anything, as a rule—and a small bottle of Purell.
Also two granola bars, my Bird Book, my sketching pencils, and Shaw's green journal.

In my head is nothing.

The fear I felt in the cab is gone. But the rumble in
my feet is still propelling me on, through the deep gray
morning mist of this endless marsh.

I'm calm now. I only think about the path. There are one hundred thousand streams, creeks, and rivers threaded through this place, but this is the path. I'm sure.

I concentrate on the path. Only on the path.

There are lots of dark green piney patches around here, according to Google Earth, but looking northeast about five miles from the visitor center (humans walk at two miles an hour times two-plus hours) I did notice a house with a green roof on a little bit of land jutting out into the bay. I figure it's got to be that house. It's the only house that fits Shaw's description for miles around.

Shaw's house.

I'm heading for it.

The trail goes from pebbly shoreline path to wooden boardwalk over marshland. Thick green reeds, what Shaw describes as eelgrass, shoot up every which way. Brown cattails stick out of the mud. Dragonflies dance in the drizzle.

A great blue heron maybe five yards to my right suddenly whooshes up and heaves himself into the sky, flapping and complaining at me, with a call that sounds like a truck's rusty brake. I guess I disturbed his breakfast. Well, he disturbed me, too. My heart is jumping in my chest now, and I realize I am the only one around. There's no other sign of humans, anywhere.

Usually, I would like this. Usually, this would calm

me. But right now, it's feeling a little spooky.

I walk for about an hour, just one foot in front of the other, not thinking too much. I just try to get closer to the area that juts out from the bay. That's all I'm concentrating on, step, after step, in my old, tired-looking Crocs.

After about forever, the mist lifts a bit. I can see something like a dark green blur that has to be a stand of pines. But I never seem to get closer to it. I'm farther off than I was when I started.

All of a sudden I hear someone talking, faint but distinct. It's a tour-guide kind of voice, and people are murmuring replies and clomping along. I try to avoid them, but somehow I walk right into a small group of birders, perched on the boardwalk. I feel scared and embarrassed, but there's nothing to do but stand there with them, at the back of their flock.

"Yes, folks," says the guide, "climate change is impacting the biodiversity of this precious place in serious ways. We have to make some hard decisions if we want to keep it vibrant for our kids and grandkids."

A lady in a khaki baseball cap nods and smiles at me. I nod back. Then she suddenly turns and points out into the reeds: there's that heron again! I nod and smile for real now.

I have to stay with this group, because we are all going in the right direction, according to Shaw's green journal. And actually, after all this time walking alone, I have to admit: it's kind of nice to be walking along behind the flock of birders. They are quiet and calm. They care about birds. I could almost feel like I could belong to a group like this.

We are getting to the spot, according to Shaw's book, where there should be that small stand of pines on the spit of land overlooking the marsh.

I peer carefully at the tree line, trying hard to find the outline of a house, any house. A man next to me notices me staring. "What do you see over there? Osprey?" He trains his binoculars.

I wish I had binoculars. "Actually," I say, "I'm looking for a house. Do you maybe see a house somewhere in those trees?"

"Well, let me look . . . Yes, I do. I see a little brown house, with a green roof," he says. "What about it?"

My stomach drops to my knees. I swear he's got to be kidding. But he's totally serious.

"Really?" He hands me his binoculars. Sure enough, there's the glint of a reflection on a red-framed window. The roof is dark green, with shiny edges.

I cry out loud: "It's really there!"

The whole group of birders gets very excited and whisper, "What? What is it?" They all train their binoculars on the stand of pines and murmur quietly to each other, trying to figure out what I saw.

The tour guide taps me on the shoulder. I jump. He has a bushy brown beard hanging down the front of his green warden's shirt.

"What you looking for, youngster?" he says.

"Can you tell me, do you know if, well, maybe, if that's Tiberius Shaw's house?"

His eyebrows shoot way up. "Tiberius Shaw? Do we have a Tiberius Shaw fan here then?" He smiles and shakes his head. "That's not his place, no. I happen to know the old lady who lives in that little house. Great location. She's a big supporter of the sanctuary. Nice old gal."

He turns to the group of birders. "But this boy asked about Shaw. Haven't heard that name in a while. Remember him? Bird guru, did a lot of work around these here parts, years ago." They nod politely.

You know when they say your heart *sinks*? I feel like mine is as low as the mud we're walking over. If Shaw doesn't even live here anymore, what am I doing in this stupid sanctuary? But if Shaw doesn't live here, then what did he mean by "*my hidden refuge within this refuge, its roof the greenest green?*"

I walk slower and slower until I've left the tour group behind. I rumble along the wooden boardwalks on my own, moving like a robot, like a droid.

There are miles and miles of boardwalks and walking

paths. And, of course, those one hundred thousand creeks, streams, and rivers. No wonder I got it wrong. Did I think it would be that easy?

The soft gray morning fog is gone now, and the sun shines harsh, leaving nowhere to hide. It's beautiful, though, glinting bright silver on the water. It has no right to be beautiful on a day like today.

I notice birds, but I don't care anymore. Wrens try to cheer me up with their tweety chirrupy songs, but it doesn't help. There are marsh birds, shorebirds, and two dark brown and white osprey, diving and soaring from nests on high wooden platforms that someone built right there, high up over the marsh.

But I can barely lift my feet.

I am slow, sluggish, heavy.

I was so sure my guess was right.

So sure that today was the day I would finally find Tiberius Shaw. So I could finally ask him my big question.

I lost my mother at birth, and my father passed away when I was twelve. It was Nature that raised me—I was a child of forest and field—and kind relatives lent a hand. Forest, field, and family. And I gained a glimmer of real wisdom, there, along the way, about how to survive . . .
—Tiberius Shaw, PhD

My big question for Dr. Tiberius Shaw, PhD, is: What was it? What was the glimmer of real wisdom you gained, that helped you survive?

My steps slow to a stop. I crouch down in a small ball, right there on the boardwalk, and put my arms around my knees, and rock. I am practically facedown on the walk. I peer through the cracks between the boards and watch a bug, a water skater, sluicing by on his long legs across the brown water. I scan the roots of reeds, my eyes close to the ground. I'm not looking for anything, anymore. I don't care about anything, anymore.

That's when I notice something peculiar.

There are some pressed-down reeds branching off from one side of the boardwalk. It takes me a minute to realize it's a path. There's a small piece of green cloth tied to a reed about a yard out, to mark the place. It's a path that's barely a path, something someone has tramped through just enough times. And perched on a branch at the far end, right before it turns, I see a strange bird. A bird I've seen only in a book. But I swear, I see it.

It couldn't possibly be. It's a little green parrot with a yellow head and red-orange patches. A bird that used to live around these parts more than two hundred years ago. An extinct bird. It's impossible. But there it is, or I am really going crazy: a little Carolina parakeet, sitting on a reed stalk and whistling at me.

There used to be millions of them back in Audubon's time. Dad said. And I read about it: They lived from southern New York and the lower Midwest all the way through the South. They were the only native American parakeets. They were pretty, and made nice pets.

But they were also stupid. No survival instinct. Farmers shot them for eating fruit, and seed, and they never learned to fly away. They'd just stick around, fluttering in the field, like, "What the heck? What's that shooting? Is somebody killing us?" Hundreds would die within minutes. The whole species got killed off within a century.

Or did they?

The yellow-headed parakeet flits from reed to reed, down the narrow, reedy path.

I follow.

I step off the boardwalk. Water squelches through the holes in my Crocs. I shudder, but I can't stop looking at the fluttering wings up ahead.

I don't think about the cold, muddy water. Or Shaw. I don't think about getting lost. I don't think about my dad, or Ludmila, or the twins, or Davis, or Tiberius, stuck all alone in Gram's hotel room. I don't think about

Gram. I try not to think about how horrible it is to wear soaking wet socks. There's nothing I can do about any of this anymore.

I don't think about anything except the little green back of the parakeet who shouldn't exist, but who is just ahead of me, flitting through the tall reeds.

He leads me through this jungle for so long, I'm starting to think the world's turned into one big reed marsh. But finally, we come to the bank of a narrow stream. It's strewn with mossy stepping-stones. Above the tinkling water, a flash of green. The Carolina parakeet, still there, whistling. I strain to memorize his song, in case I lose sight of him and have to track him by sound. *Too-wheet! Too-wheet!*

I place my foot carefully down on the first, slimy stone. It holds. I stutter my way slowly across, slipping and jerking, but I make it to the very end. By the other bank, I step off and sink knee-deep in muddy, stinky ooze.

Too-wheet! Too-wheet! sings a probably-extinct bird, somewhere deeper in a thicket of green. Am I going crazy?

In my haze, I notice that on this side of the stream, heading into the thicket, there is a path. By the path is a post. On the post is a green metal box with the outline of a gold feather painted on it in metallic paint. I don't see any house around. I look everywhere—no sign of one. Just a mailbox. No house.

I take off my backpack. I take Shaw's green journal out of it. I look at the golden feather on the cover of the little book. I remember the feeling I got the first time I saw that image, so many days ago in the Twa Corbies shop, way back across the country in Nevada. Like a lifetime ago.

It's the same image, on book and box. The same feather.

My heart is beating hard now, and not just from my slog across the stream.

I open the metal mailbox. It's rusty. There's nothing in there but a spiderweb.

Quickly, I flip through my own notebook, and find a sketch I did a long time ago, right after Dad first told me about the Carolina parakeet.

I based my drawing on Audubon's, in his baby elephant folio. They were actual real, live birds, back when Audubon was living. He painted a bunch of them all fluttering around a flowering plant. So I had taken my colored pencils and sketched a grouping of them, too.

I rip out the sketch, take a pencil, think for a minute, and write a long note on the back, making sure not to get drips of mucky water on it.

I write, and write, and write.

Then, I take the DNA brochure from my backpack— the one that lady Helen at the Field Museum gave me, with Tiberius Shaw's name listed as scientist/donor for DNA/genomic research. I fold the sketch and tuck it, and the brochure, into the Carolina parakeet page of Shaw's little green book. I put all three items together in the green metal mailbox, and put up its rusty metal flag.

I pause a minute, to say good-bye to the green journal. It's been with me for a while. It's given me much to think about. But it's not really mine. The old green journal is Shaw's.

The Bird Book is what's mine.

"Too-wheet!"

It's faint. I hurry down the path.

Tall reeds give way to more open brush, and soon I see another stand of little pines at the top of a rising hill.

What is this new place? Will I finally see Shaw's house?

My feet are still squishing and squelching water with every step. The skin on my nose and the back of my neck feels burned. I don't have any idea where I am on the map, or how I'm going to get back, but I'm not thinking about it. I just want to know where that Carolina parakeet went.

So when I reach the top of the rise, I gasp.

On the rise, there is no house.

What there is instead: a tall, thick stand of pine trees, their branches filled with the flutter and chirp of Carolina parakeets—as well as a few buntings, thrushes, wrens, and other birds of different sizes and shapes. There are flashes and flitters and winging around. There's hopping, and chirping on branches. It's a bird party.

I approach slowly, but the action doesn't stop. They don't seem afraid of me. I sit carefully down on a soft bed of pine needles, smelling the pine smell, taking in deep lung-filling breaths of it, and looking up at the birds. If you look, really look, you can see that the trees are filled with nests and knotholes, with bird-action. With Carolina parakeets, dodging in and out.

I let my ears fill with summer sounds I don't quite understand, but feel soothed by.

I think I fall asleep for a while, leaning back on my backpack. I am perfectly alone here, but not afraid. The world is so far behind, I don't have to think about it. This is peace. This is a type of house. Maybe this is what Shaw meant by his "refuge within this refuge." Maybe he didn't mean a real house, with doors and windows and such. Maybe this sanctuary is what he meant.

After a while, I get up, stretch, and explore some more, through the trees. And on the other slope, I see signs of a campsite. A circle of rocks, two metal stands hammered into the ground on either side. A bar across the middle, just right for a pot to hang over the fire. Some wooden pegs in the ground, which might have supported a tent. I sit by the empty campsite and sketch the pines, the birds, the flat silver fingers of marsh water.

My socks are still covered in black silt; I peel them off. My toes are white and pruney, covered with bits of pond matter. It was a terrible idea to take those wet socks off, because now I'll have to put them back on.

I know I can't stay here forever.

The sun was straight up when I saw the green mailbox; now it's not. It's afternoon. All I want to think about are the Carolina parakeets, those miracle birds. But Gram and Ludmila and Davis and the twins are peeking around the edges of my thoughts. Gram and Ludmila will be really worried. The world is seeping back into my head, and although I wish I could stay here in the green pine calm forever, I know I can't.

I tell myself I don't want to think about it. But part of me needs to know about Dad.

I leave. I go back through the beautiful stand of pines, make my way across the shallow stream without worrying this time, because now I know the depths of the water. I stumble along the boardwalk trails until I notice a man in a rowboat, wearing a big floppy hat and holding a fishing pole.

"Hello!" I yell. I don't even hesitate one bit. No heart-pounding or anything. I ask him, flat out, which way is back to the entrance, and he silently points.

Along the way, egrets and blue herons stare at me. I go over footbridges and wade again through even more ankle-deep muck—yuck!—zigzagging through marshland past groves of slim, black trees growing straight out of the water. I pass a beaver's dam. I watch an osprey dive for a fish.

It's dusk when I finally stumble into the clearing around the wildlife refuge visitor center, full of mud and covered in mosquito bites. My arms and legs are shaking and my throat's like cotton, I'm so tired, thirsty, and hungry.

There's no one in the visitor center, thank goodness. The first thing I do is head for the restroom. I rinse out my socks and try to dry them in the hand dryer. I duck my head under the faucet and try to rinse my hair. I scrub my face, feet, arms, legs, everything I can fit into the sink. *Soap-rinse-one-soap-rinse-two-soap-rinse-three-soap-rinse*—oh, to heck with it. I soap-rinse-one-gazillion. I stop counting.

I use up all the soap in the dispenser and have to go to another sink, and I use up all the soap in that dispenser, too. I'm kind of whimpering without even realizing it.

And as I'm combing my fingers through my slightly

cleaner hair, I notice, on my neck, something that looks like an apple seed scrambling along.

Wait.

No. Please. Of all things, no.

The apple seed has hairy little legs.

A loud shriek echoes off the bathroom wall. Was that me?

I pluck off the tick and fling it into the sink. My arms and legs are flailing, and I jump up and down in silent panic. A tick! My archnemesis insect! Most hateful in existence!

I run the water scalding hot and am just washing it down the drain when the restroom door opens. A tall, thin, very dark man is standing there, wearing a warden's shirt. He has a name tag, but I don't stop to read it.

"Whoa, now, what's all this?" he says. "I've been hearing the water running in here for half an hour! What's going on? You okay?" He doesn't sound like he is mad, though. His eyebrows are relaxed, not scrunched. His hands are on his hips. His voice is slow.

"I had a tick on me," I say. I try to act steady, without shivering and jumping up and down too much. He looks me up and down, says, "Aw, shoot," and leaves. A few seconds later he's back with a towel, tweezers, a dry sweatshirt, and a black plastic comb.

"Okay. Bend down, kid," he says. He calmly combs through my hair. I hate this, but I let him. Emergencies are emergencies, after all.

"I don't see no bugs in there. You're clean. Looks like you just had that one tiny little bugger, won't hurt you one bit. Imagine, all that fuss over such a tiny bugger." He stands back up. I shrug.

"You with anyone?" he asks. "Your parents here?"

I shrug.

His name tag says *"Rodney."* He has brown eyes, blue-black skin, and the whitest straightest nicest teeth I've ever seen on a human. "I'll wait outside," says Rodney. "Why don't you shake out your clothes, check them over good, put on this dry sweatshirt? You're shivering. When you're ready, come on back into the visitor center and we'll talk about what's what. Okay?" He winks and smiles his brilliant white smile on his way out of the bathroom. "That's why we built the boardwalks," he turns back to say to me. "You're not supposed to go bushwhacking, young man! Especially not all alone."

When I come back into the visitor center, Rodney's just putting the *Closed* sign in the window. On the counter, he's set me an orange soda.

"Well?" he says, pulling up a stool with his foot. "Now you got to tell me the scoop. Who do I call? Where's your folks? What's a nice kid like you doing in a place like this—alone, at closing time?"

It's such a long story. I think about Ludmila, how hard it was for her to tell us her long story. But, before I realize it, I'm talking more than I have ever talked to anybody so far.

I tell him about when Dad first got hurt. About the hospital. About Davis's road trip idea, then Ludmila coming, after the accident. About Wyoming, Yellowstone, Little Bighorn, Wall Drug, Wisconsin Dells, Chicago, Pennsylvania, Williamsburg. I show him my own Bird Book, which I've never shown anyone. And I tell him what I saw this morning in the hospital: my gram, who never cries, breaking down on the other side of the surgery window.

And when I tell him that I don't know whether my dad might have died today, and that I couldn't find Shaw to answer my questions about what it's like, having no parents—well, it gets to be so that Rodney has to bring out a box of Kleenex and another orange soda.

"Well," he finally says. "You're a birder, right? So you're just going to have to remember about the thing with feathers."

I look at him.

"Like in the poem. Emily Dickinson. *'Hope' is the thing with feathers*."

I tell him I do know about hope. That I walked all the way out to the marshlands and the pine island, and saw the Carolina parakeet, all because of hope. But he doesn't believe me about the bird.

"Can't be. You must've seen a flock of domestic parakeets, or monk parrots. Or pets that escaped over the years, and flocked together."

"No, no. I know the difference. They were Carolina parakeets."

"Well, I guess hope really is a thing with feathers." He slaps his knee. He has a very loud, deep laugh.

Rodney also chuckles when I tell him we have a three-legged dog from Las Vegas named after Tiberius Shaw. "I think Dr. Shaw would consider that quite an honor," Rodney says.

"Wait—what? Do you know him? Would he?" I feel hope—feathers or no feathers—rise in my chest. Or maybe it's soda bubbles.

"Never seen him myself." My shoulders sag. "But some of the older rangers have told me stories."

He hands me another soda. I don't even like soda, as a rule, but I'm so worn out and thirsty, I'm drinking these down.

"Well, now," Rodney says finally. And the room grows silent except for the clicking of the big clock on the wall.

"You've had quite an adventure. But it looks like it's

about time for you to make a phone call now. Wouldn't you say? You know the number?"

I nod. But I don't want to call. I don't want to have to hear my gram's voice. I never want to know what she is going to tell me. I want to stay here and avoid everything and become a Sanctuary Marsh ranger for life, with my new friend, Rodney.

He's waiting, and the clock is still ticking.

"I can't do it. Would *you* call," I say, looking at the floor.

He looks at me hard, with his very brown eyes with their very white whites locking lasers and tractor beams on me so my eyeballs swivel up on their own and I have to look at him back.

Then he sighs and says, "Oh well, I suppose you've spoken enough for one day. Okay, kid." And he takes out his phone.

40

Warring birds, peaceful birds, life and death, kindness and menace—birds mirror the struggling in our own nature. Both war and peace are human nature. They are the nature of many creatures. It is hard to accept that these things will always exist.
—Tiberius Shaw, PhD

Something in Old Bessie's wheezy, clanking engine is even worse than usual. You can hear Ludmila coming a mile away.

Rodney walks me down the steps and outside to wait. He puts his hand on my shoulder, and somehow I find the strength to let him.

Ludmila squeaks to a stop right in front of us. "*Charlie!*" she calls out the window to me, but not in a mad way. Just in her regular voice. Her pink hair looks rumpled and her eyes look squinty and red behind her heavy glasses. "We have half the town out looking for you."

"I'm sorry."

I don't know what else to say. I just stand there in my

new Sanctuary Marsh sweatshirt. Rodney stands behind me, waiting.

"Rodney," I finally think to say. "This is Ludmila."

Ludmila clicks the camper door open. Tiberius the dog tumbles down the steps and up into my arms. His whole body is wagging happily. He just doesn't understand this kind of sadness. It must be nice to be a dog.

Ludmila follows him out of the camper. She slowly comes over and pumps Rodney's hand up and down five times. Then she places her other hand over his hand, sandwiching it. People do this for extra emphasis. Then, I guess the emphasis wasn't enough, because she goes in for a hug. "Thank you so much for watching over him. Oh, thank you, Rodney," she says. She is teary.

Rodney steps back and salutes her. Then he turns and scratches Tiberius's ears. "Great dog, kid," he says.

Ludmila coughs. "I thought you might want to see him, so I brought him along."

I smile at Ludmila and hug Tiberius closer.

"Now, good luck," Rodney tells me. "Be strong. Remember what we talked about. Keep the faith. And keep in touch."

I stare at the dirty camper steps. I don't want to get back in. Getting back in, is like a failure. I failed at finding Tiberius Shaw. I fail at everything. I don't know how to do anything. I don't want to be with Ludmila. I don't want her to talk. I don't want to hear anything about anything that ever exists in the world ever again. The world is dark.

"Come on then," she says, looking me up and down. "Let's get you back. We've been more worried about you, today, mister, than we've been worried about your dad."

Then—everything brightens.

41

It's night now, and black outside as we cross the hospital sky bridge. We are heading toward Dad's room. He is doing okay!

"Be prepared," Ludmila says as we walk. "He doesn't look very good. But the surgery went beautifully, and he's going to do fine. They won't let us in to see him, but we can stand outside the glass window."

I stop in the hallway. "If he was okay, then why did the doctor seem so serious when he talked to Gram? Why did Gram cry? What did the doctor say to her?"

"The doctor was just telling her the surgery went well."

"But I never saw Gram cry before. Crying should mean *bad* news."

"Ohh. So you thought—"

Ludmila pushes her heavy black-framed glasses up on her nose and looks at me. "And that's why you ran? Oh, Charlie," she says. "Your gram cried because she was so relieved. It was happy-crying. Relieved-crying."

I think about Gram's slumped shoulders and caved-in face through the narrow rectangle of glass in the surgery door. Gram's visual cue didn't look like "happy" or "relieved" to me. Her face looked like "end of the world."

There are so many things I just don't think I'll ever get.

The waiting room smells like stale coffee. The Nintendo's off. On the TV in the corner, the blond anchor ladies look like they're still having the same argument.

"Davis took the boys across the street to the hotel," says Ludmila. "It's been a loooong day."

Gram is the only person there. She is fast asleep on one of the couches, her feet in their clean, white sneakers, dangling off the edge. She has her arms crossed over her sweatshirt and a wrinkled *People* magazine over her head.

Once she told me, "Charlie, maybe you should read *People*. Might pick up some tips."

Ludmila shakes her gently.

"I've got him. He's here," she says.

Gram sits up and the magazine slides to the floor. She looks around, sees me. I am standing straight as an iron pole, my eyes on the floor. On my filthy, filthy Crocs.

She gets up and tries to hug me. I step back and pat her gently on her shoulder.

"I'm sorry I was so much trouble to you, Gram," I say.

Then Gram burst into tears. I always thought that was a weird expression: bursting. But that's just what she does—water just explodes out of her eyes and she's boo-hoo-hooing and everything. I am so surprised, I reach in my pocket and offer her Rodney's comb, which is all I have in there. I don't have any Kleenex.

"You're not trouble, Charlie boy," she says, taking Rodney's comb and looking at it without even seeing it. "Don't you ever say that. Don't you *think* that. I just worry about you so dang much, and get so dang mad at you, because I *care* about you so dang much. Because I love you so dang much."

Ludmila brings the Kleenex; Gram blows her nose. "The whole dang lot of you."

"I love you, too, Gram," I say, still patting her shoulder, over and over, as gently as I can. And it's pretty much true.

42

I think about all the people along the way on this trip. All in all, there have been way more good people than bad. Dr. Joan at the observatory, showing me the owls and the stars, and lending us Old Bessie, the stinky camper. There was that kind Little Bighorn couple. The parrot lady at Wall Drug. The nurse who patched up my leg at the waterpark. Ludmila's friends Mariana and Karim, and their little kids, and Helen, the ornithologist at the Field Museum. And especially my new friend Rodney.

Dad wouldn't believe it if I told him I'd crossed the entire country and spoken with all these new people. Had whole conversations with some of them. I'll show him my People list later.

And I will show him the Someday Birds List. I can't wait to talk to him about what I've seen. Birds like he's never imagined.

Dad's out of intensive care, again. But this time around, here in this new hospital, today, he's sitting up and talking, and listening to us.

"Davis, honey." Dad smiles, and reaches out his hand. Then he falls asleep for ten minutes. Then his eyes open again. "Heyyyy . . . how're my buds," he croaks to Joel and Jake, then he dozes away again. A few minutes later: "Charlie . . ." Boom, he's out of it again. He still talks a little bit out of only the right side of his mouth, but hey, he is talking. He is there. He is back.

When we were little, we used to pile into Dad's big bed with him at night and ask him to tell us stories. Dad was working two jobs back then, plus trying to finish his teaching degree, plus trying to raise us alone, and I guess he got pretty tired by the end of the day, but he'd never turn us down for a story.

"Once there was, a, a little boy, and he lived at the edge of a beautiful forest . . ."

And then he'd fall asleep! So we'd shake him a little.

"Then what? Then what?"

He'd come to with a start, and tell another sentence or two of the story, usually about how the kid had been warned by some good fairy or something not to go into that enchanted forest. But of course the kid always went into the forest. The kid never learned! Anyhow, Dad would say a sentence, then drowse off again.

More shaking.

Huh? What? He'd invent another bit of the story.

More shaking.

Huh? Okay, another sentence.

We shook stories out of him all the way to the end. We are not shaking him now, of course, but he's talking-dozing-waking-talking-dozing at about that same old pace. And those enchanted forests of my dad's stories— the forbidden places where the once-upon-a-time kids weren't supposed to go, but always somehow did? I've always imagined them as thick, dark stands of pines, full of twittering, colorful birds.

43

"It's going to be a very long journey back," Dr. Spielman says to us, outside the door of Dad's room. "But I'm confident he'll make a good recovery. Slow and steady wins the race. Just remember, it won't be overnight."

Dr. Spielman is good. He is always here, checking on Dad, checking on his speech and motor and physical therapy. Davis says Gram has a crush on him because Gram is always saying Dr. Spielman this, Dr. Spielman that, all the time Dr. Spielman. Plus, we always catch her putting on lipstick when she thinks it's time for his rounds.

Right now, Gram pumps Dr. Spielman's hand gently

up and down, up and down, then does the hand-sandwich thing and goes in for the hug.

Ludmila hasn't been spending much time with us. It's odd. She's either been somewhere else, or hanging out in the far corner of the waiting room, reading magazines. I don't think she's even been in Dad's room since we were allowed in. So when I see her walking down the hall toward us with a paper bag full of sandwiches, I grab her arm and say, "You have to come in and *officially* meet Dad."

His hospital bed's in sit-up position, and his tray's over his lap. His hands rest on it. Davis and the twins are on the window seat, watching Dad rest.

"Hey, Dad!" I say.

His eyes yank open. At first they're dusty buttons but then they clear.

"This is Ludmila. She drove us all the way here to see you."

He focuses on my face first, and then her face, and he smiles his lopsided smile.

"She used to bring you coffee in the early days, back in your old hospital, but you probably don't remember."

He reaches out a weak hand.

"Davis used to hate her, but not anymore. Ludmila is like family or something now."

She takes his hand.

"So you have to meet her."

Dad smiles. "Not—not Amar's Ludmila?"

Then, it's *Ludmila* who does the exploding-crying trick.

44

What can we learn about being human, from watching bird behavior? Perhaps that tiny, community-spirited bird, Australia's superb fairy-wren, gives us the best example: their whole wren-world only truly flourishes when each bird within it acts in a manner that's kind.
—Tiberius Shaw, PhD

We are on the plane, heading home. Davis is next to me, the twins behind us, Ludmila across. Tiberius is in a comfy new pet carrier, under the seat by Ludmila. He's probably dreaming about chasing mice through cornfields.

Gram is staying on with Dad. I think she was glad for a little more time not only with Dad, but with that Dr. Spielman.

Old Bessie, our rattletrap camper, is kaput. It finally gave out just as we were getting on the beltway a couple days ago. Dr. Joan told Ludmila she should just donate it to a charity for foster children. Rest in peace, Bessie.

Ludmila is talking about going back to school. Finishing her physical therapy degree. Watching the therapists work with Dad, it started her thinking.

She and Davis are also talking about joining this charity that helps women and children survivors in war-torn countries. It's nice to hear Davis talking about something besides how crazy in love she is with boy after boy after boy.

We did some stuff in Washington, DC. The twins finally got to go to the spy museum. I went through the whole thing with them, including fake back alleys and secret passageways. We did it, the three of us, and it wasn't too bad at all.

Best of all, we went to the hospital just to hang out with Dad. I told him about how I tried to complete the Someday Birds List. That I'd seen almost all the birds he named, and then some—but that I missed the sandhill crane, and I wasn't sure whether I'd seen a trumpeter or mute swan at Yellowstone.

Dad says that's perfectly okay, because maybe we can go back and settle the question. Maybe a trip to Wyoming, and also to Nebraska, next spring, to see the sandhill cranes, he said. He wants to hear the weird noise they make.

Dad says we will go out birding together a lot, once he is better.

But I don't think Dad believes what I told him about the Carolina parakeets alive and hidden in the sanctuary. Just like Rodney, Dad frowned and asked, "Are you *sure?*" But I don't care. No matter what anyone thinks, I know I what I saw.

Funny—I thought that finishing the Someday Birds List was the only way I could give us, Dad and me, that good feeling of calm relief. I worried all across the country that I had to find every bird on that list. But in the end, it didn't really matter. The feeling of calm came anyway.

In the hospital, I worked on my bird sketches.

I thought.

Wrote in this Bird Book.

And just as we were getting into the airport cab, Gram handed me a FedEx envelope.

"It was delivered to the hospital, care of your father," she said. "It looks like it's from that wildlife refuge. Maybe your friend Rodney—did you leave something behind at that visitor center?"

I put the envelope in my backpack and kind of forgot, in all the airport hustle, and also because I'm really bad at opening envelopes, so I avoid them. But now, here in the plane, I take it out.

Inside the FedEx envelope is a smaller, dark green envelope marked *To Charlie.*

On the back is an imprint of a golden feather. I run my finger across it.

"Come on!" Davis says. "I'm *dying*!"

I hand it to her. Really. I cannot open envelopes. I always end up ripping in half whatever's inside.

Davis expertly nudges her forefinger under the flap and takes out a single typed sheet. She hands it to me, hovering. Joel and Jake hang over the top of our seats so they can see what's going on.

Davis's long brown hair tickles my arm; I flick it away. We read silently together.

> *Dear Charlie,*
>
> *Thank you for your most interesting letter—on the back of your exquisitely rendered Carolina parakeet sketch, no less—that you left in the box by one of my regular campsites. And thank you for your thoughtfulness in returning my old green journal! I never imagined I'd see it again, this long-lost souvenir of my youth. Astounding, how you found it—and then, found me. Many have stumbled where you have succeeded. You must be a truly exceptional and persistent young man.*
>
> *Your father's injuries and the sense of peril you write about saddens me. I can only tell you what I think you already know: life is hard. There's no one*

*right way through, but I feel certain you will find your
own path. You are clearly a keen observer. If you can
observe bird behavior, you can observe human behavior,
and learn from it. Keep at that journal. Keep trying.
There's a popular saying that "doing something that
scares one a little, each and every day, helps one grow
as a person." But I think you know that already. You
have taken many difficult new paths, faced many scary
things. I salute your bravery.*

*The Carolina parakeet! A once extinct bird, yes.
As you gathered, there have been amazing advances
in genomic research—and a top secret experiment is
underway. You must tell NO ONE. These wonderful
birds have a foothold solely in this one particular
microenvironment, thanks to a tremendous amount of
work by the research departments of several museums,
as well as my own private fieldwork. We've made a
tenuous but important start toward renewal.*

*It is so easy, cowardly easy, in this world, to destroy
things. And it takes such courage to create, to build, to
renew, to embrace life. Doesn't it? Look at the courage
you have shown, Charlie. Your letter said you don't
understand people, but it's obvious you manage to see
clear to the core truths. You have heart. When you see
trouble, you want to help, even if you're not sure how.
I have never met you, yet I can tell this about you. You*

are a creator, not a detractor. Also, I am impressed with
your artwork. Send me more. Let's keep in touch.
    —*T. Shaw*

My mouth is stretched in a smile that won't stop. It won't leave my face. I am smiling so hard, I don't even notice the takeoff.

Once we're cruising, I look out the plane window at what's down below. I see green circles, rectangles, brown squares—a constant flow of geometrical shapes. It's like we've turned Audubon's wilderness into a modern green and brown quilt.

Then we pass threads of blue in the quilt—small rivers, and bigger rivers, and before I know it, mountains.

Bird's-eye views or close-up human views: the world is confusing and surprising both ways. But I guess that has to be okay.

The plane rumbles and bumps, suddenly, with turbulence.

On second thought, maybe things are better close-up.

Davis is reading a book about growing up in Afghanistan.

The twins are kicking my seat from behind me. But when I tell them to please cut it out, they do.

My stomach flips, but in a different way. I think maybe this is a good flip.

The flight attendant comes by. She hands us each a small, cold, plastic-wrapped pellet.

"Hellooooo, mystery snack!" says Davis.

We unwrap them, and I think:

Whatever this thing turns out to be, I'm going to take a bite.

ACKNOWLEDGMENTS

When I was growing up, my school would go on frequent hikes along Connecticut's Mill River with a very special local naturalist and educator, Mrs. Joy Shaw. I lived for these hikes. Mrs. Shaw, over many decades, now, has opened up the outdoors to innumerable school kids. I'm deeply grateful that I got to be one of them. I want to publicly thank her.

Many early readers and writer-friends have traveled along with Charlie and me. They include, but certainly are not limited to, David Applegate, Dare DeLano, Paula Fitzgerald, Rachel Fritts, Terri Fritts, Anne Hamilton, Kristi Herro, Judy Illes, and Peter Mashman (who wrote the first book review, back when the book was titled

"Chicken Nuggets Across America"). Also, Judy McSweeney, Noa Nimrodi, Gigi Orlowski, Linda Rosenberg, Beth Rowedder (and all friends at Lake Country School), Ona Russell, Merriam Saunders, Debbie Schneider, Sarah Sleeper, Lisa Venditelli-Karmel, and Nancy Webb. Many thanks to the SCBWI-San Diego chapter. Many friends not named, but all so dear, know they have my love and gratitude.

Without the gift of a three-week writer's residency at Hedgebrook and the encouragement of the incredible women writers I met there, I might not have had enough faith in myself to finish this book. Deep thanks to all my Hedgebrook sisters, especially executive director Amy Wheeler. Hedgebrook is a truly transformative place.

Taylor Martindale Kean, my agent and champion at Full Circle Literary, is grace and intelligence personified. I'm grateful as well to the wonderful Stefanie Von Borstel for her excellent counsel. At HarperCollins, deep thanks to Rosemary Brosnan, Jessica MacLeish, and to Annie Berger, who first championed Charlie, and whose keen eye and warm heart made this a deeper, richer work. I'm honored beyond words to be able to work with each of them. Thanks as well to all the professionals whose commitment and expertise have made this a much better book, including designer Heather Daugherty, cover artist Julie McLaughlin, production editor Alexei Esikoff, publicist Olivia Russo, marketing director Kim VandeWater, and copy editor Veronica Ambrose.

Last but not least, thanks to all the members of my crazy, wonderful, talented, neuro-diverse, and just-plain-diverse family: Zoë, Sasha, and Todd Blank; Christophe, Catherine, Olivia, Charlotte, and William Pla; Michel et Marie-Louise Pla; and David, Ben, and Will Saxl. Above all, my parents, Carol and Albert Blank, and my beautiful sister, Cynthia Saxl. Leo, most loyal. And most dear: my husband, Frédéric, and my three sons, Alec, Nate, and Andrew. Because those boys started this journey, and they are the core reason, in my heart, for everything.

Don't miss *Stanley Will Probably Be Fine*!

Turn the page for a sneak peek!

1

I NEVER THOUGHT I'D end up trapped in Albert Einstein's dog crate tonight, teetering at the top of our basement stairs. But you know, it only proves my point. Like I always tell my friend Joon: bad stuff can pop up and trap you at any time.

I mean, even if it seems like stuff is going okay? Suddenly, wham, just like in the comics: a splash page of heart-thumping action can explode out of nowhere. Pow! One minute, you're happily eating a piece of cake. Boom! The next minute? Dog crate of doom.

It all started because my brother, Calvin, turned fourteen today. We had pot roast, gravy, and a giant vat of mashed potatoes that Cal basically inhaled single-handedly. It was just the four of us: me, Gramps, Mom, and

Cal. And Albert Einstein, under the table. That's our dog—the world's least intelligent golden retriever.

Mom got off work early for the first time in months so she could cook Cal's favorite birthday dinner. She also made this amazing chocolate birthday cake. Three layers. Frosting like melt-in-your-mouth fudge.

So, after dinner, once Mom had gone back out for a real-estate showing . . . I decided to steal another hunk of it.

But Cal must have heard me sneak into the kitchen. Because all of a sudden—wham!—he leapt out of thin air. He slammed his hand on the counter so hard, both the cake plate and I jumped.

"Illegal cake grab, Stanley!" Cal shouted. "My birthday, MY CAKE!"

I froze. Freezing was a bad choice because Cal had me in an instant headlock.

"Let me go, Cal!"

Just like certain superheroes, there are times when I have to set aside my usual commitment to nonviolence. This was one of those times. I stomped on Cal's foot, hard as I could. His grip loosened! I ducked, spun, and twisted free—I was getting away! I dashed behind him— but now I was trapped in a corner. Stupid, stupid, stupid!

An evil grin unfurled across Cal's slightly hairy face. "Got you now," he growled.

I looked around, frantic. Albert Einstein's dog crate! I flung open the wire mesh door and dashed inside. Cal lunged—but he was too late. I scrambled to the back and scrunched up into a tiny ball, as far from his groping hands as I could get.

I was safe!

Or so I thought.

Because then, the crate door slammed shut. And I was being slid along the floor, toward the top of the basement stairs.

"Stop screaming, you weenie," said Cal. "I'm not gonna push you down the stairs." Then he giggled. When Cal giggles, it sounds like the squeak of a rusty metal gate hinge: "HEEEE! HEEEE! HEEEE!" And sometimes he throws in a snort, like a pig's stuck in that rusty gate. "SNORT! HEEEE!"

"Noooo!" I hollered.

But yes.

Cal placed the back half of the crate, with me in it, on firm ground. But the front half he left hanging over the top step. So now, if I scramble forward to open the door, I'll unbalance—and crash down into the basement.

I try not to think about that. I hug my knees and stay still as a statue. My glasses are smudged with chocolate, but I can't risk taking them off to polish them. I can't risk any movement at all. I try not to hyperventilate.

Cal grabs my cake plate and brings it over near me. He sits cross-legged by my cage. "Mmmmmm," he says, spewing crumbs, rolling his eyeballs around. "Delicious!"

I have this stack of comics upstairs two feet high. In any one of them, the hero or even the sidekick would be out of this bind in a flash. Superman would melt the bars. Batman would open his crazy utility belt. The Flash wouldn't have gotten caught in the first place. Wolverine would be out with one swipe of a claw. Spidey would sling a web and drag himself to safety.

But I'm no superhero. I'm about as far from a superhero as you could find. The only thing I can do is huddle in the corner of this dumb crate and feebly croak: "HELP!"

2

NOT A MOMENT too soon, Mom comes in the back door. She stands there in her bright red real estate blazer, rubbing her nose and gaping at us. "What on earth? What's going on, here? CALVIN?" Mom dumps an armload of folders on the table, and suddenly Calvin's morphed from Mr. Evil to Mr. Helpful, lending a hand to drag the crate back onto solid ground. I keel over inside it, still curled in a ball, and wait for my heart to stop hammering.

"Why are you in that crate, Stanley? Calvin, why is Stanley in the crate?"

Mom looks exhausted. Her face is pale. She pinches the bridge of her nose with her fingers and closes her eyes. "Wait. You know what? I don't want to know."

"Mom!" I protest. "You do want to know!"

"Aw, Ma!" Cal laughs like the Most Reasonable Boy in the World. "It's just, you know, boys being boys! And you have to admit, isn't that pretty cool, how I set up the crate? See how he couldn't get out? Pretty clever, huh?"

"Calvin Fortinbras, you're fourteen years old. Next year, Lord help us, you will be in high school. And this is how you choose to spend your time?"

As Cal slinks away, she falls into a kitchen chair, sighing, and kicks off her high heels.

"Aren't you going to ground him or something?" I say, climbing cautiously out of the crate.

"I'll deal with him later," Mom says, rubbing her toes.

I start to leave the room, but Mom clamps one of her iron claw-hands down on my shoulder. She turns me to face her, and gives me The Look. The one where her eyes glow like lasers, boring into your very soul. "You're breathing fast, Stanley. How are you feeling? Really?" She feels my forehead.

"I'm fine."

Mom frowns at me for a long moment. Finally, she releases me. She struggles to her feet and goes to rinse the stack of plates in the sink. "I thought your grandfather said he'd clean all this while I was out."

"Gramps took out his hearing aids and went upstairs right after you left." I look at the empty cake plate. "I was going to clean my mess up, but then, you know." I point to the crate.

She sighs, and bangs on the broken soap dispenser. "I'm sorry that Cal put you in that crate, Stanley. It was a terrible trick. I'll punish him, to be sure. But I have to say it: I'm a little worried about you, kiddo. I wish you'd learn to stand up for yourself more."

I can't believe my ears. "Stand up for myself more? Nice, Mom. Blame the victim, why don't you."

Mom's eyes narrow. "Watch your tone, Stan."

"Mom, Cal's got thirty pounds on me. I've been the smallest kid in every class I've ever been in. And now that I'm in middle school, I'm the smallest kid in the whole place. It's not a matter of standing up for myself. It's a matter of physics. Weight. Mass. Force. POWER. Other kids have it. I don't."

I stare at the floor. It's covered in chocolate cake crumbs.

"Oh, honey." Mom reaches out and strokes my forehead with her soapy, damp hand, like she's trying to wipe my feelings away. "I know the new school's hard. I know you don't like it. But . . . maybe if you tried just a little harder. Talk to the other kids. Why don't you ever talk to anyone?"

I shake my head. I'm not a talker. I don't say much, unless it's Mom, Dad, Gramps, or Joon. My Safe People.

"I know! Why don't you join one of the after-school clubs?"

My stomach squirms. "There are no good ones."

"So start your own! No one knows more about comics than you—why don't you start a comic book club?"

Yeah, great. She might as well be asking me to start a Let's Beat Up Stanley Club.

"Well, you need to do something," Mom says. "You hardly leave your room. You need more social interaction. Where's your old buddy Joon these days? Why's he never around?"

My stomach contracts into a squirmy ball. "Dunno," I say, my voice tight. "He's around."

"Hey, I've got an idea."

Uh-oh.

"What about that new girl next door?" Mom side-eyes me. "I hear she's homeschooled. It must be lonely for her; I bet she'd just love to make a nice new friend like you! I met the uncle by the mailbox the other day. Dr. Silverberg. It's just the two of them; her mom's living somewhere else for a while. But anyway, he seems very nice."

"You think everyone is nice."

"Well, most people are." She gives me an encouraging smile. "If you give them a chance. And this niece could be nice, too. She's your age. New in town. Doesn't know a soul." Mom turns off the tap and dries her hands. Then she gives me The Look again. "I mean it, Stanley. I want you to start speaking to other kids. I want you to go over there and welcome that new girl to the neighborhood. It's an assignment. No: a command. You're going over there tomorrow, and that's final."

What can I do? I know defeat when I see it.

After we finish cleaning the kitchen, I trudge up to my room. I shut the door tight, sprawl on my bed, and stare at my wall.

We moved here when I was four, right after Mom and Dad got their Friendly Divorce. Back then, I loved rocket ships and outer space, so Mom spent a week painting planets all over my walls. She meant well, but to be honest, she's no Michelangelo. Everything's kind of blotchy. Saturn's rings pretty much look ready to wobble right out of the galaxy.

Still, Mom tries. She works really, really hard—as a real estate broker and as a tax accountant. And ever since Gramps moved in with us over the summer, Mom looks even more tired than usual.

My dad used to come over a lot, to help with house projects, and homework, and just to be with me and Cal. But now he works for this global charity, building clinics and schools in Africa. It's his dream job. But I don't like him being gone.

My dad's French, but born in Morocco, which is in northern Africa. That's why our last name is Fortinbras—it sort of means "strong arms" in French. My dad has strong arms. He's small, strong, dark, and handsome, and he's really, really good at helping other people.

He used to be good at helping us.

I, on the other hand, do not have strong arms. My arms are basically two overcooked pieces of spaghetti.

Anyhow. When I worry about stuff—like Dad being gone, or Calvin turning Hulk, or Joon drifting away—I like to hole up in my room. It's a pretty okay place, despite Mom's wacky space mural. I've got a super-tall stack of comics by my desk, and superhero posters, and a new drafting table for sketching and cartooning. The bed's comfy, and I'm at the end of the hall, so it's quiet. Quiet is of primo importance to me. I can't handle too much noise, or craziness, or stress. I get what Mom calls sensory overload.

Between the new school and home lately, there's a lot of sensory overload.

In fact, more and more, I'm starting to feel like

this room is the only calm place I've got left in the whole universe.

Even if it's a universe where all the planets are a little out of whack.